PENGUIN BOOKS

QUARANTINE

Born in Canberra in 1942, Nicholas Hasluck studied
law at the University of Western Australia and Oxford.
After completing his studies he worked in Fleet Street
as an editorial assistant before returning to Australia.
A practising lawyer, he has lived in Perth with his wife
and two sons since 1967.

Quarantine, his first novel, was published in 1978 and
since then he has written three novels, *The Blue
Guitar*, *The Hand that Feeds You* and *The Bellarmine
Jug*, which won the 1984 Age Book of the Year Award.

Also by the author

Novels

The Blue Guitar (1980)
The Hand That Feeds You (1982)
The Bellarmine Jug (1984)

Short Stories

The Hat on the Letter O (1978)

Poetry

Anchor (1976)
On the Edge (1981)
Chinese Journey (1985)

NICHOLAS HASLUCK

QUARANTINE

PENGUIN BOOKS

Penguin Books Australia Ltd,
487 Maroondah Highway, P.O. Box 257
Ringwood, Victoria, 3134, Australia
Penguin Books Ltd,
Harmondsworth, Middlesex, England
40 West 23rd Street, New York, N.Y. 10010, U.S.A.
Penguin Books Canada Ltd,
2801 John Street, Markham, Ontario, Canada L3R 1B4
Penguin Books (N.Z) Ltd,
182-190 Wairau Road, Auckland 10, New Zealand

First published 1978 by The Macmillan Company of Australia Pty Ltd
Published in Penguin, 1986

Copyright © Nicholas Hasluck, 1978

Typeset in Melior by P.P. Typesetting, Melbourne
Offset from the Macmillan hardback edition
Made and printed in Australia
by Dominion Press – Hedges & Bell

CIP

Hasluck, Nicholas, 1942-
Quarantine.

ISBN 0 14 008849 0.

I. Title.

A823'.3

Chapter 1

Most of the passengers, including me, hurried up to the boat deck where the announcement was to be made, already prepared for the worst. We assembled there in the dark, whispering, jostling about, some carrying life-jackets, some with torches which they kept flicking on and off, splinters of light appearing here and there on the deck as the Captain spoke, the engines of the old steamer idling, so that the Captain, whose English wasn't up to much anyway, kept having to interrupt himself, urging everyone to gather round, to come in closer towards him where they could hear what he had to say.

But even then, those around me — and I was guilty of it too — made only a token effort to do what he asked, edging forward a bit. No one wanting to be right there in the front row, even though it was still too dark to be singled out, with no more than a faint thread of dawn light in the distance. So that when he finally told us we would have to spend a few days in quarantine many didn't quite catch it and the Captain had to repeat himself, louder this time, leaning forward over the rail of the shadowy catwalk deck above us, one hand cupped to his mouth, saying he wanted everyone's attention ('Have your eyes up here,' he said in his stubborn accent, to be exact, poking his chest with a finger), ordering everyone to stop their talking, their bad manners.

But there was no stopping it, that sudden murmuring, that quick swell of whispering, because by then most people knew that the ship had shut down its engines during the night for a half hour. The rumour was that one of the crew had died and been put overboard for burial, the whole thing having to be over and done with by daylight — so I was told — that being the custom in this part of the world.

Whether or not a crewman had to be buried like that I never

1

found out but, certainly, I knew what it was like when the engines were cut, waking up to the silence, drowsy, not quite sure what was wrong, then knowing it was just that, the quiet, the feeling of suspension, standing at the porthole in my pyjamas, the stillness being so unusual, so pervasive, the feeling of drifting with only a glimmer of moonlight and a suggestion of water somewhere below, no sound of commotion, just the silence, as though everything had been snuffed out once and for all.

That made me wish there was someone with me in the cabin. Someone there so that, between us, we could work out what was happening. Instead of standing there alone, heart racing, feeling that if I did anything, whatever I did, rang the bell, went up on deck, it would seem like panic, like cowardice. Someone to talk to would be enough.

But there was no one. And nothing to be seen outside. Just a trace of moonlight on the water, nothing more. And though I knew we must have entered the canal, I couldn't see any landmarks, or any horizon, or even the banks of the canal; the darkness and the murky blisters of salt on the glass, clouding the glass, made my rubbing at it from inside useless.

So not for the first time, I thought that maybe my father should have been less jocular about roughing it in his own youth and just plain booked me on one of the conventional passenger lines, something ordinary, arranged for me to share a cabin, to travel with a group, some other students, perhaps. Not this, anything but this narrow cabin on my own, and the ship an ungainly kitbag of cargo and passengers, neither one thing nor the other, the lifeboats streaked with rust, and crates of rotten-looking vegetables being loaded off an old truck when we clattered down the gangplank at Bombay; the truck with buckled mudguards and dregs of water in its headlamps, a rag stuffed into the radiator cap on its bonnet; the driver jabbering to the crewmen handling the crates.

Yes, when I think back to standing there at the porthole, indecisively, waiting for a break in the stillness, for a flare to go up, a siren, some note of alarm to get me moving, my worst fears taking shape, I can see why it didn't surprise me to be told, only a few hours later, that there had been a burial. The silence had that kind of depth about it, that kind of restraint. But just as I was about to scramble into my clothes and go up on deck, the engines started up again, lumbering into action again without warning, the whole ship shuddering and then slowly moving forward, and eventually settling down to the comfortable irregularity of rattle and vibration I had become accustomed to, persuading me, after a time, to calm down, to forget it, to get back in my bunk, to try and sleep.

So when I begin to describe our quarantine, it still seems to me, even now, that there is no real start to it; nothing you can put your finger on. At a certain moment we were told we would have to spend a few days in quarantine. And yet, even before the announcement was made, we had already prepared ourselves for the worst.

As always, although many years have passed, the memory of the affair sets up an itch in my mind which wants scratching. The anomalies, the gaps in my understanding of what happened, the half truths — the memory begins to fester; it begins to trouble me like some blemish of the skin, some residual disaffection which comes and goes but never heals.

Thinking about the way it started, our quarantine, the way it just suddenly began to happen, I'm reminded that one of the few Arabic words I brought back with me from the canal is the word *faszad*. It haunts me that word. *Faszad*. A single word. And according to Dr Magro, who acquainted me with the concept, a word which cannot be exactly translated into English.

It denotes a sordid intrigue. An intrigue so complicated by the variety of motives and false testimony required to bring it to fruition, that it might almost be described as a conspiracy without a cause; a chain of events bearing all the hallmarks of a calculated plot — that is to say, a process which closes in on a victim, which seizes some unfortunate being against his will and breaks him, leaving him enmeshed in the ganglions of perjury and greed which brought about his downfall — but nonetheless, a process which in fact has no clearly defined purpose; as if the intention was simply to trigger off some iniquitous proceeding in the expectation that pickings of one kind or another would be there for nimble fingers in the end.

In short, immediately following the Captain's announcement, it was as if a *faszad* had been set in motion. The passengers scattered amidst a babble of consternation. Suitcases were bundled into corridors. Members of the crew, encumbered by packages, shouldered past each other on the stairs with raucous voices. Outside the dining room, a man planted an infant in my arms while he pacified his wife. I overheard the ship's officers being assailed by pleas of sickness and pleas of robust health. There was flattery and anger. Composure and skilful elderly charm. Money changed hands — openly; surreptitiously.

But hectic as it was, the hue and cry, one and all were handicapped by the uncertainty of not knowing whether it was safer to stay on board or safer to make for land. No one could tell me what was best.

At times, it seemed as though the object of the *faszad* was to defer the reckoning. At other times, it threatened to claim its victim forthwith. With one hand, it found me a buoyant cork-bosomed life-jacket. With the other, it offered me a berth (fortunately declined) in the first boat over the rail which listed badly on the winch and lay beneath the ladder, waterlogged, wallowing in the swell — a flotilla of suitcases bravely bucketing shorewards for a few yards, before capsizing and sinking.

And there was also the search. Downstairs, in the passengers' lounge, immediately prior to disembarkation, the chairs and card-tables were pushed aside and we were herded into a straggling queue patrolled by two Goanese stewards who kept piping out in shrill voices: 'All passengers! Hand luggage only, please. The rest will follow. Hand luggage only, please.'

The queue slowly shuffled forward towards the small plateau at one end of the room previously represented to us as a dance floor. There, the Purser, flanked by two officers, was rifling hastily through cases and rucksacks; anything in the nature of personal belongings — now and again running spatula hands up and down the clothing of whoever was at the head of the queue. All the time — intended, perhaps, as an aid to morale — a loudspeaker suspended above the floor kept blaring out a stream of foxtrots, bombarding those beneath with saxophonic medleys and dusty violins, the frayed edges of the music scuffed to the point of obliteration by a worn needle, a jaded turntable.

For me, this was the worst part of the morning; the search. The Purser was a huge, flat-faced Dutchman, his collar always grimy and, often, a portion of his underpants hitched up above the level of his belt. I didn't want his clumsy hands pawing their way all over me. I have a horror of that kind of thing. Besides, what was the search all about? What were they looking for? It didn't seem to be medical; although I could see that people were having to hold their wrists out towards him and show their papers. But no one knew for sure. It didn't make sense.

Someone said it was guns. And it's true that after an argument, they did confiscate a revolver from one of the passengers, the weapon being left casually on the table nearest to where the three men were carrying out their search, clearly visible as we filed towards them. But that was the only clue. We were never told. And all the time the music kept churning out of the metal blossom overhead and Tiba, one of the cabin boys, who was changing the records on the squat, four-legged gramophone anchored to a column near the dance floor, kept grinning in his friendly way every time someone raised their arms to be searched, saying: 'Maybe they is robbing you! Maybe they is robbing you!'

And the person being searched, rather than face the Dutchman, would usually look that way out of embarrassment and try smiling back at the boy. And Tiba, because he couldn't improve on the joke, would wink and say again: 'Maybe they is robbing you!' But at a look from the Purser, a look of cold savagery, he would hastily turn back to his records, saving his joke up until the next number was under way.

But the thing on my mind, the thing which kept bothering me the closer I came to the point of search, was the thought of those hands, rummaging into my small case, my pockets, touching me. And more than that, the fact was I had committed an indiscretion and was conscious of it; desperately aware that I might be found out.

On my way up to the lounge, because the corridor on the passenger deck was so crowded, I had been forced aside, forced into the steward's pantry to make room for a family pushing past me with a trunk. Right next to me, on the sink, there was a packet of tea-bags. I scarcely thought about it, but simply grabbed a handful and shoved them in my pocket Somewhere in the back of my mind I had the idea that little things like that, or coloured things or trinkets, might be useful to barter with when we reached shore. A crazy notion, true, But I didn't have the faintest idea where we would be going or what might happen.

5

And now, on the point of being searched, those crackling tea-bags in my pocket felt like stolen bank notes, hot goods, the crown jewels or something. The nearer I moved to the head of the queue, the more I worried; the deeper I pushed them into my pocket, keeping one hand firmly in my pocket, not daring to look down, fearing that already my perspiring palm might have made the tea leaves run, that already an ugly stain was spreading across the front of my white drill trousers — branding me as a criminal of one kind or another.

I kept looking straight ahead. Or at Tiba. Using my free hand to fan myself with the straw hat I had bought for a shilling (my own shilling) at Kandy.

I didn't want to be found out. Not in front of all of the others. A dozen plausible stories foxtrotted into my mind, swayed to and fro to the ragged music, dipped and disappeared.

'Maybe they is robbing you!' Tiba said, almost at my ear, but grinning at the man in front of me who was holding his arms above his head limply. 'Maybe they is robbing you!' Tiba patted the top pockets of his steward's jacket to emphasize the point.

The needle reached the end of the record; the loudspeaker directly above us crackling and wavering as the needle kept running on, with each whispering circumlocution, amidst the static, stumbling on a hard, repetitive crack.

The Dutchman straightened up, glaring at Tiba, flapping the open collar of his shirt with his fingers for relief from the airless heat.

The needle kept up its whispering progress, picking up the crack each time round. The man in front of me slowly lowered his arms.

'Maybe they is robbing you!' Tiba said. This time he pulled his trouser pockets inside out, and made a face. 'Maybe they is robbing you!' He stuck his tongue out and let his jaw sag, his head lolling on his shoulders comically.

The Dutchman reached him in one step, cuffing him over the head, stumbling him backwards with the force of the open-handed blows, the boy crouching and shielding his head with his arms, blundering against the record-player so that the speaker overhead gave a nerve-tingling yelp, a screech as the needle skidded off, the boy picked up by the front scruff of his jacket, the Dutchman banging him against the column and slapping his face, blood beginning to stream out of his nose, spattering his uniform. The violence of the assault caused the queue behind me to break up in confusion, some veering in towards the Purser, and Bricky, one of the roughneck Australian transport drivers, shoved in between the two of them with his chin back and his hands out in front of him, groping, like he was wading into heavy reeds.

I saw one of the officers grab the gun from the table as the whole queue began milling around me; splitting up, some going for cover. 'Oh, Christ,' I thought. 'Christ. Someone will get it. Get shot.' Almost paralysed I watched. But he didn't try and use it, just holding it up to his chest, his free hand shielding it, standing back, his friend, the other officer, leaving the other case he had just opened up, and getting across to the brawl, looking for a way in. Bricky's two reckless mates, who'd fight for a fight's sake, were in it now, the whole group of men staggering for balance and tearing at each other, the Dutchman, his face red, still kicking out at the boy, and Tiba, blood running into his white collar, on his hands and knees, crawling away from the boots, scrabbling for a grip on the column, looking for shelter there.

When the Dutchman stood back, finally, panting, knowing he wouldn't win, that even his own officer was trying to break it up, I thought he might take on Bricky or one of his friends, scowling at them each in turn, and shaking himself free of the ship's officer who kept trying to calm him down. But Bricky was ready for another go, hands dangling, backed up by his two mates, all of them big men, and not bothered too much about the boy, not even looking at him, just waiting for the Purser to make a move, sort of smiling, which made me think there had already been some trouble on board I didn't know about, some previous argument and they were just waiting for a chance to settle it. They wanted that Purser to try them out. I could see it.

A couple of seconds they all stood there like that. Until the Purser shrugged and turned back to the dance floor, as he did so, holding up a warning finger to Tiba who was peering out from behind the column, mopping at his nose with the back of his brown hand. And gradually, people looking at each other, not quite sure what to do, the queue began to form again, the transport drivers sauntering back into the line, Bricky with a slow wink to the others.

7

I took my handkerchief out to mop my brow. But couldn't
do anything with it, my hand and the cloth a pulp of tea
leaves and shreds of paper. Not that it mattered now because
the Purser and his two assistants had virtually given up the
search, just giving all belongings a cursory look, the queue
moving forward in silence now, no music, and Tiba, his face
wiped clean, but the smears of blood still on his white jacket,
at the far end of the queue, well out of reach and not smiling
any longer, saying sullenly, speaking almost to himself:
'Maybe they is robbing you! Maybe they is robbing you!'

And someone behind me I couldn't see called out: 'Don't
push your luck, Tiba.'

But that only made him raise the tone of his voice; his voice
becoming shrill and sneering. 'Well, maybe they is robbing
you,' he said. 'Maybe they is robbing you.'

No one said anything; the queue moving forward. And the
way the Purser stood off from Bricky and his boys when their
turn came, the two sides eyeing each other, one of the other
officers searching their rucksacks, made me think that once
we reached shore the Purser wouldn't be bothering to give us
much help; not the Purser. He was one person, at least, who
would be happy to see us reach the shore and rot. We
wouldn't get much from him.

Chapter 2

Our quarantine. Was it ever anything more than a bad dream? The hallucination of a feverish mind? A kaleidoscope of unreality? Eagerly, the sleeper, fresh from his bed of invention, lays his adventures before us — the island rising in the sea, the priceless gem, the pursuit, and then, the endless corridor, and then, the familiar face (but the sleeper's certainty it was really someone else) ... his voice trails off, the story peters out. Embarrassed, he lets the subject drop; the secret of reconstruction beyond his grasp — how he was affected by it, the only reality remaining.

Are memories any more reliable? Are they anything more than tortuous myths? The central image, the feeling of it, remains. But in the meantime, one has survived other tragedies. On TV screens, in films, darker fantasies flicker before one's eyes daily. Our past experience is haunted by what we have become.

How can I conjure up a picture of the Quarantine Station as it was then? The ramshackle buildings at the canal's edge; the mud-coloured water; the desert? How can I set down the essence of those days in quarantine without distortion?

'One dark morning, not long after the ship had entered the canal, they told us we would have to spend a few days in quarantine. At daybreak, not knowing what lay ahead, we clambered into three of the ship's lifeboats (the fourth having proved unseaworthy) and began the journey to shore ...'

That's the way the story should start, I suppose. Factual. Straight to the point. A professional would handle it that way, I imagine: both hands on the tiller; the narrative surging shorewards; every word a laser beam.

(Yes; every word a laser beam, pal. Exactly. Let's make for land without the excess crap. In three boats full stop. Don't swamp the action with that unseaworthy fourth. Who are you writing for? Insurance assessors? Get rid of it.)

The blue pencil descends. Boats vaporize. Landscapes disappear without trace. The man with a family to feed, a reputation to defend, briskly plies the scalpel. Slices into the fat. Who can blame him?

But I have no family, and apart from a brief history of the Law School, no work of fiction to my credit. Furthermore, you, my friend, my trusted colleague, know me too well. My textbooks, even the shortest of my articles, have all had to be trimmed by your dispassionate hand. I can only trundle out the facts as I recall them.

The real question is — am I brave enough to be frank? Notwithstanding our long association, can I dare to speak the truth; can I afford to reveal myself in this memoir — this confession, even to you?

My night in an Egyptian brothel. The only time I acted as a judge. Oh, yes; I've been dining out on one fragment or another of the story for forty years. Everyone who has ever passed through the faculty has heard some scandalous extract. A nipple here; a finger plucking the bow string there; the laurel wreath; the snake's head in the undergrowth; bits and pieces chipped out of the mosaic towards the end of an evening for good humour's sake — the vignette always shrouded in a haze of misleading gaiety, and never believed.

But when you urge me to lay the thing out as a whole, when you seriously propose that I should prepare a manuscript for publication, I draw back; I begin to worry, to shrink from the prospect. You have in mind a few jaunty reminiscences; an entertaining travelogue from an earlier day; something for my friends and former students to chuckle over. But I know better. In my mind's eye, that fourth boat will always be there wallowing in the swell beneath the ladder. The blood on the steward boy's jacket. I can't remove it. Already, the process of articulation, a lifetime's habit of inquiry, the compulsion to get the facts straight and in their proper order, begins to impose its discipline.

Some details stick. Some fade. But the main features of that disembarkation are still to hand — the boats pushing away from the waterline of the steamer and ahead of us, on shore, the Quarantine Station; the silhouette of a two-storeyed structure with clumsy verandahs at the front and side — a cluster of palm trees, a few outhouses, straggling away from it towards an escarpment, and beyond that, the desert.

My first impression was of a sombre colonial-style hotel which had been bought in a second-hand market somewhere else in the Orient, carried in by freighter and dumped on the canal's edge for re-fabrication by a bored and listless crew; a crew acting on instructions which had not been fully comprehended when received and attended to half-heartedly when carried out. Some of the verandah posts had a bow-legged look about them and the gables either jutted out too far or had been shorn off; the work of only vaguely interested hands.

A cartridge belt of steps tracked towards the main building from a jetty at the water's edge. Half-way up the slope, the steps disappeared into a concrete block-house, emerging from the breech at a new angle and without bannisters; petering out altogether upon reaching the level ground directly in front of the Quarantine Station. A stone parapet, crumbling in places, shambled along the crest of the slope.

One of our boats contained mostly luggage — a lopsided pile hurriedly heaped up in the centre of it. About three dozen passengers in all were cramped into the other two. Beyond us, the sun appearing above the desert, promised a warmth which was not yet felt. My fellow passengers were mostly silent now, the other boat slightly ahead of us, creating a wake which occasionally disturbed the muffled rhythm of our own boat's steadfast engine.

My small suitcase had been snatched away from me before boarding. Whether it had come to grief with the first boat over the rail, I had no means of knowing. I hoped not. My whites were already grubby. Apart from my hat, the only things I had with me were my travelling pouch and the Borthwick edition of *Justinian's Institutes*.

My passport was in the pouch. My visas and vaccination certificate were in the Borthwick. My father, speaking as a man who had once roughed it in his youth, had advised (nay commanded) me to put all my papers in the pouch. My mother, as a woman who had met him on his travels — masquerading as his brother, his own papers temporarily misplaced — argued to the contrary. Hence, Borthwick; a basket for a few of my eggs, a rival to the pouch, and a splendid introduction to Roman Law. All things considered, a perfect hiding place. Enough to make my father weep; my mother wonder.

11

Not that they ever knew. Borthwick was a secret then; and, containing, as it does, a few rough notes jotted in the margins describing what took place, such notes being the only record of any kind I kept, has remained a secret ever since. It rests beside me now.

As to the journey to shore, Borthwick is silent. I made no entry. But I recall distinctly that, at some stage of the journey, I looked back at our ship. That it struck me, with renewed force, just how old and out of date our steamer was; how down at heel; how dilapidated.

And seeing it in that way, gradually moving away from it, the weary steamer anchored offshore at a point where the canal opens out into one of the lakes en route to the Mediterranean, although I tried to keep cheerful, there was something about the grey bulk of the ship which kept eroding my resolution — the black stump of a funnel amidships, two mastheads; on each, ladders of rigging slanting downwards, the remaining lifeboats hanging crookedly from their slings, and a dejected canvas canopy at the rear of the vessel; and rust marks trailing from the portholes.

I kept a brave face; but I was scared. I admit it. The burial which was supposed to have taken place. The search. The appearance of the ship. All these things began to bear down on me; sitting quietly for the first time since waking, beginning to worry about what would happen to us. Worried by the prospect of entering a strange country. And worried also by the likelihood that we would be dealt with by officials. That my papers, my passport, my certificate, would be found deficient. That we were headed for some sleazy outpost accustomed to delay; where time would be wasted over meaningless formalities, and waiting for cables to be sent in respect of which replies would never be received, and there would be misunderstandings, and boredom, and corruption.

But thinking back on it, trying desperately to reconstruct our journey to shore in the absence of a written record, the one thing which troubles me, which scars my memory far worse than any of the matters I have mentioned, is the certainty that we never found out what we were suspected of. What disease. What malaise, or what infection.

Strange as it seems, on the way in, it never occurred to me to ask. And I never heard any of the others ask that question. For some reason — the extraordinary start to the day, perhaps

— we simply took it for granted that this was something we had to put up with. One of the hazards of travel. To be shoved into lifeboats and sent shorewards; the custodians, supposedly, of some virulent organism.

In later years, it has troubled me greatly that none of us was curious; that none of us demanded an answer. At some stage of the quarantine, the rumour was current that a characteristic of our affliction was that the sufferer became detached, often euphoric; disinclined to worry much about his condition.

But that was later. In the first few days of our quarantine, my recollection is that there was a simpler explanation. We were not concerned about our health. We felt that we were being deceived. Someone had heard that the shipping line was bankrupt; that the ship couldn't pay its dues; that it couldn't go on and couldn't go back. That the whole voyage had come to an end. That we were stranded.

Chapter 3

The first entry in my Borthwick says simply: 'Shewfik Arud to cable UK'. Then follows my translation of an elusive passage from the *De adquirenda vel amittenda possessione* section of *Justinian*. And, finally, the word: 'Leeches'.

I have always been troubled by that passage of the Digest. I notice that, at the time, my rendering was: 'Now one can acquire possession in person. A madman, and a pupil without his teacher's authority, cannot begin to possess, since they have not the intention to hold, however much they are in physical contact with the thing, as though one put something in the hand of a sleeping person.'

But as most of the textual commentators agree, this creates difficulties. The only way one can reconcile the singular implicit in 'non potest incipere possidere' with the plural 'Furiosus et pupillus' is by assuming that the reference to *pupillus* is an interpolation; especially as there is no ground for the suggestion that if the *pupillus* had *intellectus* he might require *auctoritas*.

I once asked a younger member of the faculty for his view on the matter. But he didn't know what I was talking about. In fact, I think he thought I had gone mad. But, of course, Roman Law wasn't his field. Tax dodges and discretionary trusts were his field. He made the point, quite curtly. And left me.

In any event, I must not presume too much. At the time I was grappling with such passages of translation at the Quarantine Station, I myself would have been quite incapable of reconciling the inconsistencies inherent in 'Furiosus et pupillus'. Indeed, my training in any form of law was very meagre; a state of affairs I tried to make clear to the other passengers when we set up our tribunal.

'I am quite the wrong man for the job,' I can remember myself saying. 'You can't expect me, with my limited training, to pass any sensible judgement.' And I went on to explain that I was really no more than a student; that I was on my way to England for further study; that my grasp of Latin was so inadequate that there was every chance I wouldn't even be admitted to the University. More importantly, so that there would be no mistake about the matter, I put the issue squarely before them, using the time-honoured language of Justinian — *justitia est constans et perpetua voluntas ius suum cuique tribuens* — his famous opening words on the nature of justice.

But nobody took any notice. They would hear none of it. They ignored my plea entirely. They were determined to have a Judge and, in retrospect, I can see that it was of no great concern to them who he was or what he did. My importance was simply this. It eased their consciences to be able to elect a man who was reputed to have some association with the law. Nothing more.

But what of Shewfik Arud and the musty tasting eggs he always served for breakfast?

Staggering up from the jetty where we had been off-loaded, some passengers bowed down by the weight of their hand luggage, we were confronted by a small, dark-skinned man dressed in khaki shirt and trousers who was standing on the front verandah of the Quarantine Station, surveying the dusty parade ground between the verandah and the parapet. He flourished a welcoming hand at the cluster of passengers trudging towards him and began smiling — turning his attention from one person to the next; a series of hospitable smiles (successive versions of the one smile, in fact), rubbing his thin hands together occasionally. He didn't actually do anything to assist.

'You are all welcome,' he called out; loud enough to encourage the stragglers. 'Most welcome. Exceedingly. Shewfik Arud and his staff have everything here for your comfort. Shewfik greets you. We have clean towels and gallons of hot water in limited quantities. Everything is here. A register for you to sign and the bathroom disinfected in the English style. Taps bright as buttons.'

One or two of the older passengers, overcome by the climb, the greeting, flopped down on the edge of the verandah. Shewfik frowned. A handbag had come to rest at his feet. He toed it to one side.

'The medical inspection and so forth,' he continued. 'That

will all come later. You have no need to worry yourselves. Let us put that out of our minds. Right out of our minds. Finish. Just like that. Phtt.' He sliced the air with a hand. 'Now, you are tourists. Tourists in the English style, yes? Enjoying yourselves all the time up hill and down dale. Your tips are welcome. Your gratuities and so forth. But one thing. This is not your Raffles or your Ritz. There will be some little points sorted out as we go. And some sharing of rooms, like your dormitories. But that is nothing. We are one team. And now — all inside, please. All inside.'

He moved to the front steps and began waving people inwards; one hand flapping to and fro in front of his face as though he was trying to get rid of a particularly irritating fly. 'Take your luggage to the desk and all inside now, please,' he commanded. 'All inside, now. Shewfik will be with you in one jiffy.'

The passengers, gathering up their belongings once again, trooped wearily across the verandah, crowding through the main door; Shewfik vigorously sweeping them inwards with his hand.

Standing aside to let the others pass, I was the last one in. Shewfik followed, urging me inwards, raising a friendly hand to my shoulder as we went through the door together.

'So there it is,' he confided; beaming a smile. (I shivered free of his touch.) 'For the time being, now, you are some god-awful tourist; yes? The Mena House Hotel knows your kind, of course. I have managed it. The ashtrays. The knives and forks all gone. Taken. The pyramids are not safe. Where is my padlock? My desert patrol? Ho. Ho. I am joking all the time. You know how it is in civilized company. Chewing the fat after dinner as it were, and the witty sayings. More soda. A slash of brandy, please. Another for the road. The tarmac, old boy. Ah, my good years at the Embassy. You will enjoy your stay here. I am at my best in the evenings. Effervescent after sunset. That is me. A night person. Shewfik will fix it. No mess. No rumours. A man of discretion as we used to say. Some of my friends, I am still writing with them. A fine season I am having in Kent, Shewfik. But not just a postcard, you understand. Still grateful.'

I dug into my pouch and tentatively extracted a coin.

'There is no need,' he murmured, removing it from my fingers and then pocketing it. 'Absolutely no need.'

'One queue at the desk to sign your names,' he shouted in a loud voice, moving away from me, taking charge of the situation again, shooing people towards the far end of the room. 'Most important. You must have your passports in your hands. Your passports, please.'

I attached myself to the end of the ragged queue which had formed in front of the reception desk. Shewfik scurried in behind the counter and gleefully slapped a small silver dome positioned beside his register. It made a pinging sound. 'We are ready for our names and our passports,' he called out to the room at large. 'In an orderly fashion.'

I put down my suitcase (which, fortunately, had survived) and glanced round the foyer of Shewfik's establishment. It was a seedy imitation of what an English hotel might have looked like in the late nineteenth century, conveying a first impression of comfort and dignity, an impression suggested by heavy armchairs, curtained windows looking out on the canal and a stately looking-glass in one corner. But on closer inspection, it revealed itself in every detail as second-rate — the mirror spotty and fly-blown, the curtains being nothing more than dusty hessian drapes, the armchairs lopsided, the whole scene laid out beneath a motionless punkah, suspended from the ceiling, which served only to emphasize the oppressive nature of the stillness and the heat.

I opened my Borthwick, checked my papers were still there, and closed it. A moment later, the word was passed along the line that there was no telephone at the Station but it was possible to send a cable. I loosened my collar and settled down to wait.

But despite the drabness of the surroundings, Shewfik was tremendously proud of his kingdom. As I found out when I finally reached the counter, chatting to him (or, rather, he chatting to me) as I presented my papers and entered the relevant details in the ledger he elbowed across to me.

'My concession,' he said, when I commented on the official crest at the top of the page, 'is under that self-same seal. And a fine concession it is. Look around you. You must have noticed. But I am not any younger.' He coughed weakly and tapped his chest with two fingers; then quickly recovered. 'I will be selling it soon,' he added. 'I am in the process. And I shall not be asking a small price. No, I shall not be throwing it away for tuppence. Not if I am still myself.'

17

Standing behind the reception desk, he shifted his weight from foot to foot as he spoke, now and again, his brown knuckles nervously drumming out short, emphatic signals on the wooden counter. But all the time he kept smiling; his black hair and moustache smoothed down, his khaki shirt open at the neck, keeping an eye on the rest of the passengers, some of whom had now sunk wearily into the armchairs in the foyer, some out on the verandah in a group talking.

There was a small potted palm on the counter. Often, as he flung a hand out sideways for emphasis, he struck the plant and there would be a rustling of leaves. He would glance at it suspiciously, and then hurry on — the small Egyptian, defending his counter, behind him, books and ledgers and papers strewn all over his desk. Between the rappings of wood and the rustling of leaves, a deck of official forms being shuffled rapidly in his hands.

'I will not be giving this away for one song,' he said, his face smiling, eager. But his black eyes reproachful at the thought. 'Not for one song, I assure you. Not if I am still myself.'

The outcome of his negotiations was a topic which was constantly present to his mind and always on his lips. Success, it seemed, was assured so long as he was still himself. These particular words, like a refrain, haunted all his utterances on matters commercial. The inference always was, that being himself, and mindful of the hard work he had put into building up his concession, he would be loyal to his own self-interest, ruthless in negotiation, ultimately rich. But at the same time, the threat existed, apparently, that some other man, some sentimental fool beneath the surface, might take possession of his faculties at a crucial moment and shunt the negotiations into an abyss; a dead end of conciliation and fatal propriety.

It was a wistful notion; the more wistful because all the indications were that it would never happen. At all times, Shewfik Arud, the outward man, the one who had lived through humiliation and adversity, the one who had been obliged to spend two full days with his uncle who was a book-keeper preparing a fresh set of figures for the purpose of the negotiations, was the one who was clearly in control. The other, the inner man, the benevolent assassin, if he existed, was never anywhere to be seen.

'Do you know what the advertisement cost me?' he asked. 'Do you know how many hours I attended the Consul? Not once. Not twice, I assure you. Me, talking to his clerk; surrounded by the all and sundry of the streets whose barrows and confectionery are nothing compared with my concession. A pretty picture it was. A pretty picture. A man such as I with important transactions in the one hand and my purchaser becoming restless and my guests requiring attention. A pretty picture, indeed. And the Consul, who everyone knows has no mind to make up, though I don't say it to give offence. Such a Consul with his pacing up and down and pointing to the ceiling. His freckled hands. And saying science shows that tiny flakes of paint from the ceiling can fall into one's coffee over twelve years and kill a person by stealth. All the time a cockroach on my side of the desk.'

Shewfik rapped the counter angrily. 'And still no approval. What am I to do about paint flaking down from his ceiling? Am I a painter? A carpenter? Ridiculous. As I said to my barber who is a friend and can mostly be trusted. Ridiculous. I am a concessionaire. Not some painter. Not one of the felaheen with a barrow load of carpets. And all the time my purchaser wanting figures about this. Figures about that. No, I shall not be selling for one song. Not if I am still myself.'

I had been smiling until then, believing this was the right thing to do. Grinning cheerfully. But now I tried to interrupt. I wanted to get a cable away to the Warden of my college; explaining the situation, apologizing in advance for my delayed arrival. I was anxious to make a good impression. To arrive at the college half-way through the first term might seem untidy. A rollicking yarn in retrospect, perhaps. But on the day, it was bound to seem a bit slack. I coughed discreetly and made the point.

Shewfik pushed some paper towards me but otherwise did not alter his stride; drawing me further and further into the web of his affairs.

'Am I to be ignored?' he asked; his hands raised and held wide in an attitude of disbelief, looking over my shoulder for some encouragement from the passengers in the chairs nearby. 'Treated with disdain? Am I to say to my purchaser — "Shewfik Arud has nothing. Shewfik Arud has spent ten years of his life putting his business on the even keel and has nothing to show for it but empty books. After all this time,

Shewfik Arud does not even have the administrator's ear. He must wait with the felaheen and the tram conductors." Am I to say that? Ridiculous. That is what I said to my barber which he agreed with. And he is one who can be trusted in certain things.'

I nodded sympathetically. Keeping an ear open for a chance to interrupt, I began printing out my message; siphoning the last of the ink out of the cut-glass ink-well which sat near to hand on the counter.

It is not surprising that such notes as I did make concerning our stay are jotted down in the margins of a textbook. Shewfik's notepaper was made of a thick cardboard-like material which was virtually unusable. It was like writing on a piece of matting; the nib of the pen frequently puncturing the surface of the material, the ink itself draining away into hidden pores leaving behind it crude misshapen lettering.

Furthermore, the paper was biscuit yellow. An insignia — being a clumsy circle with a serrated circumference which I took to be the representation of a blazing sun — seemed to have tumbled down from the letterhead and occupied a good deal of the page. Consequently, part of my message was engulfed in the stumpy black flames of the device; the words often emerging from the inferno reduced by a crucial syllable or two.

I certainly had no desire to send a piece of this writing-stuff to my tutor. Any such letter would have been rank with enigma. Suppose it arrived in the cleft of a stick? I was half-inclined to stipulate that the message was only to be sent by cable. That the original was to be immediately destroyed. But the risk of such a message being read the wrong way was too great.

As Shewfik himself explained to us many times, one of the reasons he was able to obtain the concession ahead of other competitors with far more influential connections was his command of French and English. But as he was very evasive about the way in which our cables would be sent, it would obviously be unwise to complicate the instructions. So I made my message as short as possible; printing it out in block capitals. I passed it across to him. Then, I quit the counter and walked out on to the verandah to see if anyone knew what was going on.

I never found out whether my message did get through. It

20

wouldn't have mattered much if it didn't. The suggestion contained in the message — based on the Captain's representations — that I would only be held up for a few days, turned out to be quite wrong. But, on balance, knowing Shewfik, it probably did get through.

Shewfik Arud was, in every respect, a remarkable person. He had an innate ability to get things done. Having regard to the delicate state of the negotiations with his purchaser, it may be that he was on his best behaviour. Perhaps so. But the skill with which he deployed his limited resources was masterful; a credit to the Embassy which trained him.

Assisted only by his daughter and the two servant families who lived in the outhouses at the rear of the Station, he ran his establishment along the lines of a moderately efficient hotel. The odds were against him but he coped. From somewhere, he obtained eggs for breakfast; boiled eggs with a peculiar musty aftertaste, but eggs nonetheless. And when the regular water-carrier from the city failed to arrive he made alternative arrangements. Or when the generator broke down, he fixed it. Now and again, one would chance upon him in a back room or in the yard of the hotel screaming hysterically at one of the servants, but he always had time to manage a frantic smile for the passing guest. And he was always on hand to serve drinks.

As far as I could gather — the information being gradually pieced together from intermittent conversations over a number of weeks — his family had been employed by one of the European clubs at Cairo and, with that background, as rounded off by his 'Embassy' years, he could not only speak several languages but prided himself on his knowledge of the proper standards of conduct.

'There are no true gentlemen left,' he once told me with that air of eagerness which characterized his every remark; notwithstanding that he clearly intended to sound a note of regret. 'No true gentleman of the old school.'

He implied, although it seemed most unlikely, that it was this, more than anything else, which had forced him and his wife into temporary exile at the Quarantine Station. 'But now that my wife has passed on regrettably,' he would say, becoming conspicuously crestfallen for a moment, 'a man must return to his belongings. Do you not agree?'

It was hard not to agree. He was determined to please. His

21

sympathy for our plight was boundless and frequently voiced. For this reason, as much as for any other, he was, until close to the end, remarkably popular with the other passengers. Certainly, I never heard a word spoken against him; although, to be sure, Bricky, the Australian transport driver, once confided to me that, in his opinion, for what it was worth — and he didn't appear to be seriously suggesting that it was worth much — Shewfik Arud was, in an Antipodean nutshell, a cunt.

But I hasten to add that in order to assess the true worth of that remark, to appreciate the finer points of the original, uninterpolated text, as it were, one has to know something more about Bricky and his two friends; something more substantial, of course, than merely noting their propensity to clobber the Ship's Purser good and hard when the chance offered.

They spent most of their time drinking and playing cards. There was a small table and a set of low, cane chairs at one end of the upstairs verandah overlooking the canal. The table and the chairs were directly outside the large, shuttered doors which opened on to the verandah from the dormitory which had been assigned to the drivers. Almost from the first day, they treated this portion of the verandah as being their ground.

No matter how hot it was, or whether it was afternoon or morning, they were to be found there, the three of them, sitting round the table in the far corner, lethargically dealing out their cards; a low murmur of inaudible conversation rising from the group, punctuated from time to time by clinking glasses, a bottle always presiding from the centre of the table. Three big men lolling back in their cane chairs, a thin pall of cigarette smoke hovering around them. And, indeed, they were big men. Nonchalant, muscular men. Sleeves rolled up to the elbow.

Bricky was the spokesman for the group. Standing at the verandah rail watching ships on the canal, you would hear them greeting his approach with a kind of intimate guffaw: 'How's the hangover today then, Bricky?' or, entering the upstairs lavatory, you would find the other two lounging about in the vicinity of one of the cubicles, and responding to the splintering sounds from within with a wink and a chuckling chorus of: 'How's it going then, Brick? Okay, is it?'

And a moment or so later, to the sound of flushing water, the door would open and Bricky would appear, doing up the buckle of the thick leather belt at his waist, a slow smile creasing his face, and aiming a dummy punch at one of his mates, saying something like: 'The first for the day, you bastards.' And one of the others would say: 'And not the last on Shewfik's cooking.' And then they would all laugh and begin to leave. And when you sneaked a sidelong glance at them, inevitably you found them looking at you. Whereupon their faces would go blank and surly. And someone would mutter: 'Wanker' or 'Bloody poofter'. And Bricky, pausing just long enough to scowl in the mirror and rake a heavy paw downwards through his matted blonde hair, would lead the way out; the last of the three slamming the door shut, leaving it shuddering on its hinges.

During the first few days of our quarantine, at a time when I was still trying to be polite, I had a few conversations with Bricky and the boys, strolling up to that end of the verandah; establishing contact, verbal trinkets (and tea-bags) held out in front of me, as it were. And in that way I found out something about them.

I have called them transport drivers but, more accurately, that is what they hoped to be. They were country boys from New South Wales looking for a change of surroundings. They had heard that there was an Australian-owned transport company operating passenger coaches between Haifa, Beirut and Palmyra. For some reason or other this had sparked their imagination. They were going there to get jobs. That was the basic plan. Whether they had arranged anything in advance or simply expected to obtain jobs on the spot I could never discover. It was practically impossible to prise any worthwhile information out of them.

They must have been in their early thirties, but they were like three muscular schoolboys occupying one corner of the playground. Whenever one approached they would loll back in their chairs with a half smile as if, having shared some private joke, they were suppressing their mirth in the presence of a stranger for the sake of a good laugh later. And sometimes, Bricky, with slow, indolent movements, would get up and slouch into a sitting position on the verandah rail, feeling in trouser pockets for cigarettes, appraising the visitor with derisive blue eyes.

His thatch of blonde hair was never combed. It looked as though he might have raked a toast-rack through it first thing on rising but otherwise left it alone; the hair at the nape jutting out unashamedly over his open-necked collar. And when his cigarette was lit up his free hand descended instinctively to the hip, one thumb hooked into his belt, the brawny arm slackly supported in this way, and his belly pushed out comfortably.

All questions, all attempts to draw him into conversation were dealt with in the same manner. 'Is that right?' he would say, simulating interest. And there would be a stifled chortle from his companions. 'Check that.' And there would be a wink and a nod around the group and, perhaps, the slapping of a thigh. 'For sure.' And again the answer would bear no particular relation to the question put. But, as though they were speaking in some private shorthand of their own, the group would detect some hidden meaning in the reply and guffaw, one of the others spilling some liquor into a glass, Bricky drawing on his cigarette.

I never knew what to make of them. They had an ability to cheapen every conversation. They made the minimum effort required. Any approach, friendly or otherwise, was always treated as if it was the approach of a door-to-door salesman; the words listened to with patience, tolerance — but, in the final analysis, with contempt. There was nothing which delighted them. Nothing which excited their curiosity. Nothing which surprised them. And one never turned away from them without being conscious of a faint snigger — before they went back to their card game.

I soon gave up the attempt to establish a relationship. But there they would be, day after day, lounging about in the vicinity of their table. And as the day wore on and they became drunker, they would often become playful. I remember one afternoon I was in my room working on some translation when I heard the sound of splintering glass. Walking out on to the verandah, as one or two of the other passengers did, we found that the three drivers were standing at their end of the verandah, leaning over the rail, laughing.

Below, there was a donkey tethered in the shade of one of the outhouses. The three men, swaying on their feet, were stoning the creature with empty glasses. The glasses smashing on to the ground or smacking into the wall of the outhouse

24

and splintering, the donkey, confusedly, backing and retreating, not knowing what was going on.

At that moment, Shewfik Arud, distraught, came running round from the back of the building. It took him a moment to appreciate what was happening but, as soon as he did so, he held up his hands in horror, addressing himself to the verandah above. 'Stop this form of madness,' he cried out. 'Stop this form of madness, at once. Come to your senses.'

'Shewfik, you rotten bastard,' Bricky called out jovially in reply, an empty glass held high in his hand, toasting the proprietor. One of the others lobbed a glass at Shewfik's feet, the glass tinkling into pieces.

'You have no respect for property,' Shewfik screamed wildly, shaking a fist at the verandah.

'Bullshit,' Bricky called back with aplomb. Then turned away from the verandah rail, and together with the other two loitered back to their chairs, slumping down in them, bored by the whole affair.

But surprisingly, there were no repercussions. Shewfik appeared to accept their behaviour, their occasional misdemeanours, with equanimity. They spent a lot of money on drink and, presumably, notwithstanding that they were a negation of all his cherished principles, where money was concerned it was clear that Shewfik was prepared to tolerate some exceptions to the rigorous code of proper conduct which he usually espoused in my presence.

For their part, they always appeared to enjoy his company. Appearing at their end of the verandah with a tray, he was invariably welcomed by a chorus of 'Shewfik!' and there would be jocular references to the size of his daughter's tits. And yet, despite this bonhomie, this air of apparent friendliness, there was something about Bricky and his fellow drivers which made me uneasy from the first. Behind those frank, leisurely smiling eyes, there seemed to be some element of unconcern, of brutal indifference, something capable of festering and turning sour.

And therefore, it did not really surprise me when, one night, as I came into the room downstairs where a warped old piece of board had been set up on boxes for table-tennis, that Bricky, passing one of the bats over to me said, quite directly, not intending to be humorous, not with rancour, but in the matter-of-fact tone one would use to express an opinion about

25

the weather, leaving it entirely up to the listener as to whether he made use of the information or not: 'Shewfik Arud is a cunt'.

I didn't think much of it at the time. Indeed, at the time, I can distinctly remember that I was concentrating not on his words but on his actions. Upon passing bat and ball over to a new player, Bricky had a peculiar habit, almost a ritual by which he signified his retirement from the game, of sinking one of his thick thumbs into the ball so that one was left holding a dead, indented sphere which went 'clunk' when it was dropped on the table, so that the oncoming players were obliged to scrounge round and find a new ball.

Once, angered by his lack of consideration, rather, his calculated act of annoyance, trying not to be provocative about the whole thing, assuming, for the sake of the argument, that there might be some reason for it, I put the question to him squarely — man to man — as to why he squashed the ping pong balls the way he did. As usual there was a bit of a nod and a wink amongst the group, and no clear reply. All he said was: 'Don't shit me.' And one of the others said: 'That's right.'

And the same thing happened on this occasion. I was left holding a useless ball while Bricky and his friends passed out of the room. Accordingly, although I usually try to avoid using physiological metaphors, and vaginal metaphors in particular (but by then my own standards of conduct had slipped), I couldn't help thinking that 'cunt' was a word which could be usefully employed to describe at least one person on the premises and his name wasn't Shewfik Arud.

But that is beside the point. What is more to the point is this. Although the significance of Bricky's comment wasn't clear to me at the time, I have often wondered whether, rather than being simply a passing aside by a foul-mouthed larrikin, it may not have been capable of another interpretation. I certainly made no mention of this whatsoever at the Official Inquiry which brought our quarantine to an end, but I have always wondered whether Bricky's remark was, perhaps, the forthright statement of a mercenary; an expression of contempt by one who, even though prepared to carry out his principal's will and, by the nature of his profession, scarcely entitled to moralize about the actions of others, nonetheless has a private revulsion for those who send him forth on rotten jobs.

Chapter 4

There is one part of my opening entry in Borthwick which I completely forgot to deal with. The word: 'Leeches'. It is odd that it should have slipped my mind because of all the events which took place on the first day, my conversation about the leeches is the one which troubles me most. It arose in this way.

Having lodged my cable with Shewfik Arud, I had little to do. The group of men on the front verandah were silent and moody; smoking their cigarettes, making desultory conversation, as mystified by what had happened as everybody else. I soon left them.

As we hadn't yet been allocated rooms there was nowhere in particular to go; other than to sit brooding in one of the armchairs in the foyer. But that was not really an enjoyable pastime, especially in the heat. All of the chairs were dumpy and unattractive. Past their prime. And when you sat down in one it was like being embraced by an elephant. The chair would give a quick pleasurable gasp and its two stumpy arms would swoon inwards. One sensed the presence of a rough hide and a baggy armpit. And then there would be the difficulty of extricating yourself from the situation. As you struggled out of the seat there would be a murmur of reproach, a sad popping of springs, and a hint of ruination.

I felt a certain sympathy for these old armchairs scattered about the foyer, squatting on their haunches, waiting for an encounter. But after the first day or so, I seldom went so far as to actually sit in them. Indeed, in one of my early conversations with Bricky and his friends, the point was made for my benefit that the lumpy and uneven appearance of the chairs was due to their having been stuffed with discarded bandages.

Naturally, I was not prepared to accept such an outrageous fiction. But it did colour my attitude to the chairs. Every time

27

I passed them I was reminded that this was a Quarantine Station, and a vision came quickly to mind of a procession of passengers from disease-ridden ships staggering into this same foyer and slumping into the nearest chair. Perhaps, desirous of concealing their true condition from the Doctor, furtively burying an aged sticking-plaster in a hidden crevice so as to replace it with something more presentable.

No, from the first glance, and leaving all unpleasant fantasies aside, it was clear that to remain seated in the foyer in the middle of a sultry day was not an inviting prospect. Thus, I wandered outside again, thinking I might take a walk.

I dawdled down the front steps to the jetty and watched the water slapping against the wooden piles, a thin scum of weed having formed at water level like a rim of dirt around the edge of a bath. The water itself was murky, almost mud-coloured.

The Quarantine Station stood on the tip of a slight promontory close to where the canal entered the main lake. On one side of the promontory were the waters of the lake where the steamer was anchored. On the other, a shallow bay, or inlet, almost like an estuary, which petered out into mud flats, reeds, and a ragged oasis of palm trees. In the shadow of the trees, I could just make out some rough shanties and boats, pulled up from the shore, lying on their sides.

On one of the dhows in the bay itself, two Arabs in dark robes were silently working away at the sail of their boat, the lowered boom, just visible above the hull's edge, slumped dejectedly downwards, resting on their knees.

Further out, three barges were moored side by side; black, flat-bottomed craft with a single, short funnel amidships. On the one nearest to shore, two men were rigging up a canvas awning across the deck. Faintly, across the water, I could hear them talking to each other; the voices distant, unintelligible, the guttural interchanges sporadic — unworldly; the two men entirely concerned with their own affairs; their voices coming and going softly, in matter-of-fact tones, but unreal, like the voices from the outside world a patient in a sick-room hears as he returns to consciousness after a short, mid-afternoon sleep. Disembodied, alien voices outside his window or in the corridor, going about their own business.

No one else was to be seen. Behind me, the sombre Quarantine Station, with its wide verandahs and heavy, shuttered windows; a building which gave an impression of being in need of repair although it was difficult to identify precisely what was wrong with it. The verandahs seemed to be sagging but it was hard to pinpoint exactly where they were out of alignment. Flues and piping had been fastened to the walls in various places; sometimes disappearing abruptly into a window, sometimes struggling up to roof-level. There were two pot-bellied water tanks at one side of the building, standing on iron stilts.

I left the jetty, paused briefly to peer into the blockhouse half-way up the slope — which a notice in four languages, the lettering faded, told me was a clinic used for medical inspections — and reached the parapet enclosing the Quarantine Station. I made for the gateway out of the enclosure and found myself on a dusty road leading towards the escarpment behind the Station.

As far as I could see there was no one else out of doors at all. Heaps of rock and sand had been pushed back from the edge of the road, small growths of cactus and wiry grass binding the rocks together in places. Soon, my shirt was clinging to my back. And the flies were a constant irritation. After a walk of a few hundred yards, I reached a point where a thin track turned off the road and mounted the hillside to the crest of the escarpment. The road continued on, winding round the base, and further on, narrowing to a corridor between boulders on the lower slopes of the escarpment and the reeded shore of the bay.

I took the track. It was hard going; the pathway only half formed, obstructed by chunky outcrops of rock in places, the crumbling surfaces making it difficult to obtain a firm foothold, loose stones clattering downwards as I climbed. By the time I reached the top I was exhausted. I felt drugged, weighed down by the heat, and a splinter of stone had found its way into one of my shoes, making me limp.

Struggling over the brow of the hill, I saw that someone else had come to the lookout ahead of me. But without waiting to speak to him or study the view below, I collapsed on to the nearest suitable rock and sat there panting, cursing the flies, the troublesome path, my feet; wishing that I hadn't come. I loosened my shirt collar and attempted to fan myself with the brim of my hat; wondering whether I should take off my tie, although finally I decided not to. I could see that already the bottoms of my white trousers had become grimy with dust and I knew that once I began fingering my collar, more than likely I should have finger-marks all over the limp cloth. So I sat there, trying to ignore the feeling of suffocation, trying to compose myself.

The other visitor to the hilltop didn't notice me at first. Without feeling much enthusiasm, I registered the fact that it was Burgess. To that moment, apart from nodding to him now and again while strolling on the deck, I hadn't had a great deal to do with Burgess. He had always seemed a remote figure; austere, upright at the bridge table, or moving purposefully about the ship organizing rosters for shuttlecock. I understood that he was on his way home from India on leave. Although we never discussed it, I presumed a regimental or civil service background. He was always in control of himself. He had an air of authority. After nodding to Burgess you always felt as though you had just read the editorials of at least two morning papers.

Nodding-wise, he always brought out the best in me. Meeting Burgess on the deck, my nods were always crisper, more to the point; conveying the impression that one was earnest, up-to-date, on one's way to a prearranged appointment, a young man on the move. A craven subterfuge, perhaps, but probably the only effective way of avoiding a conversation; I always had the feeling that it would be unwise to stop and talk to Burgess. It was almost certain to emerge in the course of the exchange that one was a fool. That it wasn't the editorials one should have been reading but the sports page. That there was a test match being played somewhere. Tailenders were making a mess of it. The pitch was crumbling on the first day.

Not that one could be expected to know that sort of thing on board a ship. But certainly, after nodding to Burgess, if there was a barometer handy, I usually glanced at it so as to be prepared. 'Have you read the barometer?' I would be able to say to him casually, in case I was forced into conversation, my brow furrowed with concern. I then imagined that he would take me by the arm and the conversation, commenced in undertones, would proceed, step by step, to compasses, theodolites, and some anecdote about an old schoolfriend who was now a surveyor in Macao, and then to the perilous state of the economy in Singapore.

That was the effect Burgess had on me. The look of the man was solid, dependable. Usually dressed immaculately in whites, the deep tan of his face, the prominent eyebrows and grey, penetrating, almost wolfish eyes, all created the impression of a man who was not easily flustered. A serious-minded chap. A man given to asking searching questions; skilled at detecting evasive replies. I avoided him like the plague.

At that time, not being able to read barometers, I didn't really feel that my ploy would stand up to any kind of reasonable scrutiny. As I have said, I took the basic precaution of making sure that the thing was actually working. But that was not because I intended to make any use of the figures beneath the pointer. But rather, because I knew my luck. Even then, I knew from experience, that it was inevitably my fate to tap the glass with an inquisitive finger and initiate a solemn conversation about barometer readings only to find that everyone on board knew it hadn't been working for days.

And cricket likewise. Now and again, standing up to a bar, or sharing a taxi, in order to keep up some semblance of conversation, one is often obliged to admit to, or even declare, a consuming passion for cricket. But in such circumstances, one is almost invariably found out. Feigning interest, one asks after the latest score. The only reaction is an incredulous silence. It is common knowledge that the test has been washed out. Or everyone knows that the pitch was hacked to pieces overnight by vandals in one of the most scandalous episodes in years. There is always something.

So what was I to think, finding Burgess alone on the hilltop, alone up there, one foot on a rock, staring at the Quarantine Station below, brooding?

I was puffed out. He might offer help. But I didn't want any. I didn't want any favours from him. Quite apart from his demeanour there was something about the man I didn't take to. When we went ashore at Aden, I found myself sitting across the aisle from him on the coach taking us into Crater City. It was a slow, cumbersome coach and, in the course of the journey, it came to a halt outside a cemetery to make way for a funeral procession.

Most of the passengers stopped their conversations and watched the mourners pass. Burgess went on talking to the man in the seat next to him, Mr Horwood, a city councillor from Sydney. Mr Horwood, in a dogged, but amiable way, was always ready to strike up a conversation. Neither of them bothered to look at what was happening outside. During a lull in the conversation, Mr Horwood, rummaging in his pockets unsuccessfully, asked Burgess for a cigarette.

'Why not?' Burgess said. 'People are always cadging off me.' And he held his own packet out, shaking one free.

His manner, as he spoke, was polite, but distant — as though he was making the remark for his own benefit, storing up the information. People are always cadging off me. It made me look twice at him. It seemed such an ugly, contemptuous way of referring to the request. And all the time his face remaining dispassionate and apparently friendly, Mr Horwood not the least bit concerned by the comment. But it made me wonder about Burgess, sitting there in the stationary bus, watching the mourners in their dark robes jostling past the windows, looking down into their dark weatherbeaten faces, the press of people moving along the dusty thorough- fare so thick, so congested, that in addition to the slow murmur of cymbals and drums which accompanied the throng's progress, there was the slithering sound of shoulders and costumes, the ceremonial trappings, rubbing against the coach, the coach being rocked intermittently, the crowd edging forward into the fragmented acres, the mosaic of the vast cemetery set opposite us, the avenues, the graves, the white stones and heaps of debris, open to the sun like cracks on the floor of an old kiln, the palm trees on the far perimeter, their feathered heads, lifeless, providing no shade under the pale, shimmering sky, the people spreading out into the avenues, encompassing the principal mourners, cymbals and the sad chanting gradually receding, leaving our coach stand- ing there on the roadside in the settling dust, some of the pas- sengers with cameras at the windows, and Burgess and Mr Horwood not looking at anything, Mr Horwood smoking his cigarette, the two of them still talking.

Perhaps it was just a slip of the tongue, his comment being simply an inadvertent choice of words; the sort of slip which could not reasonably be held against the man. Perhaps. But it coloured my attitude towards him; the incident, the coldness of his voice. I didn't want any favours, not from him.

'Knocked out by it, then?' Burgess asked; noticing me, he had come across to where I was sitting. His voice calm, con- cerned. And he stood beside me, repeating his inquiry softly, one hand nonchalantly rattling some coins together in his trouser pocket, his expression sympathetic. 'You look quite knocked out by it. Absolutely whacked. If that's not putting it too strongly.'

'That's not putting it too strongly,' I replied, attempting a chuckling rejoinder, trying to sound cheerful about the whole thing, suppressing my irritation at his presence, using the sort of hearty tone I imagined he was accustomed to; the kind of subalternese one falls into the habit of using at twenty-one years of age, mostly in the presence of ex-headmasters or prospective employers. 'Absolutely whacked beyond question.'

Savagely, I pulled off my shoe, hoping to locate the aggravating splinter which lay somewhere within. 'It's the heat,' I added, looking up. 'The heat is absolutely killing.'

'Yes,' he said reflectively. 'The heat. It will be a problem.'

He stopped rattling the coins in his pocket and turned his attention towards the sombre steamer anchored in the lake below. Somewhere on board, one of the crew was idly exercising a concertina. The faint, broken-down whining of the instrument could be heard drifting across the placid water, softly, invisibly. The ship motionless. The scene below utterly still. No other traffic in sight. On the far side of the lake, there was nothing but a low, continuous hump of desert set against the pale, heat-hazed sky, appearing as a dark, undulating, featureless barrier. Directly beneath us, one could see the Quarantine Station and the road winding out of the enclosure along the ragged banks of the inlet, past the escarpment, reappearing near the encampment of trees at the base of the inlet, then connecting up with a railway track and following the canal towards the distant city; a tiny outcrop on the horizon almost like a mirage.

Burgess flicked some flies away from his eyes and turned back to me. 'The heat will be a problem. There's no doubt about that.'

'You may be used to it,' I said, making a show of grumbling 'But I find difficulty coping. You walk ten yards and finish up feeling like a sponge. And in any event there's nowhere to go.'

Saying that, I took my first good look at the desert stretching away from the escarpment. It was certainly inhospitable; the uneven terrain, glittering with stones in places, spread outwards, an expanse of camel-thorn and sand.

'We mustn't complain,' Burgess said. Now, he was watching me closely. 'The important thing is to get out of here as soon as possible. And to do that, some of us will have to keep an eye on things.'

I looked up at him, curiously. 'What sort of things?'

'Contacting the authorities. Making sure we get proper medical attention. Find out exactly what's going on. All the usual things.'

'Yes,' I agreed. 'I expect you're right.'

'I know I am. I've been through this sort of thing before. Be polite if you have to but let them know from the start that you won't be pushed around. Which means we've got to act as a group.'

'Present a united front,' I said, attempting to round off the discussion; a discussion which would obviously sprawl in all directions unless brought to the point by a summary with a ring of determination in it. I put my hat back on my head, and tugged down the brim.

'Exactly.' I couldn't help noticing that my words, rather than tying up all the loose ends, appeared to have excited him. 'That's exactly it. A united front. My own thought exactly. All of us, working together. Making the proper approaches. Maintaining discipline. Doing the thing properly.'

There was something vaguely disturbing about the way he used the word 'discipline'. To me, the word 'discipline' has always been in the same category as the word 'diet'; words to be held in high esteem, flourished about the place like manifestos but, in the final analysis, not to be taken seriously. But this man did appear to be serious. He had put the word down in front of me, discreetly, politely, true, but like a pair of shoes for polishing nonetheless.

'Definitely,' I said. 'Definitely. But, of course, the medical people will probably want us to take things quietly.'

'See those boys down there,' Burgess said, interrupting, ignoring my reply, pointing over my shoulder.

I twisted round. Behind me, the hillside tumbled steeply downwards for a few hundred feet of jagged rock outcrops to meet the road out of the Quarantine Station; the slope dissipating into the marshy flats which constituted the upper reaches of the inlet. Just below the road, in amongst the swamp reeds, I could just see two boys in white robes crouching at the edge of a pool of water. They were staring intently into the water. It was difficult to see what they were doing.

34

'What about them?'

'They're catching leeches. I was watching them before I came up here.'

'Oh,' I said, without a great deal of enthusiasm and, having massaged my sore foot, began untying the laces of the shoe I had removed.

'Do you know how to catch leeches?'

'Leeches?'

'Yes. Water leeches. About that size.' Now, he was speaking eagerly. He demonstrated size by creating a short gap between thumb and forefinger.

I put my shoe back on. 'I don't know much about them,' I said, wondering what was coming next. 'Leeches aren't my line, really.'

'There used to be a lake near my home and my brother and I would go down there with a kerosene can. So did some of our friends. What you did was to put your feet into the shallow water. There they'd be, your feet, like white fish just below the surface. Then you would see the black slug come easing itself on to your skin. And as soon as you knew you had it caught, you took your foot out of the water and peeled it off. The leech. Using some spirits if you had to. You could get a drumful in a morning and sell them to the apothecary for a shilling. They still used leeches then. The apothecaries sold them to horse-dealers. For draining fluid out of bruises and so on. And now they're doing it here. Two boys. Two brothers probably.'

He stopped abruptly, having raised a hand to his chin and tapping his lips with two fingers, as if he was rebuking his mouth, conscious that too much had been said. But at the same time, looking at me expectantly as if waiting on me to respond to his anecdote in some way, to declare an affinity, perhaps; to reveal some boyhood secret of my own; a suggestion in his manner, an assumption, that all of this was relevant to what we had been talking out before.

'Well. Well,' I said heartily, but finding it difficult to conceal my revulsion. 'So that's what they're up to down there.' I indicated my spectacles and smiled confidentially. 'Bit difficult for a chap like me to see the fine print.'

But he wasn't to be put off so easily. He took my elbow, urging me to my feet. And flapped a hand at the inlet. 'Working at something side by side. Do you see the point?'

I stood up and had another look down the hillside. All I

could see was the outline of the two small figures crouching at the water's edge. But it was impossible to see exactly what they were doing. 'I can see the point but not the leeches,' I said, peevishly. My 'absolutely whacked' and 'cheerio' type voice was obviously having no effect. There was no reciprocation. There were no 'cheerios' forthcoming from the other side. Absolutely none. The conversation looked as though it would wander on. It was time to make a stand. 'I'm sorry,' I said firmly. 'I can't see any leeches.'

Burgess walked away from me to the other side of the small clearing which comprised the vantage point. He put one foot on a rock and stared out towards the canal. But it was obvious he was thinking of something else. It was so apparent that he was utterly immersed in his own thoughts that I was almost on the point of sneaking away, having seen all that I wanted to see.

I was surprised at his vehemence, his sudden outburst of excitement, or tension, whichever it was. He had always seemed such a dispassionate person. But thinking about the matter, his sense of responsibility, his sudden display of emotion, gradually, my feelings towards him became more charitable. After all, if he could see leeches, then, perhaps there were leeches. Who cared either way? I once had a friend who thought Africa looked like a foetus attached to the navel of Europe. Oscar Wilde thought Australia looked like a packing case.

Burgess came back from the far side of the vantage point and spoke again.

'No one is sure why we've been landed here, correct?'

'That's so,' I replied cautiously.

'And most of us want to get out of here as soon as possible?'

'Correct.'

'There's only one way to do that,' Burgess said. 'By appointing a spokesman to make the appropriate representations. The passengers will have to meet and elect a spokesman. It's going to be a waiting game. And we'll need patience. Internal discipline. Otherwise the whole thing will fall apart. I've seen it happen before.'

As he mapped out this strategy, as all these thoughts came together in his mind, his voice took on a firmer note. The remote quality I have spoken of became more pronounced. He was obviously excited by the prospect of negotiations, skil-

36

fully executed strategies, the ultimate success. I myself was more interested in the odd juxtaposition of ideas which made up his line of reasoning. But before I could reflect on the matter at greater length, he put a question to me directly.

'Would you be prepared to act as spokesman?'

I was staggered by the thought. 'No, not me,' I said quickly; protesting. 'I couldn't take it on. It isn't my line.' I rapidly acquainted him with the essentials of my position. I had completed a first degree in Melbourne and was about to embark upon a post-graduate course in the UK. I had a lot of work to do before term started. I was still studying. I was still trying to improve my Latin, my powers of translation. I couldn't afford the time.

'But you're a legal man?'

'Well, not exactly.' Again, I tried to put the matter in perspective; that although I had studied law, apart from a month or so in a solicitor's office, I had no practical experience. I was really no more than a student and, even then, my chosen speciality was Jurisprudence.

But he would hear none of it. 'We shall need men with balance,' he said.

'What about yourself?' I asked, seeing a way out of the dilemma. 'Would you be prepared to represent us?'

'I have had some experience of this kind of thing,' he admitted, speaking slowly, as if voicing his thoughts aloud. 'But whoever is appointed should have a committee behind him. Otherwise there's dissatisfaction.'

'That sounds like a good idea,' I said, enthusiastically, recognizing that an escape route had opened up in front of me. 'A committee. It adds weight.'

I took out a handkerchief and mopped my brow. It was not easy talking to Burgess. He seemed to be a man of very fixed ideas. On top of that, although I myself couldn't see the relevance, his story about the leeches — an anecdote which didn't appeal to me in the least — in some way or other seemed to be central to his thoughts. It was fairly obvious to me that if he canvassed support from the other passengers on the basis of that gruesome little parable, there was every chance that if a poll was held he would be defeated in the first ballot.

But all this was of little concern to me. There was only a month and a half to go before term started and, quarantine or no quarantine, I simply had to buckle down to my study of the *Institutes*; otherwise I would not even be admitted to the course. 'Shall we get back to the Station?' I asked, waving a hand towards the buildings on the peninsula below.

'Will you serve on the committee?' Burgess asked, halting my movement towards the track with a quick motion of his hand.

'I suppose so.' I shook myself free of him irritably. 'If I must. But for heaven's sake, let's start back.'

As we started down, watching our step on the narrow track zig-zagging downwards from the crest of the hill towards the road, he called out from behind me. 'On that basis I'll call a meeting. Tomorrow morning. After I've found out what I can from the Doctor.'

I made no answer because it was hard going. Trudging upwards was tiresome but my feet had been reasonably steady. Descending was more difficult, dangerous — the track precariously close to the edge of the jagged escarpment tumbling down to the road below and the swamp flats of the inlet. It would be easy to fall, one kept taking small scampering steps, feet sliding on the loose stones underfoot, and it was an effort to stop oneself breaking into a reckless trot or skidding off the track on to the rocky outcrop below. Soon, I was feeling weak at the knees.

But when we reached the road and began walking back towards the Station, I thought about the matter further. Burgess was odd; there was no doubt about that. On the other hand, he did seem to know what he was about. And presumably it would be wise to set up some kind of a steering committee, otherwise we might never get out of the place. It couldn't do any harm and it might do some good. That was how I saw it. And at least it would give people like Burgess something to get their teeth into. Better than sitting round hearing his life story if a mood of boredom set in; especially after having heard the instalment about the leeches. No, it was probably best to get Burgess busy on organizing a steering committee.

Accordingly, continuing our conversation, I asked Burgess what he knew about the Doctor. What sort of a man was he? Was he competent? All he could tell me, and I gathered that the information had been pieced together from one of the Ship's Officers and Shewfik Arud, was that the Quarantine

Station was regarded as an adjunct of the central administration and that in a few hours' time we were to be examined by a doctor who was coming out to the Station for that purpose.

By this time, we had nearly reached the shelter of the high verandah surrounding the Quarantine Station. To get out of the glare was the thought uppermost in my mind. But before I could take the last few steps that would take me into the shade, Burgess placed a restraining hand on my shoulder.

'Let me put it to you this way,' he said. 'We must act. There's no question about it. And clearly the first step is to call a meeting. But we must find out exactly why we are being detained beforehand. If you like, I'll see what I can do about that. I shall certainly be having a word with the Doctor.'

He went on talking, almost to himself. Later, I regretted that I did not listen more carefully to what he said. After all, in a general sort of way, he had recruited me to his cause. It was therefore desirable, having regard to my reservations about him, that I should keep myself abreast of his plans at all times. But at that moment, just as he was beginning to tell me what he intended to do, at that very important moment, my attention was distracted from what he was saying by the appearance of Mrs Walker and her daughter, Isobel, at the front entrance to the building.

They stood in the doorway, apparently trying to make up their minds whether to go out of doors for a walk. Mrs Walker had a parasol with her which she was offering to her daughter. But Isobel, with a vague gesture of one hand, a diffident, almost disinterested motion of the hand that was characteristic of her, declined the offer, pushing the parasol away as though it was something of little concern to her; saying something to her mother as she did so.

They were an attractive couple and such a welcome sight; the two women standing there in the doorway, so poised, and in the circumstances, bearing in mind the haste with which we had left the ship, looking so fashionable — both of them in pale cotton dresses, Mrs Walker with a wide-brimmed hat and a thin scarf at her neck.

But although at that distance the disparity between their ages was not evident, Mrs Walker having an exceedingly trim and well-presented figure for a woman approaching middle-age, naturally, my attention was drawn towards Isobel; her languid pose, her lustrous brown hair falling to her shoulders, in every way her appearance, as usual, recommending itself to me so forcibly as to make any comparison between the two women insidious and quite unreal. To me, Isobel was a tantalizing creature, embodying the fascination of womanhood to perfection. I had been fortunate enough to spend some time in her company on board ship. Surprisingly enough, in a group, or even if we happened to find ourselves alone, I always found myself quite relaxed in her presence, never tongue-tied or at a loss for words, she herself never saying much, but always taking in what was being said, smiling prettily on occasions.

Yet, seeing her from a distance, I was always possessed by something like a sense of awe. At that time, at that early stage of our relationship, I could find no fault in her whatsoever. I would readily admit that many men would not have found her so attractive; not sufficiently vivacious to be of interest. Certainly, she made no effort to present herself in such a way as to be singled out for attention. But it was this passive quality, this air of biding her time, combined with her youth, her fleeting moments of gaiety, which, as far as I was concerned, made her so intriguing.

So striking was my regard for her at that stage, watching her standing there in the doorway with her mother, still sheltered from the fierce glare by the verandah's shadow, I was inclined to run forward so as to urge her myself not to go into the sun without protection, even for only a brief period. But something held me back; some sense of propriety. And in any event, at that moment, just as they were about to turn away from the door, they noticed me, so that I was compelled to wave hastily; Isobel rewarding me with a quick flutter of her gloved hand, Mrs Walker doing no more than acknowledging my presence with a small inclination of her unopened parasol. Then they both withdrew out of sight, returning to the foyer.

As always happened after I had had any form of communication with Isobel, I was immediately conscious of a sense of well-being, a feeling of elation; a feeling which, I might add, was inevitably followed by a pang of disappointment, a sense of restlessness, dissatisfaction; a recognition that I had frittered away an opportunity. Frittering away opportunities, I often reflected in such moments, seemed to be what I was best at. And regrettably, it is a talent which can never be rewarded. To qualify for the trophy, you must, almost by definition, be the sort of person who would break a leg on the night of the presentation. And on this occasion, with Burgess beside me, still talking, still outlining his plans, crackling the blueprints, there was not much available in the way of commiseration.

At a later time, it became a matter of controversy as to whether Burgess had fully acquainted me with his plans, whether I had backed him from the start, and even Isobel herself made some wild accusations, saying that she had seen the two of us conspiring immediately after our arrival at the Station, but I am able to say quite definitely, having searched my conscience, that even if Burgess did tell me exactly what he intended to do, the sort of punishment he proposed for anyone who stood in his way, I cannot recall him confiding in me. My thoughts were elsewhere. By the time I turned back to him, Burgess, this nagging Praetorian, wishing to shake him off without further delay, to be free of him, to get indoors and talk to Isobel, he had finished what he was saying. In fact, it was he who closed the discussion; suggesting firmly, but annoyingly, that we should go inside, rather than be standing about in the sun; the sun, as he put it, being likely to affect our senses.

41

Chapter 5

I think of you, my friend, my confidant over many years, quietly working your way through the pages of this manuscript; already puzzled by it, already surprised. On a Sunday morning, perhaps; before breakfast, before the rest of the household has risen — sitting on the verandah of your bungalow in your favourite position, reading quietly at your own pace, glancing at the sea front occasionally for relaxation, watching the early morning swimmers in the surf.

What will you make of it; this memoir — if, indeed, I find the courage within me to put it in your hands? What will you think? Such a far cry from what you expected. And difficult for you to comment on because, unlike my textbooks, there is no structure to it. No beginning and no end. Disorderly. In that way, unlike anything we have worked on together before. And even I am unsure where it is leading or what the truth of the matter is.

I have mentioned Oscar Wilde. In the first few hours of his trial, the master of paradox, the creator of so many verbal fancies, delighted the court with his wit. There was, in the time-honoured words of the reporter, 'laughter in court'. But as the day proceeded, as the questions became bolder, more direct, the evidence of pederasty incontrovertible, the story, a succession of sordid dealings — the mask of flippancy was laid aside and the witness, harassed by his accusers, those who had betrayed him, was, as many saw it, at last forced to speak plainly, was made to face reality.

But is that to say that the original version of events had ceased to exist? The facts remained the same throughout. What changed was the tone of voice. He was forced backwards. Made to answer. Made to describe his companions, the hotel rooms ... But finally, compelled to look inwards, his answer to the allegations against him was not a plea of guilt, nor even any effective denial of the charges, but rather, an eloquent defence of beauty; testimony containing its own kind of truth, words which have survived the factual verdict.

Would you ever betray me? Circulate this manuscript? Pass it around the younger members of the faculty who already regard me as an anachronism; the new breed of lecturers who say that jurisprudence is out of date, a soft option, having less to do with life than probate planning and variable trusts? Would you make me a laughing stock? I could never believe such a thing. You will use your discretion. If the manuscript should be suppressed, then you will guide me.

And so I go on; retrieving the past; remembering that truth may be arrived at not merely by a study of the so-called facts but from the very process of narration. Often, the kind of lies a man tells reveals as much truth as a technical statement of what he saw or did.

For instance, at the Quarantine Station, I can recall that Doctor Magro, who had spent his early career in Sudan, told me the story, well-known amongst the medical profession in the area, of a District Officer in charge of a lonely outpost in the Dinka swamps.

Affected by overwork, fatigue, cafard, any one of those obscure complaints of the total person which seldom receive much attention in the textbooks, he imagined himself conducting a local war against surrounding enemies. He committed his vision to paper, sending periodic despatches to Headquarters. Details of skirmishes, flanking movements, pitched battles, relief of native garrisons, casualty lists and, finally, recommendations for awards; recommendations which were accepted and rendered tangible by the preparation of medals for two native officers who had for some time past been in a state of somnolence; victims of sleeping sickness. But the narrative, comprised of memorandums, certificates and despatches, fantastic in its conception, was not entirely without virtue. Not only was it interesting in itself but it documented symptoms of the author's malady; symptoms which were otherwise invisible.

'Take the case of migraine,' Dr Magro said, on the occasion of our first meeting. 'What are we to do with migraine? Laugh at it? Pretend it isn't there? Are we to tell the patient that when the man sits in front of us suffering? To him, it is the only thing which is real. And yet, there is nothing to touch.

43

Nothing to examine. But we take him at his word nonetheless. We place ourselves in his mind. We enter his world of discomfort. We share his pain. We cannot do otherwise. Surely, you agree?'

Such remarks were characteristic of Dr Magro. There was always a sort of weariness about him. Unlike most doctors, he never pronounced a verdict; stated a conclusion. He always argued the point with himself, and then sought agreement. But in the course of the argument, even when he purported to be speaking of medical matters in which he might reasonably have expected some deference to his opinion, there was seldom any reference to a scientific basis for his opinion. Always a hint of philosophy, an indication that he might well be persuaded by some explanation to the contrary even if it was based only on superstition or fable; as though experience had taught him never to be convinced by his own views.

He had established himself in the small clinic by the landing area and was examining the passengers one by one in the order of registration. He had arrived at nightfall. When it came to my turn — the last of the passengers to leave the main building and go across to the clinic near the parapet — I was immediately conscious of the gloom inside the building; a lantern hung from a rafter at one end of the room, the plank benches around the walls, the cabinets, all in shadow.

But Dr Magro seemed disinclined to light the other lanterns — one hung from each rafter down the length of the room — sitting there at a small wooden table close to the doorway, a stethoscope round his neck, his leather case opened out, a small box of index cards positioned in front of him.

I had pressed him to specify the nature of our complaint but, parrying the question with the guarded, tentative comments which was characteristic of his speech, he had drawn attention to the complexity of human ailments, how unwise it was for a medical practitioner to commit himself to premature judgements, particularly a medical practitioner such as himself who, having been trained at the Kitchener School of Medicine, had spent the greater part of a long career in the Sudan and, in respect of the region's diseases, had seen his preliminary conclusions confounded time and time again.

'Migraine,' he repeated slowly; continuing to speculate about the matter, a note of mockery in his voice. 'A comparatively simple case. Not the sort of thing one could specialize in. Not out here.' He glanced at me, briefly; dark, brooding eyes set beneath greying eyebrows, his brow creased with lines, the skin sallow.

He looked away again, his attention concentrated on an index card which, positioned between his fingertips, he was balancing on the table-top in front of him. 'It is not just a headache. In one sense it is a physical event. But to the sufferer it becomes almost an emotional or symbolic event; an involvement of his entire person. Who knows what the causes are? According to one theory migraine is a physical expression of unconscious hostility against consciously beloved persons.'

A wry smile crossed the Doctor's thin lips. And he removed his fingers from both sides of the card to test its balance; but it fell forward, obliging him to retrieve it. He looked up at me with dark, rueful eyes, pouting his lips briefly to indicate scepticism. 'According to one theory,' he added, continuing to watch me closely, 'it could even result from some simple inner tension such as that. The hostility we feel towards consciously beloved persons.'

He raised his hand in a shrugging gesture. He smiled faintly and let the card fall flat on to the table. 'Who knows?'

Doctor Magro had a tall, stooped figure. He wore a short-sleeved safari jacket open at the neck, and a pair of khaki trousers which, tucked into his boots, resembled jodhpurs although it was obvious they had not been designed as such. His face was deeply lined; pouches of weariness beneath his watchful eyes. Frequently his thin lips creased into a wry, deprecatory smile, accompanied by the slight shrug of the shoulders.

'Every ailment is possessed of its own mystery,' he continued. 'Its own contradictions. Some are more dramatic than others. The patient's condition is frequently misleading. In the case of many tropical diseases, in the weeks following infection, at the very moment when the patient is feeling his best the insidious poison is disseminating itself through his bloodstream. And then the onset of the first symptoms, the realization that all is not well. The body struggles to repel the intruder. Instinctively, the whole body joins together in revolt against the alien presence. And for a time there is a period of unrest. Am I boring you?' He looked up at me again, a glimmer of mockery in his eyes. I brushed aside his question, inviting him to continue.

'But even then there is a contradiction.' His voice ran on

45

smoothly after the pause. 'You will know that often the alien presence causing the disturbance has been introduced into the body for that very purpose, expressly with the intention of setting up a reaction, of creating an immunity. Modern man has, perhaps, accentuated the confusion. How is the body to know which organisms are acting upon it for its own welfare?'

He smiled briefly and replaced the card in his box, turning his attention back to me with hands clasped in front of him, resting on the table.

'And finally,' he said, 'how can we be sure that the immunity so created is not more potent, more damaging than the disease itself?'

'I don't follow,' I said uncertainly, as he left the question in abeyance. 'Aren't people such as yourself skilled in these matters? I would have thought so. It would disappoint me to think otherwise.'

He laughed dryly, shrugging one shoulder. He positioned his elbow on the table, the fingers of that hand gently massaging his scalp. 'What I say can be easily tested. One has only to consider disappointment itself.'

Slowly, his fingers explored his scalp at the hairline. 'Take the case of a talented man who has grown up in some out-of-the-way area. A man of some ability. One whose ambition corresponds to that ability.

'As time progresses, as he carries on his business or his profession, as he becomes acquainted with ideas and broadens his knowledge of the world, there is a short period of time, while his morale is high and his energy undiminished, during which he is the equal of any man. And it becomes obvious to him, having succeeded within the compass of his own small circle, that he must seek out the company of his equals in other countries in order to extend himself to the full.

'But when he seeks to put that plan into force, he finds that the way out is not so easy. On paper, all gates are open. But he is boxed in nonetheless. The horizon can't be reached.

'But the man we are speaking of is not easily put off. He is still young. He is determined. He applies for positions. His applications are refused. He studies harder; undertakes more work so as to broaden his experience. But still there are no doors opened to him. And all the time it is apparent from the gossip he hears, from the letters he gets from overseas, that others who are not conspicuously better qualified than he are getting on, are occupying the positions that he himself has sought.'

Dr Magro closed the lid of the card box and stood up, a strange look of sadness coming into his face. 'Think of such a man,' he said, commencing to pack up his leather case. 'Year after year pushing himself to the limit in the expectation that diligence and ability will be rewarded. Working in outlandish areas. And while as at first he sent off his forms of application eagerly, always hoping for the best; indeed, grievously disappointed on the receipt of every unfavourable reply, determined to try harder, emotionally involved with his own fate as a man should be, nonetheless you must appreciate that a time comes when such a man becomes adjusted to the continuing fact of disappointment, when he accepts the inevitability of disappointment even before his forms are posted. Perhaps, having resigned himself to the likelihood of failure, something of that tone creeps into his correspondence, possibly to the prejudice of his case.

'And such a man, although continuing to do his job faithfully, will begin to spend more time with his friends. The family he has neglected for the sake of his ambition embraces him with special warmth, sensing his need of them. And that, of itself, in addition to all else, accentuates the doubts which are gradually building up in him as to where his future lies. He cannot help but be conscious that those around him, although sympathetic, are becoming impatient; asking themselves, even if never out loud, perhaps he is just an ordinary man after all; an ambitious man but an ordinary man. And the man we are speaking of, outwardly receiving all the encouragement he could hope for from those around him, nonetheless, sees such questions in their eyes.

'Thinking back on the life of such a man, even his best friend, his wife even, would have difficulty picking out exactly at what point he changed his ways. They would scarcely remember when exactly his two drinks after work became three, or when his acquaintances, even those likely to be sympathetic to his cause, asked whether he had obtained the position he wanted, when exactly he began responding with facetious asides, uttered so wittily that only the very closest to him would have any chance of detecting the splinter of cynicism contrary to his true nature.'

Dr Magro paused, studying the contents of his bag, and then

47

looked across at me. 'A time will come when those who see that man daily, and even his closest friends, will believe that he has given up all thought of extending himself, that his ambition has been put aside for the sake of ordinary things; the things most men desire — family, reasonable surroundings, respect from those who know him well, and even as to those he has clashed with over the years, at least, tolerance.

'His friends will believe that he has become content within himself. That he is no longer restless. That he sees himself as part of a community. If asked, they would say: "He has accepted his lot. He is like ourselves. Now he is a mature man."

'And even the man himself, although continuing to harbour his pretensions, his private conceit — although not describing it as such — if it was his custom to think in such terms would say, saying the words to himself privately, because only in private can the words be uttered with the full measure of bitterness they warrant, a bitterness which must now be kept locked up inside himself entirely, because he appreciates that even to those who love him he is no longer young, no longer rich with potential, no longer rendered attractive by his enthusiasms: "I have become accustomed to disappointment. I am no longer hurt by it. Can't be touched by it. I am immune." '

Dr Magro closed his bag, giving a small shrug. 'And there it is. Of all afflictions, the final and most fascinating of all. The immunity which is worse than the initial disease. Complicated, in the case I have described, in that the sickness takes hold of ·the personality; becomes a corruption of the entire man. And is therefore invisible. There is nothing to compare him with except his earlier self. All other comparisons fail, and that earlier self no longer exists. At the very time when the signs of corruption are most evident to God who has seen all, they are most likely to be hidden from that person's fellow man. Thus, we meet a bad-tempered man for the first time. Are we so presumptuous as to say that his health has declined? Surely not. We accept him for what he is. And even those closest to him pass no such judgement. They say simply — this is what he has become. Perhaps it was his nature from the start. Yes, at the very moment when the signs are most apparent, at the very moment of his final deterioration, the fact of his ill-health remains invisible. We speak vaguely of pressure, of problems, of life, perhaps.'

Dr Magro gave a short laugh; gently drumming his fingers on the leather surface of his bag. 'But I mustn't scare you. I mustn't go too deep. That's not my function. All I say to you, my friend, is this. And I say it because I see that you are not like the others. The others! Pah! Sitting opposite me with their questions. What are those tablets and when are we leaving? Receiving my small fictions in reply as some sort of gospel. But you, such a patient young man. And quizzing me about leeches in your first breath as though that was the important thing. I can see that you are capable of receiving answers. And there, immediately, I state the obvious — what would a man such as myself be doing here if I was capable of influencing events? Would you expect to find a first-rate physician in such a place? Clearly, I could not survive without accepting the inevitability of acting on instructions. Is it medicine which saves lives in a place like this? Ingenuity. Compromise. Those are the important remedies; the need for them depending on the circumstances of the case.'

He tapped his bag. 'Naturally, I will be putting in reports. Completing the paperwork. That's what I'm paid for. But no one in their right mind would put much faith in any such reports. Not here.'

Mesmerized by his words, I had completely forgotten to follow through my original line of questioning. But now, as it was apparent he was about to leave, I was jolted into wakefulness.

'This is all very well,' I interjected. 'Philosophy is all very well. But what then? What will happen, in fact? Here, at this station. How long do we remain here? What are we suspected of?'

Dr Magro paused beside the table, one hand on his bag, studying me with his watchful eyes. He smiled faintly. 'I have already said far more than I should. I have already taken up far too much of your time. But let me tell you one final story.

'During the years I was in the Sudan, I sometimes had occasion to visit an isolated region in the Dinka swamps. And in the course of that journey, not often, but a couple of times in the space of fifteen years, I and my party came to the shores of a forbidding stretch of water called Lake No. It was not a lake at all. It was another swamp. The papyrus grass stood higher than a man so that you could never see what was ahead of you. There were no trees. And in places could be

49

seen the wreckages of rusted iron where river-boats had fallen into the snare of the lake's shallows and been abandoned.

'I am not an impulsive man. Nor am I given to vandalism. But strangely, and in an unexpected manner which always took my companions by surprise because it was quite unlike me, on first arriving on the shores of that lake I would point my rifle in the air and fire a rifle shot. A single shot fired wilfully, defiantly; an irrational gesture. And as we stood there watching the birds, the only animal life nearby, come teeming into the air, squawking and cackling, my companions looking at me, perplexed, I always knew that, despite my gesture of affirmation, my fracturing of the lake's smothering silence, nonetheless, at some stage of my visit, I was bound to find myself dragged down knee-deep into glutinous mudflats, the heat, the insects pestering us. Bound to be dragged down and saturated by that foul water, that swamp where every foothold is treacherous, until, saturated, I would begin to feel its water seeping into my bloodstream.

'My friend, you are speaking to a man who has been to the shores of Lake No many times. A man accustomed to refusal. To such a man, the practice of withholding information has become part of his second nature. A man with limited ability, perhaps; but one admirably qualified for a position such as that which I presently occupy.

'Don't be upset by my failure to answer your question or interpret my silence as impoliteness. I am simply acting on instructions although, as it happens, such instructions, which demand reticence, correspond with my own view of what is best. It is best to be silent. It is often best to allow time for the symptoms of a disease to manifest themselves. To manifest themselves so that we know precisely what we are dealing with; to allow time for the body to build up its resistance to the alien presence.

'No, my young friend, don't worry yourself. Be prepared to wait. You will be happier during your quarantine if you regard it merely as an interlude; a period of rest, of quietude; a transient migraine which will soon subside. Be assured that the facilities here are most comfortable.' He waved a hand in the direction of the Station. 'Everything you need is here. And I have every confidence that your tutor, having received your message, will have no objection to your stay.'

'How did you know about my message?' I asked quickly.

Dr Magro paused. 'You mentioned it at the beginning of our interview,' he murmured.

'I can't recall doing so.'

'I assure you that you did.'

'Could it be that Shewfik Arud lodged all messages with the authorities?'

Dr Magro shrugged. 'Perhaps so. But if that is how I came by the information I would have said so.'

'But you describe yourself as a man to whom the habit of refusing to answer questions is congenial. You are acting on instructions.'

'But that is not to say that I am deceitful. My instructions are to say nothing in respect of your confinement. To remind you of something that you yourself said at the beginning of the interview has no bearing on my instructions.' Dr Magro laughed wryly and picked up his bag. It was now so dark in the room that I could scarcely see his face. 'It has been part of my training to remember carefully what a patient says from start to finish. When we are looking at an entire person it is not only his physical symptoms which give us a clue to his condition. I assure you, my friend, that I would not mislead you.'

'But can you give us no estimate of how long we are to stay here,' I said desperately, following him to the door.

'It is not for me to decide,' he said abruptly; becoming tired of the conversation. 'You must accept my word.'

Outside, in the darkness, the air was sultry, oppressive, stifling almost. The horizon on the far side of the lake made a dark, uneven battlement against the faint sunset glow behind. Offshore, the ship rode at anchor, its navigation lights on. The sad, broken-down music of the concertina drifting across the water.

We climbed the steps to the parapet. I followed the Doctor to his car. It was pulled in at an angle to the parapet, overlooking the jetty; a black car with a long pointed bonnet, headlamps set into mudguards like snails' shells curving downwards to wide running-boards.

To open the boot of the car, Dr Magro began unscrewing a handle just above the bumper bar which projected out from the rear of the vehicle on metal struts. He had difficulty with the handle, the handle squeaking and protesting as he turned it. And when he lifted the flap of the boot it was necessary

51

also to lift up the weight of the spare tyre which was attached to it. Casually, he tossed his bag into the cavity. When he closed the lid again, I couldn't help noticing that one of the spokes of the spare tyre was broken, like a knitting needle, vibrating briefly as he slammed the lid down a second time to make sure it was shut.

As I opened the door for the Doctor to climb into the driver's seat, I became aware that he had a passenger; a silent figure seated in the seat beside the driver. In the darkness, and through the small windows of the vehicle, it was impossible to identify him. All I could see was the vague outline of a man's head and a cigarette butt glowing in the dark. And just before the engine stammered its way into existence, then shuddering into full-blooded life, I overheard a murmur of voices, a quick exchange between driver and passenger.

In the poor light and, in any event, having only a moment to consider the matter before the car swung out from the parapet and moved off, it was impossible to tell who the passenger was with any certainty. However, my immediate thought — and to this day I believe it to have been the correct inference — was that Burgess had managed to persuade the Doctor to take him into the city; presumably to make representations to the authorities on our behalf. In other words, Burgess, pursuant to his plan to summon a meeting of the passengers so that a programme of action could be laid down, had set off with a view to finding out something about our position.

As far as I was concerned, this seemed to be an excellent idea. As I saw it, making my way back to the foyer of the Station where the other passengers were assembled, this was good thinking; and certainly eliminated any possibility of my being elected as a spokesman for the group, a prospect which had been troubling me considerably ever since Burgess had first mentioned it. Yes, I thought to myself, when the meeting is convened, Burgess will come before it with an air of authority, knowing all the relevant facts. I myself will be off the hook; able to get on with some serious study.

At the time, I didn't apply my mind at all to what consequences might flow from us putting our trust in one man, putting ourselves in his hands, not necessarily because he was best suited to act as our leader but simply because he had taken the initiative and seemed to know more about the details of our predicament. All I could think of was that I myself would be out of it.

As it turned out, others thought likewise. The majority of those present were quite happy to have Burgess as our spokesman, the Chairman of our Committee. They were equally impressed by his energy; his initiative in getting hold of the basic facts and presenting the picture to us as he saw it.

But in retrospect, I was always puzzled by the fact that he never gave any explanation as to how he came by his information. Certainly, he was never closely questioned about the matter. Most of us, apparently, just assumed he knew what was going on and that, in consequence, he was in a position to make the desired representations on our behalf. And yet, he never mentioned his trip to the city on the evening of Dr Magro's first visit to the Quarantine Station, not to anyone, not at any stage.

And what if Burgess's understanding of the matters in issue, an understanding immediately transmitted to the rest of the passengers, was based on no more than scraps of information fed to him by Dr Magro in the course of a car journey; that all our subsequent actions may have been justified by no more than that?

The possibility is too horrifying to contemplate. I shudder to think of it. Dr Magro — nursing his disappointment, his grievances, concealing his true self; a man, by his own admission, quite capable of fabricating one or two stories simply as a means of putting an end to the conversation. And Burgess — absorbed in his own vision of what was needed to get us out of the mess, not likely to pay any attention to the mood of his informant.

No, it is too horrifying to contemplate. Certainly, such thoughts didn't occur to me on the night. Returning to the foyer, I didn't bother to mention my suspicion to anyone; my suspicion that Burgess had gone into the city with Dr Magro. Firstly, because it was only a suspicion; secondly, because it didn't seem important. And thirdly? Perhaps one could put it this way. Thirdly, because I was relieved to be off the hook myself. I was glad that Burgess was taking a lead in the affair and I didn't want to interfere.

In any event, such thoughts quickly disappeared from my mind when I found that the foyer was a scene of confusion. Shewfik Arud had just allocated beds to his guests. There was an air of frenzy in the room, a babble of voices, a glimpse of chaos. People were swarming about in all directions; milling around the counter, rounding up suitcases, jostling for advantage on the stairs.

A *faszad* was in progress; a *faszad*, that indescribable process of manipulation and intrigue, that gradual constriction of choice, that narrowing down, that vice.

Chapter 6

In glancing through the foregoing draft, it immediately strikes me that the way I have dealt with Dr Magro's passenger may prompt a query. If I was not certain that Burgess was the passenger, how is it that I can accuse him of failing to disclose the fact; a fact which may or may not have been true?

So as to dispose of the point, perhaps I should mention that years later I had an opportunity to question him about the events of that evening. And as a result of such questioning, even though Burgess refused, or declined to give me a direct answer, I came to the conclusion that he had, indeed, been the passenger.

It happened in this way. I was on my way to the Inner Temple to address a gathering of students who would shortly be sitting for their bar exams. It was not long after I had completed my degree. I had published one or two papers on Quantum Meruit and, as you know, I was beginning to make something of a reputation for myself in that field. At the time, I was still looking for a suitable academic appointment. I felt it was politic, from time to time, to scuttle down to London to deliver various learned papers (although basically, it was the same paper and not especially learned at that); a busy itinerary which I intended to flourish at Appointment Boards if the need arose.

It transpired that Burgess had also gone into the paper delivery business. I bumped into him emerging from a stairway on the way into the Inner Temple. We exchanged a few awkward words in the course of which he disclosed that he was now the proprietor of a newsagency at Surbiton. Or rather, was in the course of consolidating his title to it. The vendor had attempted to rescind the contract with the result that Burgess, on his solicitor's advice, had come up to London to take counsel's opinion. He had spent the afternoon in the Inner Temple.

It was certainly an unexpected meeting and not one that I welcomed. During the years which had intervened, I had tried to put the Quarantine Station right out of my mind. I was not at all anxious to revive the episode. Furthermore, I was running late. I simply didn't have time to cool my heels in a laneway off Fleet Street talking to Burgess.

But nonetheless, I have to admit that my curiosity got the better of me. Burgess, a newsagent at Surbiton! Surbiton of all places. I have never been there and, to my discredit, know nothing about it. But ever since I saw the name on a railway station, I have always been fascinated by it. When it comes to names, usually the English, or their ancestors, are to be congratulated for the richness of their vocabulary, the exciting surrealism of their imaginations. One mustn't sound patronizing, but who can remain unaffected by names such as — Elephant and Castle, Clerkenwell, Totteridge and Whetstone. Tooting Bec is one of my favourites. Who could forget Clapham? Which brings to mind Parsons Green and Upminster — and so on. Even Belgravia, conjuring up a vision of something Balkan, something for the Prisoner of Zenda to escape from; there, in the heart of London. Ah, had I been present at the creation of the Monopoly Board, I would have had a few hints for the better ordering of the universe.

But Surbiton! It is neither just nor reasonable that I should malign the place; speaking, as I have already admitted, from a position of complete ignorance. But one has to be frank.

The first time I saw the name, I was standing on the platform at Waterloo (which, incidentally, is another of my favourites), waiting to board a train to Aldershot when I saw a sign go up saying: 'Train to Surbiton'.

Once again, I stress that I have nothing against Surbiton. It is probably a very fine place. But for a moment I felt that I might have blundered on to the set of a Brechtian play. Surbiton! The word has a twentieth-century quality about it. It reeks of miles of nothingness somewhere on the outskirts of a big city anywhere in the world. And now that the academic journals are increasingly stuffed full of intractable data about life, or the lack of it, in suburbia — Surbiton must surely have come into its own.

'At that moment T. S. Eliot was interrupted by a person from Surbiton.' And the vision fled? Or did conversation of half an hour or more ensue as a result of which *The Waste Land* was written?

Surbiton. It is full of reverberation. In the contemporary jargon, it is a word situation with non-specific possibilities. Actually, now that I think of it, it could be a useful device. Suppose I am required to disguise the true location of the events of this manuscript so as to protect identity?

'One dark morning, not long after the train had pulled into the platform at Surbiton, they told us we would have to spend a few days in quarantine. A shop steward with a syringe and a bucket of iodine was waiting for us at the turn-stile . . .'

Shewfik Arud in Surbiton? No, it would never be believed. It is too heavy with symbolism. It sounds too fantastic. Or does it? In fact, it sounds like the sort of place where one of our junior lecturers will finish up: 'Today, the appointment was announced of Dr P. H. Dee as Vice-Chancellor of Surbiton's third university.'

In a mischievous moment, one fabricates such a news item simply to amuse oneself; with no purpose in mind other than the proclamation of a bizarre jest. But suddenly, even before the chance to have a good giggle has been fully realized, one recognizes, instinctively, that this is a statement with a ring of probability about it; that a stark glimpse of the future has been revealed. It's like Orson Welles broadcasting the War of the Worlds. One of our junior lecturers at Surbiton — beard, battle-jacket and all. What a wonderful stunt. Who would possibly believe it?

But immediately a vision comes to mind of switchboards trembling with panic-stricken calls, people taking to their cars in Idaho, bewildered Martians ferrying earthlings to the moon . . . No, one mustn't play with fire. The notion is too much to endure. For my unwarranted sniping at Surbiton I have been justly reprimanded. I withdraw all charges.

Sufficient to say that Burgess, with the assistance of a local solicitor and a London-based barrister, neither of whom would come cheaply, was in the process of consolidating his title to a newsagency there.

At the time, I accepted the news calmly. I gave no outward sign of the turbulence set up within me by the name of his new home. But I was curious as to what had brought him to that plight. After all, on our previous acquaintance, he had been an impressive figure with 'connections' in the Civil Service; just the sort of person to be chairman of a committee; to take control of a 'situation'. But now — Surbiton. Exchanging pleasantries with commuters and winkling teenagers off the racks of hard porn. It was beyond me. I pressed him for an explanation.

He was vague about the reasons for his exile — not that he described it as such — saying only, in a roundabout way, that the story of what happened at the Quarantine Station had crept back to his superiors in India and they, understandably, had not been pleased. Feeling his prospects were diminished, he had decided to wipe the slate clean; to make a fresh start.

It was then, the two of us on the kerbside being jostled by passers-by as we spoke, that I put to him the question which had always bothered me; a question which, notwithstanding my conscious attempt to push the period of our quarantine out of my mind, kept coming back at odd moments.

How, exactly, I phrased the question, I can't recall. But, in essence, I asked him if he had, in fact, accompanied Dr Magro to the city on the first night of the quarantine; because if he had, it was strange, and possibly deceptive, that he never told the rest of us about it, especially bearing in mind that the main ground of his complaint against David Shears was that David had made a similar journey. Had the other passengers known all the facts, they might not have been as severe and the tragedy would have been averted. That was the gist of what I said to him.

All he said in reply to that, saying it doggedly, tucking his leather satchel more firmly under his arm as he spoke, was: 'Anything I did was for the good of all.' And although he didn't answer the question directly, and it is possible that I didn't formulate it very well in any event, I took his failure to expressly deny the matter I had raised, together with my own observation on the first night, as being enough to satisfy me that he had accompanied Dr Magro. But it was clear that he had soothed his conscience over the years by concentrating on the purity of his motives; possibly by also exaggerating the role in the affair played by others.

Thus, I can recall distinctly the last words he said to me that evening in the precincts of the Inner Temple before we went our separate ways, tapping my arm briskly as he spoke. 'You mustn't worry yourself about it,' he said. 'You made the right decision. You had the confidence of every person present.' Then, he turned away from me, abruptly, making his way towards Fleet Street, as if all problems had been solved.

'I'm not the guilty one,' I shouted after him; angered by his insinuation. 'I certainly don't feel guilty.'

But he had gone. People nearby were staring at me, which made me give up the thought of running after him; knowing that I couldn't achieve anything by arguing the point. Although, admittedly, I was annoyed by his bland avoidance of responsibility.

I have never seen him again. I would give a great deal never to have laid eyes on him at all.

But the encounter I have just described is probably meaningless without knowing something about David Shears. How can one begin to describe him? Perhaps, I should begin by mentioning that he was the first man I ever slept with — a man with a marvellous sense of fun. That much I am sure of. Yes, the more I think of it, the more I am persuaded that as an inaugural bed companion, David Shears had much to recommend him. It would be difficult to find a better man for the job. But he had other qualities as well; qualities of a less obvious kind.

He was about my own age. Beneath the surface, the outward appearance of being simply a well-mannered youth with a wholesome zest for life, he was a person of considerable character. And although that was where I first got to know him properly, in bed, having seen something of him on board the ship, my favourable impression of him had already been partly formed before we even arrived at the Quarantine Station.

On board the ship, he was always the picture of good health. Up on deck, usually fitted out in white trousers and a loose shirt, he was always relaxed, and a pleasure to talk to. And when speaking to him, you could not help but be charmed by his blue, straightforward eyes and friendly manner often, when he laughed, sweeping his hair out of his eyes with a casual movement of one hand — perfectly at ease. He seemed to epitomize the best kind of young Englishman of a generation ago. I always imagined him as having a room in his parents' house (which I believe was somewhere near Taunton) crammed full of school blazers and tennis trophies. He had that look about him; the youth who had coped effortlessly with all the obstacles which schools see fit to lay in the path of their students — examinations, athletics, prefectures or whatever — and yet, he had still remained easy-going, unaffected, unruffled. A handsome person. An enjoyable companion.

But nonetheless, for no reason which could be attributed to his outward appearance, in retrospect, I must acknowledge that, from a very early stage, he was the object of deep antipathy; distrust almost. On the part of some, a brooding dissatisfaction with his presence. Where is the fault to be found, I wonder?

I must admit that jaundiced notions of a rather vague kind were in my mind on the occasion of my first encounter with David. I was hunched over a chess set in the poky little room near the Purser's office which, wittily, had been called The Games Room. Indeed, as an extension of the whimsy, it was also known as The Library; this, because there was a bookshelf in one corner with some books in it; from memory, mostly Meredith, Galsworthy and Edgar Wallace.

David was looking for a book. Until then, having only seen him in passing, his resemblance to one of the cricketers appearing in a sketch on the wall of the barber shop I had been using prior to my departure, was the only thing that I had found interesting about him. I had the idea in mind that he would be hearty, that somewhere in his cabin he had a blazer, or a cricket cap, or, at least, a school tie; that we would have little in common. But when he came across and asked me if he could join me in a game, he did it in such a friendly, thoughtful way that my fears were immediately dissipated. Quite frankly, I was more than willing to sit down to a game as the book of problems I had been working on was almost exhausted.

We were soon hard at it. I obtained the white and opened with pawn to Queen's Bishop three; a trivial gambit made with no purpose other than to see how he would respond. He had at me with a knight. I took one or two precautions. But still the knight persisted. I confronted it with a Bishop. But notwithstanding the reproving glance, the knight refused to yield; not until it was dragged from the saddle by a cluster of bloodthirsty pawns.

It was a satisfying game. The black fought well but lost narrowly; the last of its two perambulating castles being tracked down and decimated in the swampy marshes mid-field. The Black Queen, I am glad to say, although put to flight, was not molested. All in all, I gained the impression that the hand directing the pieces set opposite me was, if not subtle, at least, reasonably competent; admirably chivalrous on occasions. Not that I let such thoughts interfere with my usual Cromwellian zeal. On a chessboard, admirable chivalry has a way of transforming itself into intolerable tenacity; especially in a king. Accordingly, I lured his royal leader into the swamps, cut off all avenues of relief, and demanded terms. I may have been heard to mention chivalry at that stage.

After it was all over, David congratulated me. 'I never do well with the ebony,' he remarked with a rueful smile. I have always remembered that. 'The ebony.' I had never heard that description before; the words used naturally, with assurance, as though he was referring to a common form of abbreviation for the black pieces. But it was not an expression I was familiar with.

At the time, I was thrilled by the words. 'The ebony.' It seemed such a fine description. I presumed a sophistication on his part in regard to such matters which hitherto had not been revealed to me. But talking to him later on, I found out that there was another explanation for the phrase altogether.

His father, it seemed, was a vicar. A period of his life had been spent at a mission near Lagos. One of his proudest possessions was an ornate chess set presented to him as a gift on the occasion of returning to England. On Sunday evenings, after church, he and David would sit and play chess together. 'The Ivory or the Ebony', he would always say by way of commencement, holding two pieces concealed in fists behind his back. And the choice having been made, they would begin.

From the way David told the story, and from other remarks he made, it was clear that this was a treasured memory of his boyhood; his father, overworked, struggling to cope with a large parish, at last sitting down at the end of a week, for a brief moment, all his responsibilities discharged, getting out his pipe, and playing a game with his son. From what he said, a vivid picture came to me of the two of them together like that. But at the same time, some echo of regret attached to it. 'I never do well with the ebony.'

Nothing is ever idyllic. He never said so directly, but my understanding was that David's father, the frustrations of the week momentarily suspended, the posture of devout humility temporarily laid aside, he played to win, and did win; year after year. How relentless those tall African carvings must

61

have seemed, quietly moving about the large black-and-white board under the lamplight. How mystifying the sermons preceding the game, weaving tangled patterns of abstraction and reality, the simple truths imposed upon the human weaknesses, obscure notions of affection.

Is this what had prompted him to travel; working in Australia in all sorts of jobs — ship-hand, clerk, factory worker, up country? Impossible to tell, but I think so. He told me many stories about the jobs he had taken during the course of his travels over the two or three years preceding our meeting, most of the stories told on the spur of the moment, simply to illustrate a point, to cap someone else's story. But all the anecdotes, although amusing, suggested a hard won experience, a fragment from some general lesson.

Certainly, thinking back on it, the first game of chess I played with David was the commencement of an understanding between us; some feeling of friendship. And thereafter, in the early stages, although neither of us made any positive step towards establishing a close friendship, we were on speaking terms which was pleasing to me.

We spoke occasionally on deck. Now and again, we sat together in the ship's dining room. Thus, despite everything I have said so far, despite all the qualifications, the reservations which it is now incumbent on me to keep in mind so as to present a faithful picture of what occurred at the Quarantine Station, I firmly believe that, in the early stages, our feelings towards each other were entirely friendly.

What others thought — there's a different question. Mrs Walker certainly had her own views about Mr David Shears. I found that out or, at least, gained some insight into her attitude towards him, on the day the steamer was anchored off Quailu.

It was a beastly day. In this part of the world, apparently, some sort of a holy day. Everything on shore was at a standstill; the dock idle; no movement to be seen; virtually the whole population — so we were told — taking part in religious ceremonies. And the sun, as if presiding over this adjournment of all activity, blazed downwards through a haze of yellow cloud transforming the waters off shore where the ship stood motionless into a sultry cauldron.

Below deck, the heat was intolerable. And not much better above. Like most of the passengers, I found myself a canvas deck-chair in the shade and sat there sweltering; after a time, even the fan I had brought with me idle in my lap, lacking the energy to use it.

I felt like a waxwork on loan from Madame Tussaud's Chamber of Horrors. Some item of old stock lent out for the day to a charitable organization which had carefully put me on display beneath the sunniest window in the room — a gruesome effigy, gradually softening in the heat, becoming increasingly uncomfortable, but well aware that one's infamy was such that any look of dissipation in the features, any degeneration of the waxen smile, the lips, the nose, or the neatly-pointed shoe turning into a club-footed molten puddle, would be regarded by the worthy souls organizing the event not as a matter deserving attention, but merely as a demonstration of my inward decadence.

One knows full well that there has never been enough sympathy in the world to go round. But that day, up on deck, slumped in a stifling shroud of canvas close to the rail, clearly, there was none to spare. Almost without exception, everyone was equally afflicted; paralysed by the steamy temperature. The only thing offering was salt tablets. 'Salt for you?' From time to time, hearing these words at my elbow, I would look up — and there would be Tiba, the white-jacketed steward boy, carrying a tin tray with a jug of water, some glasses and a bottle of tablets on it. Mostly, I limply waved him onwards, preferring to die alone.

But later in the day, towards the end of the afternoon, boredom getting the better of exhaustion, I took a turn round the deck. And doing so, I came upon a strange scene. There was no swimming pool on board. But David Shears had come up with the ingenious idea of rigging up what might be called a swimming contraption.

He, or someone under his direction, had built up a barrier around one of the loading hatches and suspended a tarpaulin from it so that, in the hollow, enough water could be pumped in for a few people to splash about. The Captain, so I am told, was not enthusiastic about the proposal but had given his consent.

Thus, while most of the passengers were lolling about the decks in a state of exhaustion, David was trying out his pool on the foredeck. Whether there had been others with him in the enterprise originally, I have no means of knowing. But certainly, by the time I strolled round to that area, there were only two swimmers in the makeshift pool — David and Mrs Walker's daughter, Isobel. Which was what prompted my conversation with Mrs Walker.

I was leaning on the rail of the upper deck which over-looked the foredeck, not thinking of anything in particular, just hot, and disinclined to exert myself, mildly envying the two young people cavorting about in the small patch of water below, when I became aware of a presence at my elbow; a brief movement of shadow. I presumed it was Tiba, and was about to wave him onwards without comment. But when the shadow failed to speak, failed to utter the by now familiar invocation, 'Salt for you?' — I looked round and discovered that I had in fact been joined by Mrs Walker.

She came straight to the point. 'What do you know about that young man?' she asked. She was carrying a dainty green umbrella to protect her from the sun and, as she spoke, she delicately tipped the butt of the umbrella towards the scene below, pointing out the object of her curiosity.

I suppose I could have told her any one of a number of things — that I had played chess with him, that as I under-stood it he was returning home after a working holiday in Australia, that he appeared to be a pleasant fellow. But I wasn't in the mood to go into details, still feeling worn out by the heat. 'Not much,' I said, morosely; adding, as an after-thought: 'He's obviously energetic.' I didn't wish to sound too unfriendly.

'Oh, yes,' she replied. 'I can see that. Wonderfully ener-getic.' But the way she said it suggested disbelief; a conviction that his display of energy was only transitory — a brief upsurge fuelled by salt tablets which would soon fizzle out.

Distracted by a whoop of laughter from below, we looked downwards. Unfortunate as it may be, there is not a great deal that two people can do in a tarpaulin full of water slung between crates. The hollow created slopes inwards to the centre. Gravity, it would seem, or some other natural force, has the effect of propelling the occupants of such a pool towards each other.

The two of them had been having a splash fight, kneeling on the bottom of the pool and, with hands extended, moving their arms like pistons, splashing away gaily. But one of them must have overbalanced and, disturbing the equilibrium of

64

the tarpaulin, both had pitched forward into the centre of the pool where they lay squirming and spluttering, trying to disentangle themselves from each other's arms, peals of shrill laughter tinkling out as they did so.

Eventually, disengaging themselves from this centrifugal embrace, they sat up. And Isobel, picking up her floppy wide-brimmed hat from where it was floating on the surface of the water, crammed it back on her head smiling at her companion.

Mrs Walker did not look pleased. Far from it. There was obviously no point in discussing physics. I could see that she had other matters on her mind; softly rotating the butt of her parasol, a slight frown on her face.

I understood that her husband, before his death, had been a businessman in Singapore. Something to do with 'fabrics', so I was told. And now, having taken the decision to return home, she was obviously concerned that her daughter should maintain a proper standard of decorum. I happened to be standing next to them at the rail when the ship pulled out of Singapore Harbour. They were addressing their attention to a group of friends on the wharf below; Mrs Walker flickering a small handkerchief at the well-wishers, Isobel waving vigorously.

'Isobel,' I overheard Mrs Walker saying. 'Please try not to make an exhibition of yourself.' And it was apparent from the way in which Isobel took no notice of the remark, that it was an admonition which had been uttered many times before.

And now, Isobel was frolicking in a jerry-built swimming pool constructed by a young man about whom nothing was known other than that he had a penchant for being energetic in the heat. Through her eyes, it must have looked like a poor show indeed.

Mrs Walker leaned forward and made a small yodelling sound. 'Yo-ho,' she called, and fluttered a hand. 'Yo-ho. Darling!'

But there was no hope of her signal being noticed. The two combatants were now standing in the waist-deep water and were trying to walk from one end of the pool to the other; the spongy, trampoline-like quality of the tarpaulin making it difficult for them to maintain their footing.

'This is sheer lunacy,' Mrs Walker said, turning to me. 'To be out in the sun in this heat. Would you mind toddling downstairs and telling Isobel I want her?' In anticipation of my compliance, she moulded her face into what, presumably, she imagined to be a winning smile.

And that, of course, was typical of the mannerisms which always put me off Mrs Walker. After a few minutes' conversation with her it was readily apparent that she was a shrewd businesswoman. And further, a woman with no illusions about human beings, most of whom, it could be inferred from her comments, always had an eye for the main chance. And yet, she insisted, even when the occasion clearly did not warrant it, on affecting a kind of hearty graciousness characterized by an arch, outworn vernacular.

'I think we had better toddle off to dinner,' she would say and stride briskly into the dining room without allowing her audience an opportunity to demur. 'I managed to pick up one or two little poppets,' she told me, with an air of whimsy, as we shared a taxi back to the ship in Bombay, the seat beside her stacked with gifts and mementos. And a few minutes later, when the car pulled up at the dockside, she began haggling with the driver about the fare; afterwards, calling him a chiselling swine as I helped her up the gangway with her booty.

No, I had reached a stage when I was not easily taken in by her winning smile. I am sure that, for her, personal charm was a fabric to be unrolled before a customer with a flourish. And that having been done, a section of it was either snipped off in exchange for value, or else, in the event of the other party to the transaction expressing hesitation, the whole display was tartly bundled up and removed from sight.

But these considerations did not dissuade me from carrying the message down to Isobel. I had no reservations about Isobel whatsoever. She was a beautiful creature. I say it unashamedly. It was not by chance that I was standing next to them at the rail as the ship was leaving Singapore. I had deliberately stationed myself in that position in the hope of striking up a conversation. Seeing her at the rail on that day, towards evening, was a vision of loveliness which has remained with me throughout my life.

How can I possibly describe her? When I think back to that first glimpse of Isobel at the rail, a pale cotton frock enhancing her dusky skin, her brown hair dancing as she waved a gloved hand, thinking of that, it is not surprising that I have been so sceptical about setting down details; attempting to piece together a scene as if it was a jigsaw made up of tangible fragments. Because, in speaking of Isobel, I am trying to convey a total experience, an effect of radiance, in which my own inward agitation would be as material to the description as any emphasis upon her shapely figure or languid eyes.

But that is not to say that I was utterly bemused by her. Far from it. I knew her other side. She could be wilful. And like many pretty girls who have become accustomed to attention from an early age, she was often inconsiderate.

Accordingly, on the day I approached her in the swimming pool, having passed on her mother's message, it did not altogether surprise me that she did not even look up so as to acknowledge her mother's presence at the rail above. She just pouted sullenly, still sitting in the water, one hand fiddling with the brim of her floppy hat, and said: 'I'll get out when I want to. Tell her that from me.'

She looked at me crossly, her dark eyes shaded by the big hat which was now thoroughly saturated, raising one arm out of the water to steady herself by holding the heavy rope with which the tarpaulin was lashed into position, the tarpaulin itself still wobbling gently, the water sloshing around inside it as they moved.

But I was paying little attention to her words, utterly entranced by the softness of her arm, the golden skin disappearing into the folds of the heavy woollen swimming costume, and the beautiful curve of her bosom as she steadied herself, there at the pool's edge, sitting on the gentle slope of the tarpaulin as it curved inwards to the centre.

And David, sunning himself on the slope opposite, half out of the water, a wet vest protecting the upper part of his body from the sun, called out: 'Coming in for a dip, Professor?'

I wasn't especially amused by the nickname. He hadn't used it before and, besides, we weren't all that chummy. And the words were uttered more loudly than was really necessary. It seemed to me that he was showing off. Though perhaps it was only high spirits. I rolled the sleeve of my shirt up to the elbow and stuck one hand in the water.

As I suspected, the water was lukewarm. It was not inviting. Furthermore, the presence of Mrs Walker at the rail above discouraged me from joining them in a three-way romp, although David did not appear to be put off by her presence, lying back on the tarpaulin, propped up on his elbows, squinting at me cheerfully, the greater part of his body immersed in the water.

'Come on,' he urged. 'We'll have to take the whole thing down after dinner. It was the dickens of a job to get it up.'

'Not for me,' I said, firmly, rolling down my sleeve. 'Maybe some other time.'

'The chance won't come again,' he said, with a chuckle, making a final plea. 'Bricky and the boys have already had a go.'

I couldn't help wondering what Mrs Walker would have thought of that. I looked up at her, standing at the rail, a black ebony-like figure silhouetted against the hazy, yellow sky, her parasol, also in silhouette, set above the outline of her body like some mysterious head-dress.

'Not for me,' I repeated; quickly buttoning up my sleeve at the wrist. 'I just came down to pass on the message. Leave me out of it.'

Chapter 7

When I came back into the foyer on the first night, as I have said, it was to find myself in the middle of a confusion; a *faszad*.

We had known, since early in the day, that not only was the accommodation of poor quality but that there was not enough beds to go round. At least two people would have to share a bed. Faced with this dilemma, someone — quite possibly Shewfik Arud — set a *faszad* in motion. Lies had been told and money had changed hands. The intrigue — which was no longer under the control of any one person — was in full swing.

Jack Morley, a British journalist who was returning to London having completed a series of articles on the Great Barrier Reef, was near the main door, gathering up his bags before going upstairs. This man, who had practically lived underwater for the last few months, whispered to me that, by pleading chronic asthma, he had managed to persuade Shewfik to let him have one of the camp-stretchers which had been set up in an ante-chamber close to the upstairs landing. He bustled away; a camera round his neck, a suitcase in each hand, extremely pleased with himself.

A Rhodes Scholar from Delhi, who was also on the point of hurrying upstairs, told me, feverishly, that although the price had risen in the last few minutes, there was still time to slip a bribe to Shewfik Arud and obtain one of the beds in the dormitory at the end of the main corridor. He left me hastily, furtively; as though he had already said too much.

Everyone was scurrying about so rapidly that I became quite nervous. Having made a first and preliminary allocation, an allocation which had provoked a fair measure of controversy, Shewfik was now seated behind his counter on a high stool resolving appeals from his own ruling. I gathered from the muttered comments of those surging around him that the most common ground of complaint was that he had failed to distribute his favours in accordance with the bribes which had been showered upon him.

I fought my way through to the front rank and, under the guise of studying his plan, asked if I could have the bed next to the Indian student, pressing a crumpled banknote into his hand with the advice that in my country tipping was an accepted custom and I presumed that the same would apply. I was surprised at my own aplomb.

Shewfik, smiling broadly, told me that could be easily arranged.

'You have no need to worry yourself on that score,' he said, his tobacco-stained teeth exposed beneath his trim moustache. As he pocketed the note, the thin ruler he was holding wavered uncertainly above the floor plan.

For a sickening moment, it occurred to me that I had not been generous enough; that my aplomb had left me stranded. But after a moment's hesitation, he lowered his ruler and designated one of the beds in the dormitory as mine.

Conscious of the continuing babble of voices behind me, I thanked him hurriedly and prepared to move off. He shrugged. 'That is all right,' he remarked. 'That is all right. My purchaser himself described that room as one of the best in the building. It is one of the really great rooms on the part of the canal, my purchaser said, to use his own words. Undoubtedly, you will enjoy it.' I thanked him again and made my way to the stairs, relieved at having secured some small advantage for myself.

But when I located the bed in question, I found it was occupied by one of Bricky's friends. And he gave no indication that he was in a conciliatory frame of mind. He was leaning back against the wall with his feet up on his suitcase watching the traffic passing along the corridor; viewing the parade with an expression of the utmost cynicism. There was no one else in the room although all the other beds were occupied by humps of luggage. There was no sign of the Indian student.

'Yeah?' the truck driver said, as I paused at the foot of the bed.

I began explaining that I had been allocated this bed by the manager. Medically, there was probably a very good reason for it. That was the best idea I could come up with and I tried to make the most of it.

Half-way through, he held up a chunky hand, interrupting me. 'I got here first,' he said. 'Now piss off.'

At that moment, Bricky himself came in from the screen door opening on to the verandah, the door clattering shut behind him. He slouched over to the bed nearest the door and levered himself into a position of indolence, half-reclining against the wall behind him. He appeared to be holding a magazine in one hand. Or perhaps it was a comic.

'Any problems?' he asked; addressing the question to our side of the room.

His friend, watching me contemptuously all the time, settled himself more comfortably into his position on the disputed bed and said, simply: 'Not for me.' He put his hands behind his head, waiting for me to make the next move.

Knowing there was little point in arguing, I stalked out of the room without further comment and went down to the foyer again. Shewfik was still on his high stool but now no longer surrounded by people. He was studying a large ledger opened out in front of him, exploring the crevices between his teeth with a toothpick.

'You have lost the toss up,' he said, sadly, as I explained my predicament. 'The option is there for you to go back and argue the point of it. But that is for you to decide.' He jabbed his tooth pick into the earthenware bowl beside him containing his potted palm tree. 'I can do nothing,' he added, sympathetically. 'By regulation, I am at the mercy of my guests. And the regulations are not without wisdom.'

'What else is there?' I asked, without any real hope. It was now apparent that, by some process of natural selection, I was destined to be one of the two persons sharing a bed somewhere in the building; the sleeping quarters which had been the subject of rumour and misgivings throughout the day. Yes, I reflected bitterly. Shewfik Arud had stage-managed the whole thing very effectively. No wonder money had been changing hands.

It was now dark and the prospect of sharing a bed was uninviting. The bed, wherever it was, was certainly not going to be occupied by something soft and appetising like Isobel. Rather, it would be occupied by something hard and male and with congested bronchial tubes; a tattooed harpoonist,

71

perhaps. There it was. The *faszad* had run its course. The victim had finally been identified. The profit taken. It was all very amusing. Angrily I drummed my fingers on the counter.

In a leisurely way, and with a studious sucking of his gums, Shewfik contemplated his diagram and finally placed his ruler on a rectangle which, according to the key at the foot of the plan, represented a double bed. 'That is for your kip,' he said. 'In the opinion of my purchaser, a fine bed. An ideal situation looked at in all ways. One of the truly great beds in the building.'

There was no point in arguing with him. An appeal to fair play would be fruitless. My own banknote lay in his pocket. To be the victim of an injustice is one thing. But to be the victim of one's own rank incompetence is a piscatorial kettle of a different colour. How nice to be able to coin phrases, I thought, tramping upstairs again; enraged — the one man in the building kicked in the balls by his own petard.

Of course, there are always compensations. Over the years I have dined out many times on the story of 'my first night in bed with another man'; often, changing the location of the story for the sake of an extra titter. Sometimes, the story commences with me as a member of a three-man debating team losing the toss at the reception desk. Sometimes, depending on the company, I have excused myself from the scenario altogether, leaving the field to two anonymous friends who treat the episode as a bit of a lark.

But the essentials of the story are always the same. Two men, for one reason or another, are obliged to share the honeymoon suite in a swank hotel. No one bothers to tell the chambermaid. She enters the room in the morning to draw the blinds. An unshaven face rears up from the bedclothes and thanks her for her kindness. As sunlight floods into the room, coyly she turns to face the occupants of the bed whereupon the first unshaven face is joined by a second unshaven face which gruffly demands breakfast. Her smile vanishes and she flees.

Needless to say, the anecdote which I have told with such jocularity over the years bears no relation to the reality. In truth, the location was a sleazy room in the upper storey of a Quarantine Station — how fast the smiles would have disappeared from the faces of my collective audiences if that had been mentioned — and the chambermaid was Shewfik Arud's daughter, a slovenly wench who had obviously seen far more in life to surprise her than two unshaven faces sitting side-by-side in bed. And all she did was dump a pot of tea on the dresser together with two cups, smacked a mosquito dead against the wall, leaving a blood-spot on the plaster, and left. No, without doubt, although the substance of the story has potential, it was always clear to me that the narrative required embellishment in order to justify its telling.

Having located the fateful room, my immediate reaction, upon finding that my bed companion was to be David Shears, was one of relief; the situation could have been a lot worse.

'Thank God you're not utterly repulsive,' I thought, greeting him with a warm smile and a handshake; a handshake intended to be friendly — but not encouraging.

What he thought of me I don't know. Physically, I'm not out of the Adonis mould. But on the other hand, I consider myself a cut above Queequeg.

'It's marvellous to see you too,' he said. And we stood there, looking at each other earnestly, both simulating an air of matter of factness; a college chums' air of 'what say to a cup of cocoa, a few words on Spinoza and popping into bed to be fresh for rugger in the morning?' That kind of air. Tactful, considerate, but in the circumstances, a complete sham. I dumped my bags on the floor and went over to the shuttered doors leading out on to the verandah.

My visitation to that side of the room was entirely pointless. I did it simply for something to do. To relieve the tension. Or something like that. I made a pretence of examining the lock.

'Is something wrong?' David asked.

'Wrong?'

'With the lock.'

'Why should there be anything wrong with it?'

'You went straight over there. I thought you might have noticed something.'

'Oh no,' I said, airily; facing him with a smile. 'I was just reminded of all those books about Arabia. You know the type of thing. The two travellers in their tent sleeping. A stealthy hand slitting the canvas and fossicking amongst their belongings without their knowing. That type of thing.'

David looked doubtful. 'I don't think I've actually read that particular book.'

'I must try and get you a copy then,' I said heartily. 'By P. C. Wrensleydale,' I added, plucking a name out of the air. 'Full of adventure. Canvas slitting and that type of thing.'

He looked at me curiously. In retrospect, I suppose I did sound slightly insane. 'I'll keep an eye out for a copy,' he said.

'I recommend it. The first edition especially.'

The book now appeared to have been exhausted as a topic of conversation. We looked at each other. 'Fortunately, we're not in a tent,' David said. He dug his hands into his pockets and drifted towards the bed.

'And fortunately,' I replied, warming to the new theme, 'we've got this sturdy little customer up our sleeves.' I rattled the door handle knowledgeably to demonstrate the point, and gave the door a nudge.

The double doors collapsed outwards like canvas snatched away by a sudden gust of wind. I found myself sprawling across the threshold, having barked one shin on the high step; a door teetering on each side of me.

'Are you all right?' David asked, hurrying across. He began helping me to my feet.

'Quite all right, thanks,' I said stiffly. For some reason, I couldn't help thinking that the whole episode was his fault. Dusting down my knees, I added: 'Apparently, this is one of the really great rooms on this stretch of the canal.'

'Let's take a look,' Eagerly, David pressed past me and made his way to the verandah rail. I limped after him.

Apart from the gully of light created by the open doors of our own room, the verandah was in total darkness; a long stretch of verandah leading into the night at either end — although, at irregular intervals, small chinks of lamplight could be detected through some of the shuttered doors along the way. Out on the canal, we could see our ship riding at anchor; a ghostly apparition standing there in the dark, but made tangible by a green light burning on its masthead. Above, the clear sky was radiant with stars. From somewhere within the precincts of the Quarantine Station, there was the throbbing sound of a generator at work; a muffled, pulmonary engine working away diligently.

'It's a beautiful sight,' David said, as I joined him at the rail. In some ways, I'll be sorry to get home. To give up doing things to suit myself.'

'But are we going to get out of here?' I asked, not really convinced by his point. 'No one seems to know what's going on. I had a talk with the Doctor. He won't tell me anything. The ship's crew's out there. They're not coming ashore, apparently. The whole thing's up in the air.'

But David didn't seem to be worried, standing there at the rail, idly examining the sky. 'Give it a few days. If there's nothing definite by then, we can always walk out. I'm certainly not going to be boxed in by half-truths and nonsense about latent diseases. A few plain answers. That's all we need. What do you think?'

'I agree entirely,' I replied. 'Plain answers. We've got to have them. We mustn't let ourselves be pushed around.'

But I couldn't help wondering whether this view of the matter was too simplistic. Plain answers are all very well if you can get them. But where exactly did we stand? A group of foreign passengers such as ourselves. What exactly were our rights? My knowledge of the local political situation was nil. But as far as I could gather from Dr Magro, Egyptian political life, at present, was dominated by pressures from various sources. There were the political parties working through parliament. There was the influence exercised by the Palace. There was also the Embassy with the weight of British forces stationed in the country behind it. And the canal company. But who was best placed to render us assistance if the matter dragged on?

Dr Magro had pointed out, quite directly, that as the Embassy was on the eve of concluding a treaty with the Egyptian government which would have the effect of relinquishing British control of the area, the Embassy, at this particular moment, might not feel inclined to wave a big stick on behalf of a group of stranded passengers. It was all very complicated. Far too complicated for me. Still, I couldn't help admiring the confidence with which David spoke. Plain answers. He seemed to have no doubt that it would turn out all right for us in the end. If he thought he could do something for us by tackling the authorities, demanding a few plain answers, then it was up to me to give him as much help as I could.

'Shall we turn in?' David said.

'Not a bad suggestion,' I replied; lapsing into my cocoa-and-Spinoza voice. 'Not a bad suggestion by half.'

The two of us retreated into our room, closing the shuttered doors behind us. David left it to me to re-adjust the lock. I fiddled with the thing as best I could. But it was obvious there was no way to make it secure. The slightest pressure made the two doors swing insolently open.

'Not much protection,' I said, studying my handiwork, having adjusted the doors for the third or fourth time; still dissatisfied with the result.

'Don't worry about it,' David answered, laconically. He had changed into his pyjamas and was standing by the bed, gingerly prodding the pillows.

'Perhaps I'd best put a chair here for anyone sneaking in to trip over.' I looked round for a suitable chair.

'Don't worry about that,' David said. 'What's inside these, I wonder?' He was massaging one of the pillows; exploring its lumpen folds with tentative hands. The pillow, a small, greyish sack, crackled slightly beneath the treatment.

All I could think of was bandages. The thought made me feel faint. Noisily, I dragged the one rickety chair in the room into a defensive position immediately inside the double doors. I reinforced this barricade by placing one of my bags on the seat. The chair creaked.

'It doesn't feel like kapok,' David said. 'Still, never mind.' He pulled back the sheet and lowered himself into the bed. There was a cringing of aged springs. 'Not bad,' he said. 'Not bad.'

It was a double bed with iron railings at either end. When I first laid eyes on it, it had looked reasonably secure. But now, with one person in occupation, it resembled a large hammock. The same thought had obviously occurred to David. 'It's hard to keep out of the centre,' he said. 'One just keeps sliding inwards.'

'The interesting thing about gravity,' I said, hurriedly, delving into my bag for pyjamas.

'Yes?' David replied.

I realized that I hadn't finished the sentence and began again. 'The interesting thing about gravity,' I said, groping for something to say about the subject, interesting or not, 'basically is this.' I stripped off my shirt and singlet and put on my pyjama jacket. I felt as though I was getting changed in public.

'Yes?' David was lying in the centre of the bed with his

hands behind his head, watching me. He appeared to be taking a genuine interest in my remarks.

'Basically,' I repeated. 'Gravity,' I began pulling off my shoes, standing first on one foot, then the other, 'is one of the really great natural forces.' I began unbuttoning my trousers. 'As compared with the others, that is,' I added; cocoaing onwards.

'Take electricity, for instance.' I looked round wildly for the light switch. Discovering it near the door, I moved towards it. 'Invisible, but potent nonetheless.' I flicked the light on and off a couple of times to demonstrate the point. And left it off.

The room was in total darkness. It was very difficult to see what one was doing. Rapidly, I began stripping off my trousers, leaning against the wall for support. 'But the important thing about gravity,' I continued.

'Yes?' I could hear David muffling a yawn.

Having removed my trousers, I quickly flung them in the general direction of the chair on which I had put my bag.

'Jesus,' David said. I couldn't see him but I heard the bedsprings trembling as he sat up.

'What's wrong?'

'Bats! There's bats in here. Or a bird. Something just flew past me.'

'Is that right? A bat?' I pretended interest. But the fact was that I had more to think about than bats. I had just realized that I had forgotten to bring my pyjama pants with me to this side of the room.

'Put the light on,' David said, hoarsely. 'For Christ's sake. I can't see a thing.'

'The light?'

'Yes. Put it on.'

'Sorry,' I said, lying to my back teeth. 'I can't find it.' I began groping my way back across the room to my bag.

Unfortunately, in the confusion, I had lost my sense of direction. I blundered into the edge of the bed and sat down on it abruptly. The springs cringed again. Almost simultaneously, David's hand fumbled against my naked thigh and quickly removed itself.

'What's going on? What's happening?' he asked; the bedsprings still quivering.

'Nothing,' I replied; trying to reassure him. 'It's only me.'

I sat there for a second; trying to get my eyes accustomed to the darkness, knowing that the chair with the bag on it must be somewhere close to hand. 'What do you think about gravity?' I asked, in a soothing voice, trying to get the discussion back on an even track — playing for time. 'Natural forces and so on.'

'I'm straight, if that's what you mean,' David whispered, a small note of desperation had crept into his voice. 'My tastes are orthodox. I prefer women.'

I had a quick vision of him lying there in the blackness; eyes staring, sheet pulled protectively to his chin. But I couldn't be worried by that. I needed my pyjama pants. Until I had them I couldn't think straight.

'My tastes are orthodox too,' I snapped.

'Of course. Of course. I didn't mean to imply they weren't. Not for one second.' The voice of tolerance bravely made itself heard in the dark, inviting assault. 'Each to their own, I say. Each to their own.'

There was no point in arguing. Clearly, he had written me off as a deviant. Anything I said in my own defence would be misconstrued; would probably be interpreted as some kind of verbal foreplay; a calculated ploy. I could speak with the combined tongue of men and of angels but without my pants it would profiteth me nothing.

Carefully, I lowered myself off the edge of the bed and began crawling towards the chair; one hand outstretched in front of me, groping.

'What are you doing now?'

'Looking for the light switch,' I said, savagely, utterly fed up with the whole business.

'Do you want me to help?'

'No.'

I found the leg of the chair. Then, my bag. And finally, my pyjama pants. Legs tingling, I hauled myself to my feet and began putting them on. Properly attired at last, I moved back to the bed with renewed confidence. 'Move over,' I said, brusquely.

'Did you find it?'

'What?'

'The light switch?'

'Don't be ridiculous,' I said, and clambered in taking care to occupy no more than a narrow ridge of territory on my side of the bed. I manoeuvred my pillow into position. He had obviously done the same. The hollow of bed space between us was a yawning pit.

'Goodnight,' he called across to me.

'Goodnight.'

'It's been a long day.'

'Surely.'

'Well, goodnight then.' The commander of the distant hilltop yawned ostentatiously. 'I'm just about all in.'

'So am I,' I called back; wide-eyed in the darkness but fabricating a suitable yawn for the occasion.

Whether he went to sleep straight away, I have no means of knowing. For myself, I lay there in a state of semi-paralysis for several hours; determined not to be the first to slide into the abyss, conscious that I had already been unfairly branded as a libertine; that my good name depended upon my remaining entrenched upon the hillside.

For several hours, at least, we maintained our respective positions. There was no move from his side. Nor from mine. From camp to camp, through the foul womb of night, only the sound of regular breathing. Deep, rhythmic, conspicuously natural breathing. By God, it was difficult to keep it up. And the mosquitoes were murderous; spiralling invisibly out of the dark, attacking viciously. Eventually, I pulled the sheet over my face and lay there mummified, at last, knowing what it felt like to be a Pharaoh, lying petrified in some ghastly tomb, harassed by intruders; the centuries dragging on interminably.

Weary and fitful was their rest. Weary and fitful was their rest. Weary and fitful was their rest. Over and over again I repeated the words. Eight syllables. Twenty-six letters. Endlessly I repeated them. The opening lines from the second chapter of P. C. Wrensleydale's fourth novel. The first edition. Weary and fitful was their rest. Weary and restful was their fit. Wrensleydale and doleful was their fitful. On and on it went, the pleasing variations of the one refrain . . .

And then the words became circling birds; birds rising in profusion from a lake's surface at the sound of a gunshot. Again and again the lonely figure on the shores of the lake, almost hidden by the overhang of jungle, and the musket raised, the certainty that a shot had been fired although no sound could be heard, and the lake's surface splintering upwards into a vast canopy of wings, a billowing tapestry of clamorous wings revolving in kaleidoscopic patterns. Ragged birds taking to the air. Summoned into flight, and settling downwards into the water, disappearing, becoming part of the water itself, the lake, transforming themselves. Such a dream. And the mind struggling to identify the marksman, there, in the shadow of the trees, knowing him but unable to make out his features, conscious of him following his own purpose, shouting to him across the water, recognizing the havoc wrought by each gunshot, the transformation, the lake opening, the sky darkening with wings, distressed and yet feeling separate from it all, unable to intervene, one's own face dissipating into feathers, the sun's eclipse.

Chapter 8

'Also things captured in war, and an island arising in the sea, and gems, stones, and pearls found on the shore become the property of he who has been the first to take possession of them. Now one can acquire possession in person. A madman, and a ward without his tutor's authority, cannot begin to possess, since they have not the intention to hold, however much they are in physical contact with the thing, as though one put something in the hand of a sleeper.'

Such an enigmatic passage of translation. I believe it is not by chance that the first entry I made in my Borthwick occurs in proximity to the opening words of the title *De adquirenda vel amittenda possessione*. And yet my entry, a notation intended to serve as a record of the previous day's events, a form of diary, says no more than: 'Shewfik Arud to cable UK. Leeches.' One can scarcely imagine a more inadequate summary of what had taken place.

Could it be that even then, as early as the first day, I had recognized the futility of attempting to maintain a detailed transcript of events — knowing that, like an object placed in the hand of a sleeper, the Quarantine Station and all its inhabitants could never be possessed by a ward without his tutor's authority, or a madman; such persons not having the intention to hold, lacking the training, the intelligence, to cope with the reality?

But who can ever claim to be in physical contact with the thing? Who can take possession of a time and place? I have heard the story of that distinguished British diplomat who, having spent many years in China, was acknowledged to have acquired at least some understanding of the ways of the Orient. And yet, his memoirs, an expensive volume bound in embossed leather, consisted entirely of blank pages bearing the title: 'All I know about China.' Was this less revealing than the lucid diary of a traveller with an energetic and attentive pen?

Or could it be that I simply lacked vitality? That my attention was drawn to the passage simply by the circumstances of my awakening — finding myself curled up beside David Shears in the centre of the aged bed, responding lethargically to my surroundings, coming gradually, and pleasantly, to a state of wakefulness; the shadow of my nightmares receding, being slowly but effectively erased by the appearance of sunlit walls shifted drowsily into focus, eased into position by the tapping of the shuttered door leading on to the verandah which had come adrift during the night and now uttered a diffident reminder of its presence; the random tap-tapping finally waking me and keeping me awake but without being insistent enough to make me move, noticing, without discomfort, that David's hand lay loosely clenched on the pillow beside his tousled head, firm but vulnerable, a bracelet of pale skin at his wrist marking the usual situation of his watch.

We lay there, side by side, and there was no inclination on my part to move; conscious of his warm body motionless beside me, and for a moment feeling secure, at ease, knowing that the moment I moved the spell would be broken. A strange feeling of tranquillity; of peace, almost. A kind of bondage; our bodies touching, our minds pacified, not yet bothered by the anxieties which would beset our waking hours, the friction of being human.

Lying in this bare minimum of a room. Nothing but grubby walls, and a ceiling. An old wardrobe in one corner and a couple of chairs with our clothes upon them; in my case, my trousers slung awkwardly over the back of the chair and the chair standing in a small shaft of sunlight which fluttered slightly as the door nearby went on with its tapping. Outside, somewhere below the verandah, I could hear the faint sound of kitchen noises and the muffled sound of the generator still throbbing quietly.

Everything which had seemed ominous the night before had now become mundane; innocuous. The light bulb hung down from the centre of the ceiling on a length of twisted flex; a pale bulb sheltered beneath a dusty light shade. Ah, the magic of daylight. The reassurance of it. You wake up — and there it is. Neutral territory waiting to be occupied. Still linked to the days which have preceded it to be sure, the weeks, the months. But a fresh chance. A new beginning.

Yes, a new beginning. Languidly, I stretched my arms above my head and yawned, drinking deeply. At the same time, I shifted my position in the bed. Beside me, David stirred restlessly. He hunched himself into the pillow and snorted impatiently. Once he had settled himself again, so as not to disturb him further, executing the movement as delicately as I could, I swung my legs out of the bed and padded across to my bag, foraging among the contents until I located my Borthwick. Then, without upsetting David, I returned to the bed and began reading.

It did occur to me that, as a prospective recruit to Burgess's action group, I probably should have been doing something more constructive. Indeed, as a concession to that feeling, I believe it was then, in a business-like way, that I made my first entry in Borthwick. But sitting up comfortably against the pillow, reminding myself that I was bedded down with an athlete who was obviously conserving his energies until later in the day, the mood soon passed. As far as I was concerned, the Burgess committee, the so-called action group, could wait. The opportunity to do some undisturbed reading was too good to be thrown away.

But I made very little progress. I had scarcely been reading for more than a few minutes when suddenly, and quite rudely (regrettably, there is no other way of describing it) the door from the corridor was kicked open by a dark-skinned girl carrying a tray. She was barefooted but obviously accustomed to putting in the boot. The way in which the door smashed into the wall of the room in response to her abrupt appearance suggested that somewhere beneath the crumpled smock she was wearing, there was a good deal of muscle.

But the detonation caused by her entry didn't seem to concern her. Sulkily, she dumped the metal tray on top of the chest of drawers with a clatter and unloaded two pannikins and a plate with some whitish briquettes upon it resembling bread.

'Tea,' she said hoarsely, looking towards me for the first time, the tray, containing the pannikins, having resumed its position between her widespread hands.

David, awakened by the commotion, was struggling into a sitting position. I felt myself blushing; embarrassed by his presence, wishing he would disappear. The girl stared at the two of us impassively. I had the impression she had seen worse sights but I felt flustered nonetheless.

'What's going on?' David asked. A reasonable question but I resented his tone of voice. The implication was that I had been up to something behind his back.

'A spot of breakfast,' I replied. Heartiness was becoming a habit. 'The old Arabian kipper.'

'Tea,' the girl repeated, stonily. Presumably she had been trained to say it. Then, she turned on her heel. But, at the doorway, noticing something on the wall, briefly, she raised one knee to support the tray and, steadying it in that way, smacked at something on the wall with her free hand. And went out, leaving the door wide open, a small bloodspot on the wall behind her. Through the open doorway, across the corridor, I watched her force an entry into the room opposite, one decisive movement of the foot again being sufficient.

'We'd better close the door,' David said, swinging out of his side of the bed, crossing the room cautiously on bare feet. He shut the door and inspected the bloodspot on the wall. 'A mosquito,' he said, indicating a position near the light switch with his finger.

'Is it dead?' I asked.

But David had the kind of sponge-like curiosity which mopped up facts and fatuous questions indiscriminately. 'Seems to be,' he replied thoughtfully, before moving over to the dresser where he tested the heat of the pannikins with a tentative finger. 'Cold,' he said, bringing them across to the bed. 'But I suppose we'd better drink it.'

I agreed with him, being quite dry in the mouth. And together, we sat on the bed and sipped our tea, gingerly sampling fragments of the bread-biscuits which the girl had left with us. They were hard and salty, these fragments, and tasted like leftovers chiselled out of a sunbaked trough. Certainly, there was something of the desert in them; something of the spirit which, in the mind of the crazed traveller, can transform brackish water into wine and make cold, flesh-coloured tea drinkable sitting up in bed. Which is what we did; raising the pannikins to our lips, munching the biscuits, slowly and religiously.

'I'm going downstairs,' David said, at length, brushing a scattering of crumbs off the sheet beside him. He returned his mug to the tray. 'We've got to find out what's going on.'

Morosely, my earlier mood of contentment having dissipated, I watched him clamber into his shirt and trousers. The thought of action repelled me. The thought of Burgess more so. Perhaps it was the tea. Weakly, I lay back against the pillow. The bed cringed faintly. Borthwick slid on to the floor with a gentle slapping sound of the kind which in books usually betokens a minor whip-lash injury. Borthwick, I observed, was obviously getting sick of the whole business; was setting the stage for a spot of malingering. As a rule, I'm rather disgusted by that sort of thing. But then again, I reflected, to decry any aspect of human behaviour is to put a bullet in the foot of progress. It was something I wanted to think about alone.

'I'll be down soon,' I called out. 'You go on. I'll be right down.'

At the time, I meant what I said. I had every intention of going downstairs without delay. Indeed, I don't think the intention, as such, ever changed. No conscious decision was taken to do otherwise. But certainly, I lay in bed without moving for a long time after David left the room.

The sounds of activity in the corridor — voices, the muffled sounds of doors and suitcases opening and closing, cutlery clanging, water gurgling into basins — gradually subsided. Even the light breeze which had been gently agitating the verandah door of my room died away. The door stopped tapping and the room, which had been pleasant, became hot and drowsy; a haven for the occasional itinerant blowfly which blundered in now and again, skidded about between the ceiling, the wardrobe, the door-slats, the ceiling again, before going on its way.

There seemed to be no point in making a move. None whatever. I was quite happy where I was. Downstairs, there was nothing but Burgess and rallying to the minute book. I might have stayed in bed indefinitely had it not been for the delayed effect of the tea and biscuits. Shewfik Arud obviously had his own methods of prising people out of their beds. As time went on, I became increasingly conscious of a need to find a lavatory; a mood of inquiry which, once having been implanted in my mind, was quite rapidly transformed into a fixation. There was nothing for it but to get up and to do so quickly. Hastily, I rolled out of bed and scrambled into my clothes.

It was a near thing. I found the ablutions at the far end of the corridor just in time. Afterwards, bruised and shattered by the experience, I decided, at last, to go downstairs. There was something about the long upstairs corridor, the chafed and colourless walls, the grey, threadbare strip of hessian matting down its length, which prompted one to look for company. I didn't want to die alone up there while the last stomach pump in the building was trundled towards me, bumped to pieces on the stairs by one of Dr Magro's disinterested assistants. No, I decided, better that death's suction find me in the foyer amongst my fellow passengers where my absence would be noticed, my passing minuted, and the appropriate apology recorded with regret.

Sure enough, when I reached the foyer I found that the meeting was underway. It was, perhaps, the first time I had seen all of the passengers assembled in one place. On board the ship, the steamer's dining room was so small and cluttered that meals had been served in three sittings. Boat drill likewise. And leaving the ship, and arriving on shore, with people milling about so much, it was difficult to tell what the passenger list looked like *en masse*. But here they were. My fellow passengers. In the flesh. About thirty people in all, standing and sitting, distributed around the foyer, the chairs formed into a rough semi-circle facing the small desk at which Burgess was sitting as chairman, his back to one of the tall windows overlooking the canal, behind him the rough hessian curtains pulled back to reveal a narrow glimpse of grey water and brown landscape.

Immediately to the right of this central desk, comprising a small, inner semi-circle of their own, were the two Derbyshire sisters, two elderly ladies who were travelling back to England, on their brother's arm. He, of an equal age, a pale man dressed as always in an ill-fitting suit was sitting beside them, perched uncomfortably on the arm of a chair. As Burgess spoke, he nodded in agreement. Nearby, hunched up in a small steamer chair which must have been dragged in from the verandah, was the young Indian student, staring intently at the speaker, as if deriving some special nourishment from his remarks denied to the rest of the audience.

Further back and to one side, seated in a cluster around one of the main columns in the room were the planters; two couples in their mid-thirties who were travelling home on leave accompanied by children and several companions who were either members of their household or close relatives. Certainly, they all went about together as a large, noisy group; children, mostly young boys, gnawing at the knee of the women, and being disciplined in tones of uniform jollity by all members of the group. Beside them, sat Mrs Walker and Isobel. The former, sitting erect in one of the aged armchairs, had one hand on her upright parasol as if using it for support. Knowing the uncertain quality of the chairs, I suspected that she was keeping it to hand for safety. Isobel, looking bored and sulky, was slouched in a steamer chair, her legs inelegantly stuck out in front of her. As always, she looked divine, a pale blue dress, a ribbon in her hair.

Quite close to her there was a large chair occupied by a planter's child. I was tempted to move in that direction; to establish a presence in the area. But I resisted the temptation. There was something about the pudgy knuckles gripping the edge of the seat. The child was looking towards me already and I knew that digging him out of the chair wouldn't be fun. Not for me, at any rate. I knew the kind of situation too well. The stubborn child. One's initial ingratiating smiles disintegrating into anger and tight whispers. The parent, knowing how to cope, intervening with tact and understanding, floodlighting one's own imperfections. The child finally surrendering in tears. The meeting halted. The possibility that at the end of it all the chair would collapse beneath the weight of an adult, which is why the child had been anchored there in the first place, as they had tried to point out. And so on.

No, thank you, I decided, I would leave my approach until later in the day. Accordingly, pushing past Bricky and the boys, who were loitering in a row along the wall near the stairway, I quietly slipped into a vacant chair next to Jack Morley, muttering an apology to the occupant of the chair in front, a retired businessman who, in my experience of him on board ship, spent most of his time sitting round leafing through a scrapbook of ancient press cuttings.

Burgess was winding up his remarks; lips bent to the winch. 'That is what your committee will be aiming for,' he was saying; his grey, wolf-like eyes levelling themselves at various sections of the audience in turn. 'To find out what it's all about and put up a submission to the proper authorities.

87

Hard-core information. That's what we need first. The basic facts. We're not in our own country. Just remember that. We're strangers and we don't want to go blundering in without knowing what we're doing.'

There was a general murmur of approval from the audience for the wisdom implicit in the remark. 'We must know what we're doing,' Burgess repeated, emphasizing the point with a small gesture of the hand, his gaze concentrated on someone in the front row. 'But once we know where we stand, whom we should see, then we can start demanding a few answers.'

Again, at this, these last defiant words, there was a small groundswell of approbation. 'Exactly,' one of the elderly sisters in the front row said, smacking the butt of her walking stick against the palm of her free hand in a brief representation of applause.

Burgess held up his hand for silence, turning his attention to those in the seats further back, obviously sensing that he required more than the mandate of an aged woman in the front row to carry him through. 'But you'll have to be patient. It's a sticky situation. You can't expect us to pull rabbits out of a hat. Most of us suspect that this quarantine is all nonsense but we've got to take things step by step. Which is where your committee comes in. We'll be doing our best. You can be sure of that. I can't promise you we'll be out of here by tonight but it shouldn't be long after.'

Clearly, these brief but fighting words had set the elderly sister with the walking stick tingling. She thumped the floor with her stick and activated a small ripple of clapping amongst the planters. The scrapbook man in front of me, pink and balding, looked around and said to no one in particular: 'He's right, you know. Damn right.' Out of the corner of my eye, I noticed Bricky, slouching against the wall, wink at one of his mates, making a blubbery, blurting noise with his lips as he did so. On the far side of the room, Isobel, looking bored, twisted in her chair restlessly.

At the front of the the the meeting, the elderly brother clambered off his perch and tottered forward to the desk, whispering something to Burgess; the lower hem of his dark blue blazer riding a little way up his back, his trousers revealing the outline of a withered buttock. Burgess, startled, nonetheless listened intently. Then, nodding vigorously in assent, fended off his aged visitor with one hand.

'I've been asked to confirm that our proceedings are not in camera,' he said. 'In other words, you are free to discuss the matter with outsiders.' Someone in the planters' group clapped politely but was silenced.

'Before I take questions,' Burgess added, 'it might be as well, while we're all here if the secretary of our committee could find out whether Mr Arud has any up-to-date news for us.'

I shrank into my chair. But it was no use. In my absence, quite clearly, a vote had been taken; the ballot box, conscious of its cleft palate, had spoken — courageously, but in erratic undertones. Disastrously. There could be no mistake about it. Burgess was beckoning to me; the rapid, slightly irritable upward movements of his schoolmaster's speech-day hand (up, up) making it clear that now was the time for 'a certain member' of the class to be upstanding and come forward; heart and soul, supposedly, brimful of congenial verse — fresh from the teat of some bovine anthology.

'Steady on,' the pink-faced scrapbook man muttered as I squeezed past him to confer with Burgess. 'No need to scramble.'

'Find out whether he's had a reply to my cable,' Burgess whispered as I leant across the front desk, staring into his expressionless eyes, wondering whether my buttocks were under scrutiny. 'What we need is concrete information.'

'Concrete information,' I said, echoing the incantation under my breath. 'I'll see what I can do.'

'While our young friend is away,' Burgess said, dismissively, speaking around me as I straightened up, 'I'll take questions. Some of you may have some points you want to bring up at this stage.'

I certainly had a question — namely, how did one go about getting concrete information out of Shewfik Arud? But plainly, Burgess's invitation wasn't intended to include me. Instead, I made the best show I could of departing with a purposeful stride. It wasn't easy, particularly having to push past Bricky and the boys. No, it wasn't easy — one of the boys whispering to his mate as I went past; a lewd, audible whisper which smeared the word out into one extended syllable, *basso profundo*: '*Wanker!*' And the three of them sniggered a bit, Bricky lounging back against the wall, thick hands clumsily positioned on his hips, his eyes smiling contemptuously beneath a thatch of blonde hair, legs crossed so that I had to step carefully over the upraised boot of his forward foot in order to pass.

I found Shewfik Arud in the laundry; an out-house made of concrete blocks which had been clumsily pushed into a position beneath a flight of sagging steps at the rear of the Station. I was lucky to find him. His daughter, rinsing out glass jars in the kitchen, in answer to my inquiry as to his whereabouts, had only been able to point vaguely towards the backyard of the building. And even when I tracked down an elusive whistling sound to the out-house, it was difficult to see what was going on inside; the one window of the structure being clouded by grime, a pall of steam rising from a large vat in the corner of the room, the whole atmosphere being one of heat and Hadean gloom, bed linen piled up in random heaps throughout; on the shelves, on the floor. Rows of hessian bags, presumably containing soiled clothes, were hanging from the rafters like lumpen punching bags, obscuring any complete view of the room.

'Mr Arud,' I called out. The whistling stopped. But I still couldn't see him. I took a few cautious steps forward, fending off one of the punching bags which kept nudging my shoulder. 'Mr Arud,' I called again, a clammy lacquer of perspiration beginning to make its presence felt at my collar.

Abruptly, beneath a shelf piled high with sheets, a panel in the wall opposite me slid open. Looking anxious, almost furtive, Shewfik Arud's face appeared in the aperture. Lifting his hands to the side of the hatch for support, he craned forward to see who was calling him. For a moment, a bundle of sheets directly above his head, it seemed as though he was trying on some gigantic turban; his hands fumbling for a grip.

'Who would that be?' he asked; his voice edgy.

I shouldered my way through the linen bags, finding, when I reached the end of the row, that Shewfik was speaking from behind a wooden partition, a small door giving access to the storeroom in which he was standing. As I entered the compartment, he slammed the hatch shut and came to meet me.

'It is only you,' he said; a sense of relief entering his voice, but wringing his hands nervously, his manner agitated. 'From Dalton College.'

Even if he hadn't sent my cable, clearly, he had read it. 'How nice to see you inside, this fine day. Shall we leave?' He took my arm, as if to move me towards the door; at the same time, casting a fleeting glance at a small wooden crate standing beneath the hatch.

Obviously, whatever it was that he was putting into it or taking out of it, was not for the eyes of others. 'My foolish daughter,' he added, hastily regaining his composure. 'She has only to ring the kitchen bell.' He tugged at an invisible cord by way of demonstration. 'I have told her one thousand times. Ring the bell and I will come running from wherever. Oh, that foolish child.' He smacked the palms of his hands together for emphasis.

Like myself, the girl was probably not quite clear as to whether Shewfik intended the bell to act as a summons or as a warning of an approach. But it was not my place to resolve this ambiguity.

'Please,' I said, wriggling free of the hand which had resumed its hold on my elbow. 'Please don't let me interrupt.' I explained that the passengers were having a meeting and that I was to find out whether he had any news for us.

'Ah,' he exclaimed, throwing up his hands. 'A meeting. Some news for the meeting.' He sat down suddenly on one of the packing cases nearby and became passive, fingering his moustache, like a caterer contemplating a range of menus for a social function sprung upon him at short notice. 'Yes,' he repeated. 'Some news for the meeting. There must be something.'

I looked around. There was an old wash-tub in one corner of the room but otherwise it seemed to be mainly furnished by packing cases and a variety of upended steamer trunks, faded lettering and remnants of old labels visible on the exposed surfaces. Chilled by the thought, I couldn't help wondering whether these were the belongings of travellers who, in other years, had arrived at the Quarantine Station but never left.

'If there's none, it doesn't matter,' I said, helpfully, conscious that Shewfik was ransacking his imagination so as to be able to lay before his guests a quick but wholesome smorgasbord of information; something to keep them going for the time being.

'You can tell them that the cables are on their way,' he said, after a further moment, triumphantly. 'I handed them to the water-carrier myself. Took them out to his truck and stood

91

upon his running-board myself with personal instructions for delivery. And my credit with him is still good. My credit is sound. The cables are in a state of transmission.'

'The water-carrier?' I asked, seeking clarification.

'Yes. Yes.' Shewfik replied, impatiently. 'For delivery to my uncle in the city. And my uncle, as I have told my purchaser many times, is a man of influence. A man of great influence. A man of weight. He will get the cables sent. Every one of them. There can be no doubt. No doubt at all.' Shewfik had now become quite excited by the prospect of cables radiating outwards to every corner of the globe. Watching me with eager eyes, in a crass imitation of the American-style smackeroo, he pushed a cluster of fingers towards his lips then let them explode outwards to the detonation of a succulent, kiss. 'Dalton College,' he said, with an air of rapture. 'All okay. The authorities have been communicated with.'

I looked at him aghast. Burgess, I reflected, isn't going to find this funny. He won't be amused at all.

'Anything else?' I asked, perspiration soaking into my shirt and crutch like acid.

Shewfik looked crestfallen; somewhat annoyed. He looked around him for further inspiration. 'What do you think of this?' he asked, with a sly wink; changing the subject, pointing to an ornate box, a small casket really, which was standing on one of the packing cases; a jewel-box, perhaps.

'Here is something for your interest,' he declared, with a flourish of one hand towards the box, but quickly qualified his words. 'For your own interest that is to say. Not for your meeting.' He chortled at the absurdity of having to state the obvious — but glanced at me nervously nonetheless.

'Have you heard of the false bottom?' he whispered. Delicately, he leant over, his hand groping for something at the side of the box. He found his target. A length of carved wood at the base of the box popped open half an inch or so. Shewfik drew it out to its full measure, exposing a shallow drawer corresponding with the dimensions of the box.

'That is nothing,' he confided, his eyes gleaming, searching mine for an answering light. He tapped the side of his head with one finger. 'That is a drawer for purchasers and imbecile policeman.' Gracefully, he slid the drawer shut, touched the side of the box and popped it open again. 'That is nothing,' he repeated.'That is next to nothing. Not the main thing at all.

92

Your wooden duck as the English say.'

'Your wooden duck?'

'Bringing birds to their death.'

'Decoy?'

'Ah. Your "deecore",' he exclaimed, smacking the palms of his hands together excitedly. 'The very word on the top of my tongue. Your "deecore".'

Shewfik stood up, slapping the pockets of his khaki trousers, finally, digging into his back pocket, and producing a sheet of yellowish paper very similar to the form on which I had written out my cable the previous day. He folded it in half to obscure the writing, touched the hidden spring and, having eased the drawer out to its full position, slipped in the piece of paper. 'Your "deecore",' he said, pointing to the paper, and closing the drawer again.

'Now, we look closer,' he continued, beckoning to me to come forward. 'Now, we find out what the box really holds.'

The top of the box consisted of two wooden leaves secured at the centre by a wooden catch. He undid the catch and pulled each flap outwards to reveal the interior of the box. The box was empty but the walls of the interior were curtained with folds of blue silk; the silk being attached to the two flaps comprising the lid so that, with the flaps opened outwards, the folds of silk concealed the hinges which presumably attached the two flaps to the body of the box.

Shewfik invited me to feel the inside walls of the box. I did so. Beneath the folds of silk they seemed quite solid. I withdrew my hand. Shewfik then, one by one, prised off the five buttons fastening the silk to the central line of one of the flaps until the silk fell away in a heap in the centre of the box. The inner wall of the box thus revealed was somewhat thicker than expected. Sure enough, Shewfik then proceeded to slide off a strip of wood along that edge, revealing a cavity perhaps half an inch wide running the full length of the box. He groped in his pocket, produced another sheet of yellow paper and posted it into the cavity. 'Three hundred English pound notes, for an example,' he said with a sly wink. Then, he slipped the strip of wood back into place, buttoned down the silk, shut the two flaps and looked at me triumphantly.

He held up his finger, grinning broadly. 'The police,' he said, commanding my attention. Miming the part of a stern, sour-faced official, he began snooping round the packing case on which the casket stood, eventually picking it up and examining it carefully.

'Whacko,' he boomed, pursing his lips, turning towards me, pointing at a button comprising the centre of a sunflower carved into the side of the box. 'Whacko. Whacko,' he cried again.

Quite obviously, at some stage, a dangerously infectious vaudeville act had been cast into quarantine.

'Whacko,' Shewfik said again, pressing the button. The drawer popped into sight. Shewfik snatched the cable and began threatening me with it. 'Ho. Ho,' he said, waving the paper at me. 'What have we here? Let us be frank. Let us make our confession.'

Throwing his hat and cane into the wings, Shewfik resumed his normal voice. 'The "deecore".' He waved the piece of paper at me again. 'A love letter. A bank statement.' Then, he rapped one edge of the box with his knuckles knowingly. 'But in there, undiscovered, three hundred English pounds,' he said. 'A passport, maybe. Some precious stones.'

He pushed the casket to one side and came down to business. 'You want to buy?' he asked. There was nothing obvious about it, but I had the impression that he was blocking my way out of the room.

'Perhaps,' I stammered. 'Perhaps another time. But right now, I have my meeting.'

'Ah, your meeting,' Shewfik said, clicking his tongue, reminding himself of the point of my visit. 'Of course. Of course. Your meeting. Forgive me — I clean forgot it. Always the meetings. They are so important. And the League of Nations. I am all in favour of it. Totally in favour. I have never wavered. Never for one minute. If there is anything more I can do for your meeting you will certainly let me know.'

He took my arm and led me to the door, all thoughts of his mysterious box apparently forgotten. 'My uncle is the one for meetings,' he said, confiding in me. 'A great one for meetings. In the English style. Except that he must make his living, I think he would spend all his times at meetings. Sometimes, in the family, we worry for him. He is not an idle man. Believe me in that. We tell him he is giving up the remains of his life when there is work to be done, problems to be attended to. But still he goes to his meetings. It is a kind of sickness in him. We have not the heart between us to stop him. He is so happy there, hearing speeches and counting up hands in the English style and so on. Sometimes I have heard him say he will do what the others at the meeting say. What can you do? It is a kind of sickness. Like the croquet and your bridge table.'

Shewfik walked me to the door of the laundry, the two of us dodging the linen bags as we went. 'A jug of water,' he said as we reached our door, a startled look of dismay crossing his face. 'For the Chairman. Of course, a jug of water. And clean glasses. I will send the girl. How foolish of me. How forget-ful.' He moaned slightly. 'Everything buggered up. Good and properly. What will my purchaser say?' He looked at me wildly and hammered his temple with a fist. 'A jug of water in the English style. He must have noticed, your Chairman. He has reported me! That is the trouble with your meetings. They are full of hidden traps. General business. That is the one to watch for. My uncle knows. But me? Good and proper-ly up the spout.'

Sensing his mounting hysteria, I tried to calm him. It was difficult. I told him that there had been no complaints so far. I promised to summon him the moment things looked like getting out of hand. He thanked me; attempted to hug me in fact. Ultimately, I was able to shake myself free of him and stumble out of the laundry into the dazzling brightness of the sun, wondering what on earth I was going to say to the meeting. 'Concrete information', I reflected, the door leading into the kitchen corridor slamming shut behind me; it was hard to come by.

Chapter 9

Back in the foyer, I found that the atmosphere of the meeting had changed. David Shears was on his feet speaking. I could tell from the way that Burgess was hunched forward over the front desk, the knuckles of one hand pressed into his gaunt cheek, the fingers of the other hand drumming impulsively on the top of the desk, staring at the speaker, his grey eyes intent and brooding, that some kind of debate was taking place between the two men. All eyes were watchful. There was no movement anywhere else in the room. Even Bricky and the boys were following the proceedings attentively, making no attempt to obstruct me as I sidled past them on the way to the front of the room.

'I don't think we're going about things the right way.' David was leaning forward as he spoke, his hands positioned on the padded shoulders of the armchair immediately in front of him. 'What have we been told so far? Nothing at all. The ship's crew won't talk. Probably been told not to. And now they're sitting out there having nothing to do with us.' He gestured towards the canal. 'And as far as I can see, Dr Magro is up to something we don't understand. I found him pretty evasive. Very polite but basically evasive. Suppose what we've heard is true. Suppose there is no question of disease here. That the shipping company is in trouble. If that's the case, then this quarantine is just a fraud. We're being detained against our will, and we should be taking action straight away to put it right. That's how I see it.

'I know the political situation here is dicey. All up in the air at the moment. Frankly, I don't understand it and don't pretend to. But there must be someone else to deal with besides Magro. That's why I say let's send a deputation into the city. Find the top British official. And put the case in front of him. It's the only way we'll get anywhere. There's no sign of anyone falling ill at the moment. That shows in itself this quarantine is crazy.

'But the longer we stay here, all crammed up together, water being brought out in a truck, food coming from God knows where — the more likely it is that people will start getting sick.' David paused for a moment, his gaze travelling round the room as if looking for support, and then slowly resumed his seat.

The room was silent. Absolutely still. The kind of stillness which can take possession of a concert chamber a brief moment before the violinist lowers his instrument; the audience attentive to the final, quivering note, the filament of sound extending itself to a point of disappearance, invisibility, perfect concentration.

Burgess broke the silence with a dry cough. A chairman's cough. A small, unhurried sound. But with the crackle of an agenda in it. Delicately, he scratched the bridge of his nose. 'Thank you for that valuable contribution to the debate,' he said, carefully placing his pencil beside the pad in front of him and settling back in his chair. 'I think we're all indebted to Mr Shears for his comments.' The members of the audience, sensing that there was going to be no confrontation, no sharp clash of opinions, began to relax. One or two people shifted the position of their chairs.

'Speaking personally,' Burgess continued, surveying the room, his voice conversational, 'I found everything that Mr Shears had to say was very much to the point.' There was a small murmur of approval. 'My only regret is,' Burgess said, smiling indulgently, 'that Mr Shears isn't a ·medical man. Then we'd really know where we stand.'

Again, there was a murmur of approbation. But this time Burgess cut it short by holding up his hand for silence. 'Of course, that's the point, isn't it?' he said, the tone of his voice becoming serious. 'Dr Magro is, indeed, a duly qualified medical practitioner. Trained at the Kitchener School of Medicine, I believe. Your committee can vouch for it. We've already made one or two inquiries in that regard as a matter of course.'

Burgess leaned forward and took up his pencil again, and looked directly into the eyes of his audience. 'I think we have to be a wee bit careful before we start treading on toes. We've got some children here and some old people.' He flapped a

97

hand at the elderly sisters. 'If some of us do start getting sick — and I don't say for one moment that we will — we're going to need Dr Magro.'

These remarks had obviously touched a responsive chord. A faint whisper of assent could be detected throughout the room. I sat down on a spare chair near the front, waiting for a chance to come forward, rehearsing, beneath my breath, what I was going to say; wondering how, in a few words, I could get the message across to Burgess that Shewfik Arud was totally unreliable; that if we wanted to open a line of communication to the outside world we would have to look further than the proprietor of the Quarantine Station.

'And, of course,' Burgess continued. 'There's the problem of getting into the city. I don't quite know what Mr Shears had in mind concerning transport. In extreme circumstances, I would agree, one sometimes has to take unorthodox action. Probably one or two of us here have had to commandeer a vehicle when there's been a spot of "trouble" brewing.' Directing a sympathetic smile to the corner of the room occupied by the planters, Burgess was rewarded by a ripple of nods and murmurs. 'But I think we want to avoid illegal action as far as possible.'

'Quite right,' I heard the scrapbook man mutter from somewhere behind me. 'Quite right.'

'The political situation is difficult,' Burgess said, testing the strength of the pencil he was now holding between his hands. 'I mention that simply as a matter of plain fact. It's very difficult. And changing day by day. Not quite the same as parliament, you know. Not the same sort of thing at all. There are all sorts of groupings and factions which the newcomer couldn't possibly hope to understand. Not in a month of Sundays. But don't think for one moment that I blame young David Shears for not being familiar with it all, as he says.'

Burgess forced another smile. 'I'd be the first to admit that when I was his age I had my mind on other things.' There was a shy titter from the elderly ladies and one of Bricky's mates guffawed loudly. Out of the corner of my eye, I couldn't help noticing that this caused Mrs Walker to direct a look of unmistakeable hostility towards David; probably attributing the flutter of merriment provoked by the chairman's last remark to David's association with Isobel on board the ship, especially the episode in the makeshift swimming pool. 'But the fact is that we can't afford to appear in front of the authorities like a gang of hijackers,' Burgess concluded, speaking firmly.

'That isn't quite my point . . .' David blurted out, springing to his feet, his manner agitated.

Burgess tossed his pencil on to the table with a clatter. He held up a hand for silence, compelling David to resume his seat. 'I know the last twenty-four hours haven't been easy. And when tempers get frayed there's a tendency to want to do things impulsively. In that respect David Shears has my sympathy entirely. I know how he feels.'

'But my point . . .' David began again. He sounded shrill, petulant almost.

'Sit *down*, young man,' one of the elderly sisters said furiously, rapping the floor with her cane.

'Perhaps the secretary of our committee has some news for us,' Burgess interposed, inviting me to come forward to the front desk, introducing a diversion.

I tiptoed forward and leaned across the desk to speak to him. 'There's not much to report,' I murmured. 'Not in the way of concrete information.' Somehow or other, I knew I had to make it clear that Shewfik was like something out of a comic opera more than a person in real life. That was the one thing I knew I had to make clear. 'Shewfik knows less about cables than a novice in a nunnery,' I whispered, paraphrasing a line from the Major-General's song in *Pirates of Penzance*, assuming Burgess would take the point.

'For God's sake,' Burgess hissed at me, a venomous splash of saliva stinging my cheek. 'Get on with it. What did he say?'

'Nothing really.'

'Nothing.' The face of my confederate at the front table abruptly became a mask of loathing. 'Get a grip on yourself. Did he say he was in touch with the authorities?'

'He *said* he was.'

With that, Burgess waved me away and turned his attention back to the meeting, quickly regaining his composure. 'Our secretary has gone into the matter,' he said. 'Very thoroughly as a matter of fact. As some of you probably know, soon after we landed I took it upon myself to make some representations to the authorities by cablegram. The latest reports we have suggest that our submission is under consideration as a matter of priority.'

There was something bland and compelling about the way Burgess spoke. One had to admire his performance. What I couldn't fathom was why he was so determined to have his own way. Did it always happen like this at meetings? That simply because a query was raised as to the wisdom of following some course of conduct the original proponent of that course felt obliged to defend his position even at the expense of truth?

'And in addition to that,' Burgess continued, 'following a personal plea to the ship's captain, I myself have made personal contact with the spokesman for the relevant authorities on your behalf. Therefore, summing up, I think we can safely say that negotiations through the proper channels are under way and are likely to bear fruit in the near future.'

'Whom exactly have you spoken to?' David called out.

The question hadn't been asked in an especially provocative tone but it was interpreted that way. 'Keep quiet, *please*,' one of the old ladies said crossly.

'You've had your say, young fellow,' the scrapbook man commented, endorsing her remarks. Mrs Walker looked prim and the planters stirred uncomfortably, embarrassed.

'I'm afraid I haven't kept a diary of every minute,' Burgess said, ostentatiously slapping the pockets of his shirt as if reminding himself that he was honour bound to keep a record of his movements. 'I can't honestly say that I've kept a record of every single thing I've done. But if that is the wish of the meeting, I will certainly do so.'

'Of course not,' Mrs Walker called out; intervening in the debate for the first time. 'No one expects you to.' Her voice was crisp and determined.

'Absolutely ridiculous,' the scrapbook man exclaimed. And there was a general murmur of approval.

'Nonetheless,' Burgess said, reverting to a tone of solemnity. 'If we are going to conduct our affairs in a democratic way, I think I'm duty bound to treat the remarks of Mr Shears as a motion of dissent. Can I, perhaps, treat the motion before the chair as being — that the negotiations presently being conducted on your behalf be abandoned. Does that seem to sum up the spirit of the motion? That the various things we've tried to do for you be called off? If that's the motion, then, I think we'll put it to a vote. We've had enough discussion. Everyone knows what the issues are.'

Burgess looked round the room for sign of objection. Finding none, in a mild, somewhat jocular undertone, he asked: 'Is there, in fact, anyone in favour of the motion?'

A lone hand rose from the body of the audience. Surprisingly, it was not David's hand. He himself, realizing the odds were against him, must have decided to throw in the towel. The hand belonged to Jack Morley. He had taken no part in the debate but held his hand up resolutely, almost defiantly; suggesting that some quality in the debate had convinced him that he must support the so-called motion of dissent.

Burgess nodded sympathetically, making a small clicking noise with his tongue. Then, leaned forward, pencil hovering above his pad to record the landslide. In a much louder voice, he put the serious question: 'All those *against* the motion?'

Nearly all the hands in the room rose in unison except those of David Shears, Jack Morley and my own. Isobel, I noticed, also wasn't voting. Burgess turned and looked at me. His grey eyes were difficult to avoid. I raised my hand. Then, he counted all the hands and declared the motion lost. As he explained to the meeting, he took this to be an indication that those present were happy for the committee to go on representing the interests of the passengers as a whole; to keep on 'negotiating' for our release.

There was no further disagreement. I wished there had been. Even then, at the meeting itself, I had a premonition that things were heading in the wrong direction; that for no real reason at all we were setting ourselves on a course which would involve misunderstandings and disaster; that some people, knowing only half the facts, would make mistakes and miss the point; that others, believing they did know all the facts, would regard any opinion contrary to their own as in the nature of a personal attack upon their probity, prompting them to retaliate in kind. That others again, because of some perversity in their nature, would seek to impose their wills upon the rest regardless of the facts. That for all these reasons, rumour and suspicion, like rank undergrowth concealing some impending catastrophe, would thrive and spread in all directions.

'Ask him again,' I wanted to call out across the floor of the meeting to David Shears. 'Ask him whom he's dealing with. What he hopes to achieve. For all we know, he's a stupid man. He may have left the whole thing with Magro.'

Surely, I thought to myself, surely common sense must prevail. Surely amongst these people there must be someone bold enough to look dispassionately at the matter; to find out the facts and make a balanced judgement. None of the great assemblies of the past, or even of the world today, would let things ramble on into the undergrowth without taking some steps to set things right.

These feelings gnawing at me, how I waited for someone to rise up from the floor of the meeting — to speak calmly, without anger, in a way which would be acceptable to all sides, to review the whole position, to set us straight. Jack Morley, perhaps. Someone with special insight, someone able to see through people such as Shewfik Arud and Dr Magro and to put the situation in perspective.

But I waited in vain. No one spoke. Not in that way. The meeting moved on to consider other matters. The *faszad*, that strange conglomerate of misunderstanding, self-interest and meaningless intrigue, was beginning to run its course. And looking back to that day over forty years, I remain conscious of the same turbulence within me. Knowing now how the disaster would manifest itself, the urge to shoulder my way back through time, to take up a position in the front row of the meeting and to speak my mind becomes unbearable; an agonizing itch which pervades my whole being. Why did no one speak? Why did everyone assume someone else knew better?

Older now, a little wiser, I know full well that even the kind of speaker I had in mind would have been greeted with initial scepticism, the line of his thought resisted, he himself assailed for his lack of evidence, his motives called into question; yes, he would have appeared before us in the loincloth of a pygmy, dressed like ourselves. But at least it would have been said; there would, at least, have been a display of courage, something to look back on without shame. Ah, courage, that much despised but infectious quality!

But why waste time on courage. In fact, the motion having been declared lost, the floor of the meeting was being rapidly infected by something equally contagious. I refer, of course, to boredom; that persistent malady, that lethal disorder of the tongue, a painless but latent septicaemia, the carrier never being conscious that he has it, boredom, embodied, in this case, by the person of Mr Horwood.

I think mention has already been made of Mr Horwood. You will appreciate, my friend, my patient censor, that having been about this enterprise for many days now — and mostly before breakfast — it would really be far too wearying to go back and find out what exactly I have written. But I believe Mr Horwood has been mentioned. He must have been. Conscientious bores, those with a dogged aptitude for their work, seldom escape notice — especially on a ship.

Yes, Mr Horwood, ex-alderman of one of Sydney's less fortunate city councils, the incredibly, if not criminally, inappropriate chairman of the council's Art and Leisure Committee for thirteen years and seven months precisely, cartage contractor and former runner-up in something similar to golden gloves, whose father once had dinner at the Embassy on Steamer Point, this luddite of the inner ear, a thumb buried in his paunch at the belt, his heavy jowels, gleaming with perspiration, being mopped at with a handkerchief — was on his feet; lecturing the meeting on the subject of personal hygiene, the kitchen, the communal bathroom, reminding those present that the locker room at Surry Hills football field in 1927 had been plagued by tinea for months on end, principally because of carelessness. Beside him, in a floral dress, his exhausted-looking wife nodded approvingly, recalling those frightening days; the long campaign, the nights, the mugs of tea, the men locked in conference, the final victory, the jock-straps buoyant again.

Methodically, his words sinking into the meeting like a slow poison, Mr Horwood let us have the benefits of his experience. At first, out of a misguided sense of politeness, the passengers listened attentively. Even I, as protective of the clefts between my toes as the next man, always prepared to learn new skills, to pit myself against the treacherous undercurrents of the intestinal tract and bowel, sat upright in the early stages of the discourse, receiving all.

But in the second aeon, my spirits flagged. Like others present, I found that my chair began a stealthy evacuation from beneath me so that, constantly, I finished up slumped in apathetic poses. From time to time, sternly reproving myself, I immediately sat upright again. But gradually, deadened by inertia, the will to resist the process disappeared altogether. Like a fish, one glazed eye pressed to a crack between planks of the jetty, weakly drawing breath, I went on listening to Mr

Horwood's voice; all hope gone, my despair heightened by the knowledge that, not far away, cool and slumberous, weathered pylons glistening with barnacles disappearing downwards into the green depths of it, lay the rapture of another world; if only one could reach it.

Whether some respected scholar has written a treatise on the subject of boredom, I simply do not know. Quite probably. The tendency of all research is to magnify the problem requiring resolution; to expand it into something worthy of a grant, a doctorate, a professorial chair. And why not boredom? A spate of textbooks on the subject could turn the problem into a real threat. Stimulate a demand for a School of Advanced Study. A seminar in Rome, at least. Yes, why not ride the glacier? Mr Horwood having flickered into view, it would be foolish of me not to jot down a few notes towards a definitive definition.

For some reason, people often have the absurd belief that bores are immediately recognizable. That they never travel in disguise. Nothing could be further from the truth. Oh, without doubt, one frequently encounters novices; those who ply their trade on the outskirts of the dinner table, tedious souls who fiddle about with platitudes and pluck at your attention with cricket scores or recipes just as someone in the centre is on the point of revealing what he overheard Churchill say to Roosevelt at Yalta. There are plenty of that kind about, to be sure.

But we are speaking now of veterans; grand masters in the craft. They are invariably in disguise. How can they hope to extend the torture over many hours unless they first disarm you with a brief display of affability and a simulation of interest in your views?

Take Mr Horwood, for example. I have to concede that when first we sat together on deck, legs propped up on the ship's rail, I listened to his dissertation on desert travel with more than passing interest. He knew the desert. He had been a soldier. Post-war, he had helped to quell the riots on the Nile Delta in 1919. He seemed to know what he was talking about. His suggestion that light roads could easily be established across the desert by simply hardening the existing tracks with a fine spray of bitumen smacked of common sense. And my own contributions to the dialogue were heard attentively.

But then time dragged on. Our glasses were emptied and filled again. But then, while my interest in the theme diminished, his increased. We crossed the deserts of the world in tandem. The Sahara. The Nullarbor. The Simpson. His spirits never flagged. In fact, his enthusiasm mounted. Restlessly, my feet explored the rail for new positions; seeming to be hitched to the horizon. And on we went. My excuses quashed with jocularity. My attempts at escape restrained by avuncular hands.

This, then, is the first proposition of consequence. Boredom proper is induced not so much by the tedium of the words uttered in one's presence but by the realization that one is doomed. That the speaker, nourished by his own language, is growing stronger while one's own self is steadily becoming weaker. True boredom, then, as distinct from mere superficial feelings of impatience, is marked by a kind of horror; a desperation; a sense of being surrounded by fields of impenetrable energy; a recognition that one is in the grip of alien forces; forces with fantastic powers of endurance. One wriggles. One squirms. One gropes for a chunk of krytonite. One reminds oneself that Bonnie Dundee, who was rumoured to be impervious to ordinary bullets, ultimately, at Killiecrankie in 1689, had to be shot with a silver button from his own coat. And one gazes longingly at the bore's necktie, dreaming of strangulation.

Yes, if I am ever to map out a thesis on boredom, Mr Horwood is worthy of attention. And further, whenever he spoke, one was conscious that a different language was being spoken: a language of irrelevancy, chuckling footnotes, disjointed stories and punch lines in splints. Matters of importance were bluntly pushed aside, shouldered out of the scrum, until finally one felt that nothing of substance whatsoever was being said. And the sense of weariness engendered thereby was final proof that one was in the presence of a master.

It was this quality, this sense of words being utterly remote from matters at the forefront of my mind, this habit of being quite oblivious to the effects his words were having, which finally, in addition to his energy, persuaded me that Mr Horwood could justifiably claim to be in the very front rank of crashing bores. Because, by the time we got to know each other, by the time we began to have our rail-side conversations, we had left the Quarantine Station behind us. And although, for a short time, it was a relief to talk of other things — desert travel, building roads; indeed, an escape from the memory of our unhappy experience to talk of such things — after a time, it became oppressive to hear him go on and on when the rest of the passengers were weighted down by the shadow of what had occurred; by the fact of David's death and all its consequences.

And when that mood came upon me, when his words, although anchored in reality, dealing only with the actual world, true events, nonetheless seemed to have nothing to do with what had come to be most real, the inner world of love and fortitude, and justice, the things capable of betrayal, corruption, matters of the most significance, then sometimes, even in Mr Horwood's presence, breaking into his self-indulgent monologues, I would lurch to the rail and be sick; sick with a complete abandonment of the body, exhausting myself with vomiting. And even at the moment of nausea, the bile rising in my throat, the white lather of the ship's track flashing away from the flanks of the ship beneath me, wondering, deep inside me, whether the lassitude I have described as boredom was something more than boredom — self-disgust, perhaps; remorse, or bitter grief.

Chapter 10

Isobel. The very name, the mere sound of it, seemed to activate some hidden zone of pleasure within me, making me prickle inwardly. Isobel. Murmured softly, the syllables themselves would float away from one's lips forming an image in the surrounding dark of smooth limbs and loveliness somewhere just within my reach. Isobel . . . Isobel. At night, struggling into wakefulness at odd hours, there being no pattern to it, her name seemed to haunt my lips incessantly being, at once, a plea for the dream of her not to fade but also, in part, an involuntary murmur of despair.

So many nights broken in that way. The hours of darkness, a lonely chamber, a rack. If David and I had been obliged to go on sharing the same bed after the first night, life would surely have been intolerable.

When dreams of Isobel came to me in the night, flickering before my eyes in tantalizing glimpses until I lay wide awake, tossing and turning, my mind would be seething with voluptuous shadows, but gradually transferring its attention from private fantasies to a desperate rehearsal of what I would say to her in the morning, how I would approach her, what I had said to her the day before.

When my mind was occupied in that way, utterly preoccupied with memories and aspiration, active, but at the same time, longing for rest, the bed seemed scarcely large enough for a single person. Yes, it was, indeed fortunate that we had been able to make other arrangements — obtaining a camp stretcher from Shewfik Arud and David volunteering to set it up at the end of the upstairs corridor, making it his permanent bed. So very fortunate. His presence would have been unbearable.

Sometimes, lying awake, turning the pillow this way and that, trying to banish all thoughts of Isobel from my mind, trying to subdue my desire for her — a hard, compelling desire that left me sleepless, exhausted by daybreak — I envied him his camp stretcher, knowing that, on my way to the bathroom in the morning, I would see him there, the outline of his head visible beneath the pale gauze of his mosquito net, sleeping peacefully, untroubled, utterly relaxed.

Was there some magic in it, I wondered, lying in the darkness, moonlight through the shutters of the verandah door casting a grid of slanting silver rods on the floor beside my bed? Was I heir to some abnormality, some hereditary mania, that I should be racked by visions of the girl? Were my responses human or debased? Others seemed to be able to control themselves, passing before my eyes daily; their voices rational, occupied with worldly things — their income, their health, their relatives. Why not I? Never before had I been gripped by such fierce uncertainties. I longed to take up the moonlit grille beside me and tear it apart; to buckle up the silver rods, to fling them at the wall. They seemed so tangible; the shadows between the rods so sharp-edged.

But then, I would turn again to the pillow, stretch out in a new position and compose myself. Address my mind to my studies; remind myself that Borthwick was a better man than Isobel — turn a passage of translation over in my mind, persuade myself that this was my vocation, my chosen course, renouncing all other pursuits. But even then, even when I had finally managed to settle myself and achieve some peace of mind, hovering there on the edge of sleep — the slow, irresistible fantasy would begin to seep into my thoughts, dominate my mind — Isobel, the two of us alone together, the room, wherever it was, seeming to be soundless except for the pleasant murmur of our voices, the walls insulated by vaguely perceived but richly decorated tapestries, her loose garment in the candlelight, her nightdress dissolving beneath my touch, my kisses . . .

And then I would be wide awake again, punching the pillow into new positions restlessly. Isobel. The name, at once, a pleasurable reminder of what was taking place before my eyes but, in the same breath, an invocation, a call for reality to reassert itself, to make its presence felt, to rid me of the dream. And all the time, my despair heightened by the knowledge that in the morning, if I met her, if I was fortunate enough to have a moment with her, conversation would be polite but desultory, taking place mostly within her mother's earshot; but even then, even within that framework of decorum, my night-time infatuations would still be chafing at the back of my mind, making the daylight actuality seem remote and meaningless, the stilted conversations as ephemeral, as difficult to anchor in the mind, as images from a dream.

But in the days following the meeting, all activity at the Quarantine Station had a similar quality; a feeling of remoteness, of time held in suspension, of listlessness overshadowed by an ever-present sense of concealed tension, foreboding; the steamer itself, riding offshore, the visible evidence of dislocation — being always there, a sombre outline motionless on the water. Whether one stepped on to the wide upstairs verandah or strolled out of doors, or even if one was just reading a tattered magazine in the foyer, the grey steamer, its weathered flanks stained with rust always seemed to be within view; a mote in the corner of one's eye, at anchor, a reminder of our isolation.

The sultry days, the brown landscape, sapped our energy. People gave up talking about how we were going to get out, how long it would take. The general assumption was that Burgess was working on it. That Burgess would pull something out of the hat. And for that we were thankul. Myself included.

Although I was supposed to be on his wretched committee, he certainly never sought my advice. Since my failure to produce 'concrete information' when required, apart from a few words in the corridor on odd occasions, I had little to do with him. I wondered how he was getting on with Shewfik Arud. Presumably, Shewfik had simply told him whatever was necessary to keep him satisfied.

In my experience, Shewfik would regard a lie told to please one of his guests as being no more than an elementary courtesy; one of the duties incidental to his management of the concession — a notion which Burgess, on the other hand, would find so fantastic as to be scarcely worthy of consideration. To Burgess, in accordance with the European tradition, a lie was a serious business; something you saved up for important moments and used only when it was absolutely necessary to deceive. But even though I suspected that they were working at cross-purposes, that Burgess, proceeding through the agency of Shewfik Arud and Dr Magro, was making no real progress, I left matters alone.

For my part, I spent most of my time in my room — grappling with Borthwick. The dresser, the only other item in the room apart from the bed, the wardrobe and the rickety chair, was too high to work on. But I managed to persuade Shewfik to let me have one of the old bridge tables I found stacked away under the main staircase and this became my desk.

Not that I accomplished much, sitting in the stuffy room in the afternoon heat, my clothes damp with perspiration, my arms itching from small sores which, having been scratched, began to fester, and never seemed to heal. A rash beneath my wrist-watch was particularly irksome. And unsightly — a red flush of peeling skin beginning to spread up my arm. The heat, the small but bothersome irritations made it hard to work. And overall, one was conscious of a lack of vitality.

Fortunately, I had been able to borrow some paper from the scrapbook man, and therefore had something to write on, although I took care to use it sparingly. But more often than translation, I would find myself using it to make sketches of Isobel. Profiles. Sketches of her hands. She and her mother walking. Isobel reading. Then, guilty, realizing that I had idly covered almost an entire page in this way, I would crumple up the scrap of paper and resolutely try to settle down to my work again.

But it was never any use. The mood of lethargy which seemed to have penetrated to every corner of the Station was too oppressive. I would become restive, fidgety. And the slight murmur of voices from the verandah outside, the random chinking of coins and glasses as Bricky and the boys at their end of the verandah, were occupied by the endless card game, their methodical drinking, a distant ripple of noise which, upon first sitting down at my desk was only a background movement, a faint distraction, but which soon became an intolerable disturbance, obliging me to quit the room and go downstairs; irritable, annoyed with myself, my fellow passengers, wanting to be alone, but, at the same time, hoping to find Isobel, to sit and talk with her, any conversation, no matter how stilted, being better than none. But knowing all the time that she would probably be with David or, if not with him, that she would find an excuse to slip away and join

110

him. And probably leaving me talking to Mrs Walker, engaged in a polite but long conversation, chiefly concerning her experience of business houses in the East, which would leave me feeling more exhausted than ever, more irritable, feeling that I was surely ridden with some debilitating palsy.

And yet, if I didn't spend time in their company there was nothing much else to do downstairs. The scrapbook man had set himself up in one corner of the foyer and sat there, day after day, jotting down notes and pasting things up. By this time most of our luggage, such of it as was accessible, had been brought in from the steamer. Hence, now fully equipped, he was able to sit there sucking on his pipe while he made notes and studied the faded clippings and photographs which he leisurely extracted from the two or three large shoe-boxes he had positioned around him.

Now and again, having nothing else to do, I came and peered over his shoulder, watching him as he pondered over his scraps of paper, sometimes holding as many as four or five clippings in his hand before sadly discarding the bulk of them and applying his glutinous paste to the one that mattered.

He didn't object to my presence. In fact, as often as not, I was one of a small gallery of spectators watching him at work; the most frequent attenders being the elderly sisters and their brother, sitting in a row behind his shoulder, being most careful to speak only when spoken to.

I gathered that the scrapbook was not just a scrapbook. It was to be the foundation for an autobiography; the consummation of a lifetime's work. The scrapbook man had been something to do with the manufacturing of mining equipment. Most of his photographs were of hillsides blackened by coal dust or gaunt derricks standing on ridges. Many of the clippings made reference to mining disasters. There were obituaries extracted from company reports and union broadsheets. Obituaries of mine managers and respected foreman — the secretary of a social club. All written in the stately prose of a bygone era. 'Many will lament his passing ... He has been snatched into the shadows ... May the sand rest lightly on a good sport.'

Such wistful phrases, repeated time and time again in the faded newsprint — acquaintances, presumably, of the scrapbook man. Certainly, he was in no rush to complete his work.

111

It often took him a long time to decide which of several items was worthy of the paste; the decision process being assisted by a good deal of pipe cleaning and experimental suckings.

It was impossible to tell what criteria he applied in making his selection. Sometimes, without discomforting himself by turning round, he would hold up a photograph for the gallery to inspect. Perhaps, a picture of a miner holding a drill. Or a sporting team standing in solemn ranks, the captain nursing a trophy. Sometimes, photographs of a regiment.

'That's nice,' one of the sisters would say. 'Isn't it nice?' inviting her sister to comment. 'I like it,' the other would agree. 'There's something about it.'

The bald head in front of us would nod slowly. 'Hard to come by these days,' the scrapbook man would say, by way of summary, but still without looking round. 'If you don't put them aside at the time, they're gone forever. You won't find pictures like that in the history books.' Then, having pondered on it for a while longer, sadly, and usually after a few tentative retrievals, he would place it in what I understood to be the shoe-box full of rejects.

No one ever questioned or commented on his decision. Quite possibly this was because the older hands knew they would have a further chance; that the decision wasn't necessarily irrevocable. It was not until I had been watching the process intermittently for several days, and happened to notice a miner wielding a distinctively-shaped drill identical to one I had seen a few days before, that I realized that the reject box was periodically brought up for review. Clearly, in the final analysis, if the years were merciful, everything would receive the paste.

Why exactly he had embarked upon this sisyphean labour was impossible to tell; the motivation behind it was never really disclosed. Once, in my presence, one of the sisters coyly asked that very question. 'I don't know how you keep at it,' she said. 'You must have been born with a special talent.'

'We've never had anyone creative in our family,' the other sister chipped in, tactfully, indicating the reason for their mutual interest.

The scrapbook man sucked his pipe, contemplating the issue set before him. 'It's the daemon,' he said, at length, almost sadly, releasing a clipping, the frail paper softly fluttering awkwardly into a shoe-box. 'It never lets up.'

112

'The *Daemon*.' A breathless hush descended upon the gallery as the word was whispered aloud, the speaker looking into her sister's eyes, being rewarded by a wide-eyed humility equal to her own. 'The *Daemon*.' And nothing else was said. As if the sisters, fearful of penetrating to the core of mystery, were satisfied to have caught a glimpse of the forces of creativity — the sombre, unrelenting compulsion which, like dark battlements in silhouette above Childe Roland's slughorn, lay forever beyond the reach of their family and themselves.

But strangely enough, it was in consequence of a visit to this quiet corner of the Quarantine Station that events were set in motion which brought me closer to Isobel. I can remember the particular morning distinctly. It was the morning Shewfik Arud's purchaser came out to the station for what, according to Shewfik, was to be his final tour of inspection.

'Today he will give us the once over for the last time,' Shewfik said to me with an air of confidence.

Coming downstairs early, wondering whether to take myself for an after-breakfast walk to the vantage point on the escarpment, I had found Shewfik in the foyer peering out of the window overlooking the approach to the Quarantine Station, nervously fingering the rough hessian curtain which he had drawn back from the window-pane, casting anxious glances over his shoulder at the large clock set in the wall above the entrance to his office. 'We can afford no mistakes,' he confided to me, managing a harassed smile. 'Not today. Not when all is in readiness for the change-over.'

'First, I give him a big breakfast.' Shewfik began ticking off his tactics on the fingers of one hand, all the time keeping an eye on the road. 'A decent breakfast. An example of goodwill. My friendship. Any time he has come he has always wanted a good meal. That is the way it is in business. A working meal. And this purchaser is a man who knows the ways of business. And has contacts. Titterington, the King's chemist, for example. He is a personal friend of my purchaser. A bosom friend.

'Then, after our meal, I will show him that the heating is in total order. All beyond repair. He insists it must be. And then, if I am still myself, the bargain is struck. Put together, just like that.' Shewfik smacked his fist into the palm of his hand to demonstrate the point.

113

While we were speaking, the scrapbook man had been setting himself up nearby in his usual corner, opening up his large album, putting out his paste and distributing his cardboard shoe-boxes in a semi-circle around him. He fumbled for his pipe, staring morosely at his effects.

'Do you see his car?' Shewfik hissed at me, tightening his grip on the curtain, narrowing the size of the opening so as not to be seen.

Sure enough, rounding the shoulder of the escarpment where the road passed between the swamp flats of the inlet and the foot of the ridge just below the vantage point, a car had appeared; a black car with a long snout of a bonnet and a spare tyre strapped to the runningboard, dust blowing from behind its rear wheels. 'He is here,' Shewfik said, dropping the curtain. 'He is within earshot.' He smoothed down the collar of his khaki shirt and darted off towards the entrance.

'He's an odd chap, that one,' the scrapbook man said to me, casually looking up from his work. 'Can't make head nor tail of him m'self.'

Idly, still wondering whether it was worthwhile going for a walk, I strolled over to my usual position behind his chair.

'Do us a favour,' he said, half-cocking his head towards me, speaking in a matter-of-fact way. 'I've left one of my boxes behind. What about slipping upstairs and fetching it, eh? There's a good chap.'

I was happy to oblige him. He told me where his room was and gave me elaborate directions as to how to find the box. Purposefully, I set off, mounting the stairs with my usual double-step stride, having long ago been told that vigorous climbing of stairs was good for the heart and excused all other forms of physical activity. Naturally, I made as much use as I could of the bannister.

The scrapbook man's room was about midway down the long corridor. I was still panting when I got there. His room was much like my own. There was a bed, a wardrobe and a shuttered door leading on to the verandah. The only difference was that whereas mine was a complete room, this was smaller and had a makeshift quality about it. One wall consisted of a high wooden partition. The partition only went about two-thirds of the way towards the height of the ceiling. The space between the top of the partition and the ceiling was occupied by a long curtain suspended on a cord running from hooks in either walls and some hooks driven into the ceiling. The room having been divided in two in this way, the side in which I was standing was really quite small. The bed, pushed up against the partition, took up almost the entire length of available space. The old wardrobe beside the bed was smaller than my own. Someone had run another length of cord from the partition to the end of the wardrobe to serve as a washing-line. A row of handkerchiefs hung from the line limply.

I found the missing shoe-box, not at the foot of the bed as predicted by the scrapbook man (or the shoe-box man — whichever you prefer; I myself was certainly beginning to wonder which description was the most apt) but pushed under the head of the bed, the lid beside it. Obviously, before turning in the previous night, the Daemon had taken hold of him and persuaded him to delve into this particular shoe-box while sitting up in bed. Having found what he wanted, he must have put it away in the wrong place.

Just as I was straightening up, fitting the lid of the box to the body, through the partition, I heard a short cry of fright and the sound of something clattering to the floor. This was followed by another sharp cry. Instinctively, I clambered onto the bed which just gave me enough height to raise the dividing curtain and peer into the next room.

Isobel, dressed only in a loose, cotton dressing gown, was skittering from foot to foot in the corner of the room nearest the verandah door. She had scooped up the lower folds of her garment almost to waist height and was uttering quick yelps of anxiety, side-stepping, trying to dodge some menace on the floor nearby. The one chair in the room lay overturned at the foot of the bed, a heap of clothing beside it, suggesting that this was what I had heard falling.

'Quickly,' she called out, catching sight of me, and almost in the same breath giving another startled 'whoop' of fright. 'Two rats. *Two* of them.' There was a note of indignation in her voice. 'Help me.' Then, she yelped again and made a scrambling dive for the bed.

I tried to haul myself up and over the partition. I wasn't quite sure what I was doing. But with the shoe-box still tucked under my arm and the curtain brushing my face, I wasn't doing very well. And with some measure of weight upon it, the partition began to sway precariously.

'Use the door,' Isobel bleated, now bundled up on the bed and alternating quick peerings over the edge with unsympathetic glances towards my performance on the Matterhorn. 'Quickly. Quickly,' she yelped.

'Coming,' I said, sliding off the partition to an upright position on the scrapbook man's pillow, noticing as I jumped down, that I had left smudged footprints on the grey linen, footprints which I hurriedly smacked at with my free hand, turning the pillow over and heading for the door.

I raced into the corridor and up to the next door, barging in to find Isobel still scrambling round the bed on her knees. 'They've gone under,' she called out, now flattening herself out along the length of the bed, face downwards, leaning over the edge of the bed for a better view. I caught a quick glimpse of smooth, golden legs flashing out along the bed, flailing about for balance. A breathtaking sight. I nearly swooned. But then she was kneeling up and turning to the other side of the bed.

'One just went under the wardrobe.' As I reached the bed, she snatched the shoe-box out from under my arm and hurled it wildly at the space between the wall and the wardrobe. Clippings and oddments went everywhere. At that moment, a brown scurrying thing came at me from the foot of the bed, charging past, crouched against the wall opposite for a second while I tried to kick the chair at it and then went desperately in a straight line for the wardrobe.

'Force them out,' Isobel yelled.

I looked round and picked up a jacket from the heap of clothes beside the chair.

'Not with that, you idiot,' she exclaimed, tearing it out of my hands. 'The parasol.'

Sure enough, a dainty parasol which must have been hanging from the back of the chair was sticking out from under the clothes. I grabbed it and went for the wardrobe, crouching there, flourishing it about between the short stumpy legs of the wardrobe, rattling it about industriously, Isobel calling encouragement from the bed, 'Anything?' she kept asking. 'Anything?' As though I was likely to straighten up with something impaled on the end of my weapon for her inspection.

'Nothing so far,' I said, breathing heavily, rattling some more.

'They must have gone,' she said as I stood up and went to the back of the wardrobe, looking along the wall. 'Escaped.' There was a note of reproach in her voice.

'Well, at least they're gone,' I replied, preferring to state the case in terms of positive achievements. I picked up the overturned chair and hung the dainty sun-umbrella from the back of it. Then, I restored the clothing to the base of the chair.

'Can't stand rats,' Isobel said, shivering briefly, and sitting up cross-legged on the bed, her dressing-gown still up around her bare thighs. 'They're revolting. Like toads and spiders and things.'

'And lizards,' I joined in, wanting to keep the conversation going. I bent down and began picking up the papers off the floor.

'Yes, lizards,' she agreed, but doubtfully. Clearly, I was slightly off the mark.

'I can't stand rats either,' I said, returning to safer ground.

Isobel reached into the pocket of her dressing gown and produced a handkerchief. She blew her nose and tucked it away again. The movement caused the crossover lapels of the gown to open a little way. As far as I could tell, she had nothing on underneath. In a mood of abstraction, I went back to my collecting. The pieces could have been banknotes or pages from the Domesday Book. I wouldn't have noticed; mechanically stuffing them into the box, my mind on other things.

'I've never liked things that take you by surprise,' Isobel said, reflectively.

'I can't stand them either,' I answered over my shoulder. I wasn't really clear what she meant but I was prepared to agree with anything for the sake of the conversation. Although I must admit the words 'You idiot' still echoed in my mind, rankling slightly. But not enough for me to make a fuss about it. Not while things seemed to be going so well.

'I'm getting sick of this rotten hole,' Isobel said, crossly. 'Rotten food. Rats in your bedroom.' She looked round the room. 'The whole place smelling sour. Smelling like garbage.'

Picking up the lid of the shoe-box, I sat down on the edge of the bed and began sifting through the contents of the box, shuffling the papers into a more orderly appearance.

'Sorry,' Isobel said, her voice softening. 'I didn't mean to mess them up. I panicked. It was the nearest thing.'

'That's okay,' I replied. 'Don't worry about it.' I gave her a comforting smile. And she smiled back. She really was attractive, her dark hair loose but wavy, the collar of her dressing gown open at the neck, exposing the healthy suntan beneath, the curve of her breasts. She must have only just got out of bed, looking so rumpled, but so healthy.

'What are you doing?' She edged forward slightly and studied the papers I had put beside me on the bed while I began re-arranging the contents of the box from the bottom up. As she moved closer to me, I felt self-conscious about the unsightly rash spreading outwards from the vicintity of my wrist-watch towards the elbow. I wished I was wearing a long-sleeved shirt. 'What about that?' I said, to distract her attention, showing her an old postcard, a picture of three rosy-cheeked young ladies stepping out in their summer dresses, arm-in-arm on an amusement pier, inviting her to share the joke.

'A Mabel Lucie Attwell postcard,' she whispered aloud, turning the postcard over and reading the inscription on the back, 'The three friends.'

'I bet they had a good time,' I said playfully, amazed at my daring.

But she seemed to respond favourably to the sally. 'I bet they did,' she said. 'I'm sure I will when I get to England. What else have you got there?' She moved closer to me to look at the papers inside the box. I could feel the soft pressure of her body against my arm. I didn't dare move my arm. I didn't want to move my arm. I peered intently into the box.

'They're not mine,' I said, hastily. 'I was just fetching them for the scrapbook man. He's got all sorts of things.'

I picked out an old menu and held it out for her to see. It was a ship's menu. Clumsily printed, the upper portion was dominated by a graphic design of a steamer moving through choppy seas towards a headland. There was a lighthouse on the headland — a few strokes of the artist's nib radiating out from it depicting iridescent beams. Beneath the drawing was a quotation from Kipling:

Swift shuttles of an empire's loom
that weave from main to main,
the coastwise lights of England
give you welcome back again.

118

For several minutes, we studied the menu together. 13th August 1921. Calf's Head *en tortue*. Braised leeks *au beurre*. Girton pudding. Savarin *des Fruits*.

How could I ever forget such names? Sitting beside Isobel, her shoulder, her breasts, leaning in towards me, just touching my arm. Quietly, almost magically, these perfectly ordinary words seemed to have been transformed into the names of exotic spices. Gently, moving no more than a fraction, I leaned towards Isobel, the pressure on my arm increasing ever so slightly, making me tingle inwardly. The stillness between us persisted. She didn't draw away. I was breathless, lowering the menu so that I could hold it steady.

Girton pudding. Leeks *au beurre*. Mind racing, I pondered my next move. The lighthouse beamed out at me encouragingly. Was she as conscious of our closeness as I was? Surely she must be. I had only to take her hand . . . A vignette from one of my night-time fantasies flickered into my mind. I immediately suppressed it. But it kept lurking about. This is ridiculous, I thought, steadying myself. This is simply a case of two people looking at a menu. Two adult people. Two rational adult people. And the calf's head *en tortue*.

What would she do if I tried to put my arm around her. My arm with a rash to the elbow. My leprous arm. Two rational adult people reading a menu at a Quarantine Station. It was madness to even think about it. But the soft pressure against my arm remained and an inward voice — a pleasant, conversational voice with no hint of hysteria in it kept saying: just do it. Just put your arm around her. Casually, just like that. See what happens. I will, I replied stiffly. That's what I intend to do. I'll be getting on with it in just a moment. But from somewhere deep in the earth a magnet was anchoring my hands in the one position. It was so pleasant to be with her, so thrilling, but at the same time I wished I was toying with a slice of Girton pudding somewhere off Dover on the 13th August 1921. This is ridiculous, I thought to myself for the final time; and made my move.

But just as I made my move she yawned sleepily and moved away so that my arm, detached from the magnet, clumsily floated upwards and bumped into her ribs.

'Sorry,' she said, yawning again.

'My fault,' I replied quickly, blushing, disguising my embarrassment by reaching for a clipping.

'They're fascinating, all those old cards,' she said, her words lengthening into another yawn. 'Excuse me.' She muffled the yawn with a hand and moved away from me, drawing the lapels of her dressing gown together absent-mindedly. 'I really ought to keep a scrapbook myself.'

'Perhaps we could work on one together,' I suggested, tentatively, shuffling the rest of the papers into the box, grateful that she hadn't noticed my discomforture.

'That's a thought.' Her tone of voice was matter-of-fact; not promising anything but, on the other hand, not rejecting the proposal out of hand. 'I'd better get dressed.' Gracefully, she swung her legs off the edge of the bed and stood up, the dressing gown settling itself down almost to ankle level. 'Thanks for your help.'

Warmed by her smile, I stood up, fumbling with the lid of the shoe-box, at a loss for words. 'Well, I'd better push along.' I stood there, awkwardly, for a moment, trying to think of something else to say. 'I enjoyed our talk,' I said, at length, looking into her eyes for some answering response.

'Yes,' she said, non-committally. 'I'd like to look at some more things some time. There's so little to do here while we're waiting.'

'But without the rats, next time,' I ventured.

'Without the rats. Definitely.' She smiled. 'Wait until I tell David about the rats.'

'If I see him first, I'll tell him.' I was a little put out by David's sudden and unsolicited appearance in the conversation. I wanted to make it clear by implication that David was the sort of chap who received rat stories from all quarters as a matter of routine. In short, there was no need for her to make any special effort to submit a report on the incident.

'See you later in the day, then,' I said, casually, moving to the door.

'Probably,' she said, 'As long as mother doesn't get into one of her moods.' She pouted and tightened the cord of her dressing gown, but giving me a final smile.

Almost in a daze, I went downstairs and delivered the box to the scrapbook man. The sisters were in their usual place, tactfully seated behind him, but on this occasion, I didn't join them. I needed time to think; to go over what had just taken place.

I went to my room and lay down on my bed. I removed my

spectacles and placed them on the chair beside the bed. Carefully, I reviewed the evidence.

Isobel and I had talked together privately for the first time. Leaving the rats out of it, and also the lizards, our conversation had gone quite smoothly. She had made no effort to break it off. It was fair to assume that she found me reasonably 'interesting'. Or, to put it another way, not altogether repulsive. Could I take it beyond that? In my experience, she was, basically, a very polite person. Had she been obliged to, she probably would have carried on a cheerful conversation with Svengali or Mickey Mouse without revealing any sign of inner reluctance.

No, not Mickey Mouse, I decided after a moment, retracing my thoughts. Not after the rats. Although polite, she was strong-minded. Quite capable of terminating a conversation upon finding out that her companion was in fact a member of the same detested species as the rats. So therefore, I finally concluded, I could draw some comfort from the knowledge that our conversation had been lengthy, and almost intimate. But could I take it beyond that?

It was true that she spent most of her time in David's company. But he wasn't encumbered by Borthwick. He had more time available for mooching about. It didn't necessarily follow that she was attracted to him. And she had seemed quite comfortable, quite relaxed, the two of us sitting together on the bed, suggesting that there was something physical between us.

Recapturing the moment, again, quite vividly, I felt the warm glow of her presence beside me, the soft pressure on my arm. I touched the spot, expecting the feeling to disappear. But it didn't. The pleasurable sensation remained. She was, without question, a beautiful creature; someone a man could really respect.

The more I thought about it, the more I was glad that I had not disgraced myself by trying to embrace her. I shuddered at the thought. It would have been disastrous. Quite out of character on both sides. Here was a woman accustomed to courtesy. Surprised in a moment of disarray, admittedly. But that, in itself, all the more reason for observing the proprieties.

No, any move on my part clearly would have been premature. As I saw it, our relationship would progress from a mutual interest in various things — I couldn't specify exactly what, as by this time I was becoming quite drowsy, but I had a vague impression of the two of us standing together in the nave of some lofty cathedral, fingering wood carvings on the portal and so on, animated conversation over a carafe of wine, a book of poetry open between us, the book having quite possibly been written by myself, the dedication in her favour being personal but discreet, Mrs Walker joining us for a drink ... It was all imprecise, but the general shape of the thing was quite clear in my mind. A relationship based on mutual interests, a growth of trust and respect; and if, in the course of time, the physical compulsion between us could be resisted no longer — well then, that would be natural and inevitable and no cause for shame.

With such thoughts slowly swirling through my mind, I drifted into a comfortable sleep; the first unbroken rest I had had for quite some time.

I was awakened by a medley of voices coming from somewhere outside the verandah door and the sound of a car's engine being revved madly, rising to a crescendo and falling away, and then coming back again with a feverish whining sound. It was impossible to go on sleeping through such a racket. Adjusting my clothes, I stepped out onto the verandah to see what was going on.

The white glare out of doors sprang savagely at my eyes. I raised a hand for protection before moving to the rail. Down below, between the verandah of the Quarantine Station and the parapet, still within the main enclosure, a vehicle was bogged in a patch of loose sand; the rear wheels of the car churning up sand and dust, the car lopsided.

Shewfik's purchaser had apparently tried to turn his vehicle round in the narrow space and had got himself into difficulty. The black car was slewed round, pointing towards the verandah. Bricky's two friends, Murph and Johnno, as I now knew their names to be, had set themselves behind the car and were straining to move it forward as the wheels spun. Bricky himself, I presumed, although it was difficult to tell at my distance, the face of the driver being obscured by the poky little windows of the car, was in the driver's seat.

The purchaser was standing near the car, a lean man in a black suit. Everything about him was thin and black. He had black, glistening hair which came forward to a narrow peak above his brow. A pointed moustache. A black tie making a thin line down his shirt. He stood there with one hand tucked into a trouser pocket watching the machinations of his car dispassionately, his black shoes set at oblique angles like the pointed hands of a clock.

He was smoking a cheroot. Shewfik, wringing his hands, was darting from the car to his purchaser, backwards and forwards; imploring the driver to extract the recalcitrant vehicle; placating the purchaser with expressions of optimism. Faintly, I could hear his two voices working together in harness. 'It will be all right. Step on it, Breeky. It will be okay. You will see.' But the purchaser took no notice of him, flicking away ash from the end of his thin cheroot.

'Take it out with a "whoosh",' Shewfik called, scampering back to the edge of the car and demonstrating his heart's desire with shunting motions of the hand.

As if in answer to his plea the car lurched forward a pace or two, the two men still straining at the back, the engine howling, only to sink into another pot-hole — a fresh shower of dirt spraying out behind the rear wheels. 'Step on it and out with a "whoosh",' Shewfik called again, scurrying to the back of the car to collect some pieces of wood which had been laid down for the wheels to get a grip on, and running forward to fling them wildly into a new position.

'Out with one "whoosh",' he screamed into the driver's cockpit, simultaneously mounting the running board to urge the chariot onwards.

'Shewfik, you bloody clown,' Murph yelled out from the rear, standing up in disgust, his hands on his hips. 'Keep out of it.'

Shewfik skipped nimbly off the running board but otherwise paid no attention to the remark. 'Think nothing of this,' he called out, returning to the purchaser, his face contorted into a smile. 'A trifle of a thing.' He waved a hand dismissively at the scene behind him. At that, as if by magic, the car staggered on to the hard surface of the road and came abruptly to a halt, catching Murph and Johnno, the two pushers, at the rear, off balance, both of them rebounding briefly off the back of the car and tottering to an upright stance.

'There it is,' Shewfik said triumphantly, hurrying across and wrenching the driver's door out wide to receive the purchaser.

Moodily, Shewfik's purchaser butted out the last of his cheroot with a pointed toe before moving across to step into the car, allowing Bricky to slide out of the driver's seat without comment. He ignored Shewfik's outstretched hand. A moment later, the door was dragged out of Shewfik's hands from an interior force and the engine revved. 'You will make your decision?' Shewfik shouted at the narrow window. 'We will hear from you?' And nodded in response to some muffled reply from within.

As the car pulled away, Shewfik turned towards Bricky and his mates, commencing to congratulate them each in turn with feverish handshakes.

Sheepishly, the three muscular men shook his hand, Bricky mopping his brow. 'That's okay, you old bastard,' I heard one of them say, as the entire group moved towards the Station, Shewfik in the centre, dwarfed by the others, his face alight, a hospitable hand placed on the shoulders of the two men nearest him.

'You are most objectionable,' he commented cheerfully. 'You are the most offensive men I have ever met.' And the group guffawed loudly, Shewfik's eyes beaming with pleasure.

I stayed at the verandah rail, looking towards the desert. The purchaser's car, which had disappeared from view behind the knotted ridges of the escarpment, had now re-appeared, some distance away, soft parachutes of dust billowing out behind it as it headed for the tiny mosaic of city buildings on the horizon. The car lurching and butting its way forward along the uneven desert track, now passing the swampy oasis of the inlet, a few rough fishermen's shelters visible among the scattering of trees and camel-thorn, now beyond it, and gradually diminishing.

I was still at the rail when Bricky and the boys came out on to the verandah to take up their usual positions at the table near where I was standing. They were in high spirits, laughing among themselves. In one hand, Bricky was carrying a large flagon.

'Hey, Professor,' Bricky called out. 'Come and 'ave a drink.'

'It's on the house,' one of the others said.

'On the station y' mean y' bloody prick,' Bricky said. And they all laughed uproariously.

By this time Johnno had uncorked the half-empty bottle on

the table, swilled the dregs out of a spare glass and brought it across to me. 'Here,' he said. 'Take it. 'ave a drink.' Johnno was usually the more reserved of the three. There seemed to be an air of gruff, almost apologetic, friendliness in his gesture.

Reluctantly, I took the filthy-looking tumbler, the glass clouded by fingerprints, the brownish fluid looking as though it had been drained out of a sump. Unappetizing. I sidled a few steps closer along the rail as a half-hearted indication of goodwill. They, slumping themselves into their chairs, rapidly dished out a liberal portion of brandy into each glass. Bricky put down the flagon he was carrying and examined the inch or so remaining in the bottle of liquor. 'Did someone tell Shewfik to send up another?' He cradled the bottle into the crook of his brawny arm, waiting for a reply.

'Yeah,' Murph said, lighting a cigarette. 'I did.' Casually he threw his empty cigarette packet over the side of the verandah rail.

'Well, Professor,' Bricky continued, putting the bottle back on the table and raising his glass to me in a mocking toast, his eyes smiling, a smudge of dust across his forehead, his blonde hair damp with perspiration. 'Here's to ya.'

'Yeah. Up yours,' one of the others said. They all chortled again and knocked back their drinks at a gulp. I took a sip of mine, watching them warily.

'What do ya think this is, Professor?' Bricky continued, wiping his mouth with the back of his hand. He picked up the flagon he had been carrying and held it out to me for inspection.

'I don't know,' I replied. 'A bottle of wine.'

As usual, my words seemed to activate some chord of latent hilarity.

'A bottle of bloody wine,' Bricky said, with a smirk.

'A fucking bottle of wine,' said Murph, echoing him. And the two of them burst into laughter, smacking their thighs. Johnno sniggered a bit, but did not seem to enter into the joke with quite the same gusto.

Bricky leaned forward and distributed the last of the brandy equally between their three glasses.

'That's perfume,' he said, pointing to the flagon. 'Essence of perfume. Shewfik gave it to us. Add pure alcohol to it and you can make eau de cologne. Bucketfuls of the bloody stuff.'

125

'You can sell it all over the world,' Murph volunteered. 'Put it in bottles and sell it all over the bloody world. Women go off their faces about it. You can make a fortune.'

'Bloody Shewfik,' Bricky said, contentedly, putting down his glass and beginning to unscrew the cap on the flagon. 'What a bloody card.'

He took the cap off and smothered the top of the flagon with his handkerchief, upending the flagon into it, and taking it away to show a damp patch on the cloth. 'Have a smell,' he said, holding it out to me.

I leaned forward and had a sniff, not wanting to look too closely at the handkerchief itself. The odour was vaguely medicinal. 'Marvellous,' I said, straightening up.

'Marvellous,' Bricky chortled. 'The Professor thinks it's fucking marvellous. Here, have a smell.' He offered the hand- kerchief to Johnno.

'Bloody good,' Johnno said without much interest, passing it on to Murph.

'What about giving Shewfik's daughter a whiff,' Murph whooped, noticing that the girl was coming towards us with a bottle on a tray. 'A taste of Dad's own perfume.'

Bricky took back the handkerchief and upended the flagon into it quickly a couple of times. 'Hey, Delilah,' he said, as she leaned down to put the bottle on the table. 'Get a whiff of this.' He shoved his hand out at her, dabbing the handker- chief at her neck.

The girl dropped the bottle on the table and drew back defensively. She was not noticeably frightened but defensive, not protesting but simply trying to escape. She stumbled against Johnno's chair behind her, losing her balance for a moment, her tray dropping to the ground with a clatter. She put her hand out protectively as Bricky stood up still menac- ing her with the outstretched handkerchief and saying in a crooning undertone — 'Have a dash of the old eau de cologne' — and forcing her to retreat towards the verandah rail. She was now looking alarmed but still made no sound, trying pas- sively to protect herself, one arm put out limply in front of her as a barrier.

'Give it to her Brick,' Murph called out, reaching for the bottle on the table. 'Give 'er a sample.'

'Too right,' Bricky said, his voice tightening, forcing her right to the rail. He was still smirking but his eyes were now

126

hard and unfriendly. Following her, saying almost under his breath, 'Just a bit of a sample', he lunged at her. His arm at her waist, and the handkerchief smearing wetness on her face, she squeaked with fright, her face bobbing from side to side to avoid his touch, leaning out over the rail, but his arm tightened around her, holding her in, and his body was now pressing into hers against the rail, the handkerchief working at her face, her chin, her throat, his hand beginning to maul her body, until she was trembling and beginning to whimper. It was all happening so fast that it took me an age to move along the rail and try to part them, my glass smashing as it fell from my hand. All the time Murph was cackling away to himself saying: 'Give it to her Brick. Give 'er a sample.'

'Cut it out, Professor,' Bricky said, brushing me aside easily. But with his attention distracted in that way, causing him to relax his hold on the girl, he himself lost interest. 'Don't get your knickers in a twist. It's just a game. Just a bit of a bloody game.'

He let his arms drop and the girl slipped out of his hold, and, with an apprehensive glance behind her, collected the fallen tray. Sidling a few steps, she moved away from us, her pace quickening as the distance increased, still without having uttered any real cry for help or assistance.

'What did ya do that for, Professor?' Bricky asked, stuffing the handkerchief into the pocket of his dungarees and swaggering back to his seat. 'Just a game. No harm in it.'

I was trembling all over and found that I couldn't reply. I gripped the verandah rail for support, knowing that I didn't even have the strength to walk away from them.

'Have a drink, Brick,' Murph said, leaning across the table and pouring him a splash. 'Get it into ya. That's the spirit.'

Bricky took a gulp at it and rolled the liquid round in his mouth. 'You can't bung on side,' he said, turning back to me. 'I've seen the way you've been sniffing round that Isobel. Sniffing round her like a bloody dog. We've all seen that.'

'It's not the same,' I blurted out, struggling for words. 'It's nowhere near the same thing.'

'Bullshit,' Bricky said. 'Bloody bullshit. She's a real hot pants, that little bitch, Y' can see it a mile off.'

I nodded disagreement. I couldn't speak. My throat seemed paralysed. I just kept nodding disagreement. Nodding and nodding, refusing to listen to them.

127

'Not for you,' Bricky said contemptuously. 'Don't worry about that. She isn't a hot pants for a little fart like you.'

'She and that David Shears,' Murph broke in, ramming his glass on to the table and reaching for the bottle. 'We've seen 'em having a go. Haven't we Johnno?'

Johnno nodded without saying anything, reaching for his packet of cigarettes.

'Down in the Doctor's office,' Murph continued, nastily, jerking his finger towards the rail and Dr Magro's clinic close to the quay below. 'A bit of the old slap and tickle. She's no angel.'

I felt the perspiration break out all over me. I couldn't accept it. I couldn't bear to listen to them any longer. Their crudity. Their malicious lies.

But at that moment Johnno broke into what was being said. 'Look at his arm,' he said, affecting a hearty laugh. 'He's got the same trouble as me. That'll be nice for her.'

They all stared at the rash of peeling skin on my arm. 'Yeah,' Bricky said, breaking the silence brutally. 'But he hasn't got it between his legs like you.'

Johnno flushed and looked down at his glass. I noticed that Murph was embarrassed and wouldn't look at him. There was another uneasy silence.

'Well, it isn't my fault,' Johnno said, taking a quick sip of his drink. 'It isn't my fault.'

'It bloody well is,' Bricky said ruthlessly. 'Because we told you not to.'

'It isn't my fault', Johnno said stubbornly. 'It isn't my fault. How was I to know?'

'Well, let's live with it,' Murph said, lighting up a new cigarette. 'In the clink at Maitland, shit. Everything was going round. Bloody plague proportions. Y' had to have iron balls. There was more clap there than at a bloody concert. Tough as nails, that's what y' had to be. Shit. Getting into the sick bay was a bloody art. There was a bloke up there one day cut his bloody finger off with a bayonet. Just sat there in the yard. Right there in front of us. Used the bayonet we'd been hiding under the workshop. Chopped one of his fingers off like a bloody carrot. Just put a handkerchief over the stump and went to the sick bay. Said he'd had an accident. Took a sickie for two weeks. Toughest bloke I ever saw.'

Bricky gulped down the rest of his drink. 'We've heard that

story before,' he drawled. 'About three million times.'

Again, the group lapsed into an uneasy silence. 'I'd do anything to get out of here,' Johnno said, after a moment, slamming his glass down on the table fiercely. 'Any damn thing at
all.' Dark crescents of perspiration were spreading out from
his arms; the fist of one hand clenching and unclenching
compulsively.

But the others wouldn't look at him. Murph and Bricky
glanced at each other across the table, for the first time a hint
of uncertainty appearing in their eyes.

'You just keep taking Shewfik's medicine,' Bricky said after
a moment. 'You'll be right, mate. You'll be okay.'

But they kept on staring down at their glasses. They
couldn't bring themselves to look at him. He was crying;
knuckles pressed to his eyes.

Chapter 11

Once, on one of our walks along the beach front, you said: that in an age of increasing scepticism, to speak of inner truth is a sign of abnormality; to make a stand, a symptom of ill-health.

You were, of course, only trying to console me (just as you are trying to console me now by encouraging me to write this book) suggesting that my quarrel with the faculty would never be patched up so long as I kept harking back to the old days and the need for independent minds; students with a background of jurisprudence and philosophy. And what you say is true. No one listens to that sort of thing any more.

The television camera, the magnetic eye, tracks outwards, indiscriminately picking up details, ceaselessly recording the surface, the here and now; the ambulance and the shattered flesh. The traumas of the mind are becoming too fantastic to be revealed. Urban man sits, bleary-eyed, in front of an aggressive screen; a spectator and, simultaneously, because of his own apathy in a darkened room, his inability to resist events, a participant, a barbarian at the gate, a horror-stricken protagonist in all that happens anywhere on earth.

I remember having the same sort of feeling. The feeling of being involved, but at a distance from it all — the day David and I set off together for the city, determined to find a solution to the impasse, determined to obtain the release of ourselves and our fellow passengers from the Quarantine Station. David was certain that we could do it. That we could achieve something. I myself couldn't help wondering whether it might not complicate matters; plunge us further into the depths.

He had come to me with the proposal the previous day, explaining that in the course of a talk with Bricky and the boys he had found out that they had already sneaked into the city on several occasions, even though it had been made quite clear to us that nobody was to leave the Station except by authority of Dr Magro. They had, it seemed, bribed the water-carrier to take them. David was intent on doing the same. His plan was to make representations to the Consul.

I was aghast. 'You'll be going behind the decision of the meeting,' I pointed out. 'We agreed to leave things with Burgess. Everyone will see this in the wrong light.'

It was hard to find the right words with which to express my unease. 'They'll see it as some kind of treachery. That you're taking the law into your own hands. Suppose we get picked up and everyone is prejudiced by us breaking the regulations?'

'They won't bother about that if we get them out,' David replied.

He had come to my bedroom to discuss the matter, and now began pacing up and down the room beside my bed like something caged, his face tense. 'We've got to do it,' he said. 'Burgess. He's a fake. I've seen his type everywhere I've been. In every country. They've got all the front. They get the top positions. But they never know what's really happening. Managers who don't know why they're managing. Ambitious little men. They're always pushing into the driver's seat even when they don't know where to go. They just feel they can drive better than anyone else. And their manners, their air of authority, of knowing it all, lets them get away with it. But this is serious. We can't let the thing drift.'

I had never seen him so vehement. It was most unlike him. He was usually so good-natured, so obliging. But over the last few days, everyone at the Station was becoming increasingly restive, angry inside. A child belonging to one of the planters' families had fallen ill and at odd hours, at night or during the day, its screams could be heard throughout the building, reminding us that our situation was getting worse.

Dr Magro had come out to treat the child but not, apparently, with much success. Its cries were still heard. The child's parents, the Staceys, had a violent row with Shewfik Arud in the corridor outside the kitchen, accusing him of not boiling the water as he had been instructed. And even though most people were sympathetic to the young parents, none-theless, there was a rumour circulating that the child was the real cause of our confinement; that it had been contagious from the first. But no one was prepared to discuss such things openly.

Even the scrapbook man had given up work. He still sat in his corner, his shoe-boxes spread out around him, but now, for long periods, he simply sat there, his album in his lap, staring listlessly out of the window. And the heat, the stifling heat, the sense of claustrophobia, was always present.

'I know what you mean,' I said, replying to David, marking the page in Borthwick I had been working on with a paper clip. 'But we took a vote. We placed our trust in Burgess. Perhaps we were wrong. Perhaps we made a mistake. Perhaps nothing is getting done. But isn't it going to be worse for morale if everybody goes their own way? Even worse than nothing getting done? The place will fall apart, nobody knowing who's in charge. I think we'd better call another meeting.'

'Another meeting,' David said bitterly, turning to face me, silhouetted against the verandah, the glare outside visible between the shutters. 'All right, let's have another meeting. But before we do, let's get some basic facts to put in front of the meeting. To rub their noses in it. I need a witness. You heard what happened last time. Nobody will believe me.'

I found it hard to argue against him. I put the case for discretion, of course. I suggested that despite everything he said we should still get some sort of approval for our actions; not knowing where my loyalties should rest, remembering, after all, that in some way or other the passengers had elected me as one of their representatives. But it was hard to be convincing. Burgess was ignoring me. Furthermore, a recent meeting with Dr Magro had done nothing to strengthen my faith in our medical adviser.

Having treated the sick child, Dr Magro reluctantly agreed to see Burgess and myself for a few minutes. Burgess didn't say so directly, but I had the distinct impression that he also saw the wisdom of having a third party present during the discussion. The interview took place in the small clinic near the water's edge. Dr Magro sat behind his table. We sat opposite him, fanning ourselves with thick pieces of cardboard, the kind of makeshift fans which most of the passengers had, by now, devised for themselves. Outside, just within view, the dilapidated steamer lay at anchor. One of the squat barges from the inlet had pulled alongside it. I could see a couple of men in dark robes shuffling about on the deck of the barge; the barge hovering there like a blunt-nosed parasite attached to the flanks of its giant host.

'Please. There is no use becoming excited,' Dr Magro said, parrying the first question Burgess put to him. 'You have received certain assurances. You know that I myself have presented my findings to the authorities. But here is a land where all must depend on patience.'

Looking at us across the table with dark, brooding eyes, he gently tapped his black fountain pen up and down in front of him, creating an irregular syncopation as a background to his words. 'What can an active man achieve in this country? Your enemy will always fade into the desert. Direct action is seldom possible. I have made certain findings. Now it is a question of a word here. A word there. A mild reproach. A hint. Some small favour, perhaps. Then, a note of impatience in the right places. In this country, to be active is not to be seen. You must keep in mind that I have had many years of experience.'

'But we have rights,' Burgess said, sharply. 'We can't be dragged into some political thing which isn't our business.' Impulsively, Burgess thumped the table. 'It's days since we last spoke. You must have some information. I have to be able to tell my people something.'

The Doctor smiled wryly. 'Tell them anything you like. Tell them that the authorities have authorized your release. Does that mean you will actually go? Decisions have a habit of being reversed at some other level. I was once appointed to the staff of a school of medicine. Does that mean I am there? Nothing is ever tangible.

'To understand this country, Mr Burgess, you must look at the night sky. Here is a country where at night the sky blazes with a special brilliance, bringing into view the faintest fragments of space matter which are seldom noticed elsewhere. And always, beyond it, the hard blackness of the outermost dark. Think of that, Mr Burgess. Here, obscurity is not a matter of clouds or English rain which you can brush away with ingenious umbrellas.'

'Dr Magro,' Burgess said testily, indicating no interest whatsoever in this speculation. 'Where do we stand?'

The Doctor shrugged contemptuously. 'I have submitted my findings,' he said. 'That is all I can say. I am making represen-

133

tations. I am doing what is in your best interests. I have no cause to hinder your progress. If that is what is prescribed, it will be a matter of personal convenience for me that you should go. I am not your nemesis. Believe that. I am working in your best interests.'

'We have a sick child.'

'I am working in your best interests.' With that, he rapped the table one more time and put the pen away in his pocket. 'Think of this,' Dr Magro added, almost as an afterthought, smiling crookedly at the notion which had entered his mind, apparently recalling some personal joke. 'In the Sudan, one always had to be careful about keeping a native in hospital too long. If he died there, his relatives naturally thought the hospital was the cause of his death. Sometimes, looking to the future, it was better to let him out during a period of temporary recovery.' Dr Magro shrugged one shoulder, splaying his hands out in front of him expressively, and balancing them gently to indicate that he wasn't preferring one side of the question to the other. 'Surely you understand that quarantine is always a matter of waiting?'

He left the question with us for a moment, his hands suspended in mid-air, palms upward. Then, he let his hands drop and stood up abruptly, signifying that the interview was at an end. 'I must go,' he said. 'I have other cases, other matters to attend to.'

Without further comment, he scooped his leather bag off the table and climbed the steps towards his car which was parked alongside the parapet; an old and dusty beetle standing in the white heat of the sun. He walked with a careful precision, wearily mounting the steps, as though every step required a special effort.

'You never know what to make of them,' Burgess said, bitterly, watching him go, appearing to be speaking as much to himself as to me. 'All these people in the tropics. Whether in Asia or here. They're all the same. If they spend their lives here, something gets to them. The heat probably. And then they start spouting their ratbag philosophies. And they're all the same, these philosophies. Always an excuse for doing nothing. For standing still. For waiting until tomorrow.'

He turned and looked at me. 'When he started that business about the night sky I nearly took to him. I've heard it everywhere. In Kuala Lumpur it was just the same. Talk to a

134

beggar or some drunk in the club. They'll all finish up talking about the night sky. Their precious philosophies.' He jerked his thumb towards the Station. 'And we've got a sick child in there.'

'Then, let's forget Magro,' I said. 'Try something else.'

Burgess pulled at his lip, standing awkwardly in the one position without moving. 'I don't know,' he said, obviously unwilling to discuss the matter but recognizing that some explanation was called for. 'We can't. Not yet. I always dislike what they say, these people. But despite everything, do business with them, and you often find they get things done. They're devious. And they approach things from an angle. But they often get things done.'

He paused, still standing in the one position, one foot turned inwards slightly, searching my eyes. 'I haven't given up on him altogether. And the main thing is to keep our people from falling apart. We've got to keep order. That's what we've got to do — whatever the cost.' He groped for the edge of the table to steady himself. 'We must have unity. Whatever the cost.'

I tried to give David some account of what had taken place at the interview with Dr Magro. But beyond satisfying himself that nothing of substance had been said, he wasn't really interested.

'Dr Magro,' he said. 'You keep talking about him as though he counted. Would you take your sister to him for treatment? He's a fake. The same as Burgess. Middle-aged men speaking like oracles and not getting on with it. What do they care if there's a sick child upstairs? They've seen people die before. They know they can live through it one more time. How do you think wars are started? How do you think politicians go on being politicians, walking through slums, inspecting disaster areas? Let things take their course. That's the voice of experience. But that's not good enough for me. Not here. Not right now. Not in this place. Things never take their course unless someone begins pushing.'

I thought about his words on the journey into the city, the truck lumbering along the broken road, the spare cans attached to the two huge drums on the back of the water-carrier's vehicle banging about behind us like makeshift instruments in some weary percussion band. The water-carrier himself dressed in soiled white robes crouched over the steering wheel, an old fez squashed on his head, the two of us sitting beside him, scarcely able to distinguish the uneven road revealed by his headlights from the surrounding terrain.

There was a glimmer of light at the horizon and as we travelled, slowly bumping our way across the desert, the sky began to pale, the flush of dawn across the distant tracts of sand and waste becoming more and more evident, the stars dimming, the higher reaches of the sky, finally, becoming blue. We came to an intersection where a track led in from a cluster of low bungalows at the canal's edge and joined the road we were on, heading towards the city. Past the intersection, the road mounting a rise, it was possible to see the distant lake, a blue reflection of the sky set into the beige-coloured desert.

Two camels came towards us, lurching methodically along the road's edge, the weathered faces of their riders staring at us impassively. The water-carrier paid no attention to them, all the time the outline of the city gradually becoming closer, until it was possible to make out the scattering of bungalows and rough shelters on the outskirts, then, in turn, giving place to the blocks of stucco buildings with their heavy shutters and lofty three-storeyed latticed verandahs. Everything looked down at heel, in need of repair, but having a kind of sullen grandeur about it nonetheless.

The truck bumped its way across a double line of tram tracks, the cans at the back jangling wildly, and turned into a broad boulevard running parallel with the track. It was like a boundary established between two different territories. On one side of the street, looking towards the desert, the direction from which we had come, there was a large market area; a jumble of stalls and canvas awnings, alley-ways of canvas and wooden crates piled crazily on top of each other.

Although it was still early, already the merchants were preparing themselves for business; some of them setting up stacks of earthenware jars. A man and his son, both in identical robes, hanging up clusters of saucepans around the walls of their stall. Nearby there were two men arguing beside the scrawny flanks of a donkey piled high with rugs and mats, their hands spread out in gestures of expostulation and complaint. In one of the rough alley-ways, two men in baggy trousers, white aprons around their waists, were trundling a large wooden barrow into position, the back of it piled high with chicken-coops, the wire cages jumbled together precariously.

As I watched, a gang of street urchins came careering out of an alley-way, rattling sticks against the wheels of passing carts and barrows, flicking the hindquarters of a donkey before disappearing into another alley, drawing after them sporadic volleys of threats and abuse from irate traders.

But on the other side of the boulevard, the scene was less cluttered; the walls of the imposing stucco buildings beginning to receive the warmth of the early morning sun; the overhead verandahs, the verandah posts casting hard-edged slanting shadows on to the white plaster, the struts at the top of each post forming geometric outlines on the walls.

A number of horse-drawn landaus had begun pulling into the kerb, their black, umbrella-like hoods often torn or noticeably patched, the drivers standing in the street beside their vehicles, obviously not expecting any custom until a little later in the morning. Standing there. Gossiping.

As our truck sidled past each cross street one caught a fleeting glimpse of a straight avenue, almost deserted, bounded on each side by the squat, grimy buildings, and narrowing down — sometimes to a distant parapet, sometimes to a set of stone steps turning the street clumsily in a new direction, or even into a mere shadowy emptiness; in all cases, the perspective effect being accentuated by the lines of street-lamps ranging down the streets, glass and metal helmets fixed to the top of rigid black poles.

On one occasion, looking down a side street in that way, a street slightly wider than the rest, there was a tram coming out of a block of shadow, lumbering towards us; an old tram with an open, wrought-iron front to it, the faded green roof of it like the lid of a rectangular casserole dish, the passengers, some in robes, some in suits, abandoning their bench seats and stepping lightly off the slow conveyance without paying any apparent attention to whether it was moving or not, the driver, disdainfully, sitting up front and not deigning to notice what was going on behind him.

It was only a brief glimpse, but there was something so matter-of-fact about that tram poking its snub nose out of the shadow and trundling forward into the sunlit street, something so ordinary about it, so routine, that it almost made me

137

forget the purpose of our mission. Here was a city coming to wakefulness, people going about their business. It seemed almost fantastic to remind oneself that we had come from a place where nothing was straightforward; where nothing was certain.

But here, everything seemed so ordinary. Could we get our message across? Would the Consul and his subordinates simply regard us as overwrought travellers unaccustomed to foreign places? For my part, I was glad David was the one who would do the talking.

The water-carrier turned off the boulevard into a side street. Without ceremony, he swung the truck towards the kerb and brought it to a grinding halt. He pointed to the pavement, indicating that this was the place we were to get out. 'Merci,' David said. 'Merci,' the driver replied with an air of indifference. But it was more likely he was referring to the money we had given him at the start of the journey than to our companionship. 'El salaam 'aleikum,' David added. The driver looked momentarily surprised but then forced out the time-honoured response: 'Wa 'aleikum el salaam wa rahmat allah.' And revved his engine, waiting for us to complete our evacuation of the driver's cab.

'I'll find out where to go from over there,' David said, as we stood together on the footpath, watching the truck pull away from us, the bulk of its two large, black water-drums resembling the humps of some mechanical camel, the smaller cans attached to them still jangling and crashing against the sides.

He was pointing to a café across the street. The proprietor was moving amongst the tables and chairs, spreading them out ready for the day's business. A pergola projected out from the front of the premises, the ceiling of the shelter being comprised of dried palm fronds laid across each other. There was a wooden bench against one wall of the café. A small boy was sleeping on the bench, a woollen scarf wrapped around his head so that, lying there in his robe motionless, he looked like a rag doll.

David darted across the street to speak to the proprietor; the latter reaching for his broom propped up close to hand against one of the tables almost defensively as he noticed the approach of a visitor. I sauntered over to a wooden bench on my side of the street and sat down with my back against the wall of a building, glad to feel the sun beginning to warm my bones. It had been cold out in the desert, especially waiting for the water-carrier to pick us up from the foot of the escarpment — the place where Bricky had told us we should wait — and I still felt chilled all the way through.

I sat there, fatigued, watching David and the proprietor talking; David lean and athletic beside the stooped figure of the proprietor who had now put aside his broom and was demonstrating something on the table-top in front of him. As they spoke, the boy on the wooden bench sat up, fumbling small hands into the folds of his thick scarf, leisurely rubbing his eyes and then standing up and stretching.

We found our way to the administrative quarters of the British Consul eventually, walking for several blocks. Sometimes, at the end of a street, we would catch a glimpse of the distant lake shimmering in the day, the morning now quite hot. The number of people in the streets and on the kerbside was growing. Shouldering past them, we threaded our way through the tables and chairs of the sidewalk cafés. The tables, even at this early hour, were already beginning to be occupied, and, I noticed, at one, two chess-players gravely studying their pieces, the strength of their respective positions, suggesting that they had left their armies out all night, locked in combat. And all the time, the sounds of the city beginning to become familiar to us, the street trams lumbering past, bicycle bells, sometimes a street musician with a tambourine and a shallow drum at his waist crouched under the awning of a shop, a blanket to receive coins spread out in front of him expectantly.

But once inside the consulate everything was different. The waiting area was crowded, even more crowded than the streets, but there was a pervading silence about the room; men and students standing about in clusters and talking in whispers, whispering excitedly sometimes, but even then always being immediately subdued by the reprimands or severe looks of their neighbours. Overhead, one fan in a crowded room, the broad blades turning sluggishly, encouraging those below to loosen their collars and, from time to time, to step outside on to the steps of the building for some fresh air, or to squat in the shadow of the portico.

David and I joined a queue which was shuffling towards a rough table manned by a young man in khaki uniform. I didn't envy him his job. He was taking a brief note of the subject matter of each person's business and, as often as not, the mere request for information seemed to provoke the applicant to an outburst of rage. Patiently, he would pacify them and send them off into the body of the room to wait their turn. Now and again, in a loud voice, he would call out a name from a clipboard he had in front of him and the lucky applicant would come eagerly pushing his way through the throng to be conducted up a small flight of stairs by an orderly, disappearing into an inner sanctum, the crowd closing its ranks behind him with a murmur.

Not knowing exactly whether we were in breach of some regulation, we had agreed that it would be unwise to state the true nature of our business until we had actually reached the presence of someone in authority. Accordingly, when we finally presented ourselves to the official at the desk we said no more than that we wished to see the Consul on 'a matter of business'. 'A franchise,' David added, rendering our story more plausible. 'We are seeking a franchise.'

The young man behind the desk looked at us keenly, hesitating. 'What sort of franchise?' he asked, but his eyes kept drifting to the length of the queue behind us. Before David could answer, an Arabic messenger scuttled across to the desk and passed over a note. The young man read the note, frowning. Still holding the note, he abandoned his earlier question, and simply said: 'Names?' We told him. He noted them on his list. 'Wait till you're called,' he said, curtly, waving us aside, and almost in the same breath commenced to read out some names in a loud voice, addressing the room at large: 'Mr and Mrs Razek. Fariq Shelqani . . .'

Moving aside from the table, it was almost as though we were being enmeshed in the foliage of the proverbial grapevine. 'Meester Razek. Where is Fariq?' Amongst those close to the table, there was a murmuring and jostling, a pressing forward, a transmission of rumour and nuance from tongue to tongue.

'Does anybody know Shelqani?' Already two or three people had presented themselves to the orderly at the foot of the steps claiming to be the applicants in question or, at least, closely related to them. They gabbled at him without avail. He stood there, impassively, until, by some process of selection or survival, the crowd parted and ejected from its midst the rightful claimant.

'Fariq Shelqani?' the orderly said to an elderly white-robed figure who emerged from the throng as we shouldered our way through the cluster of anxious applicants. The old man nodded in answer to the interrogatory, and although it was a mystery to me as to how the orderly was able to recognize the validity of his claim in the presence of a bevy of other candidates all of whom were prepared to force an entrance into the administrative offices of the building by fraud or by any available crookery. Nonetheless, the orderly appeared to be satisfied and, with a dignified stride, led the old man up the short flight of steps.

On the outskirts of the room, things were much quieter. Merchants, many of whom were dressed in baggy Turkish-style trousers and waistcoats, stood in clusters gossiping. Other applicants, resigning themselves to a long wait, sat patiently on the hard wooden benches attached to the wall. We managed to find ourselves a place on one of these benches, and settled ourselves down to wait, hoping our names would be called without too much delay.

At first, we were optimistic, confident that we would obtain an early hearing. But as name succeeded name — even the young man at the desk who had been calling out the names being himself eventually succeeded by some other subaltern who arrived to take up a tour of duty in the front line — our hopes flagged. The bench was unconscionably hard. More-over, the frustration of the wait was exacerbated by not know-ing where one stood in the scheme of priority; assuming there was one.

I have always despised queues. I have a philosophical objection to them; an objection based on a rigorous linguistic analysis of the concept inherent in the word. In short, I have a tendency to arrive late at places and am, therefore, usually on the end of them. Hence, my objection. On the other hand, if by some miracle one occupies a forward position in a line of people, provided you do not look over your shoulder, by my definition, it is not a queue. My objection disappears.

But it now became apparent to me that the cluster system of attendance on earth, the hamburger-bar style of pressing one's suit, was fraught with uncertainty, injustice even. I had previously regarded this system with some favour, vaguely imagining from the way people spouted penances and called for the priest that heaven must be organized in that way; that

141

there was some quasi-official method of queue-jumping in force which would permit someone such as myself to scramble through the Pearly Gates in the end. But as the hours lengthened, as our names resolutely declined to be mentioned, as one contemplated the possibility of struggling into robes and burnoose and being Fariq Shelqani or whoever for a few exhilarating minutes beneath the stairs (Lawrence, perhaps?) — the attraction of the cluster system palled.

I recall from childhood days some Arabian legend about the genie imprisoned in the bottle. In the first thousand years of his captivity he resolved to bring half the treasures of the earth to the one who released him. During the second thousand years, the mood of generosity was still upon him — had become even more pronounced, in fact. He resolved to confer the remaining two-thirds of the world's treasure on the one who released him. (I pause to mention that, as to the bounty which was to be distributed, I have long since forgotten the precise figures but they were certainly enormous and, at that age, fractions, far from forming part of the vulgar language of a later day, were rich with imprecision; fraught with mystery.) But in the third thousand years of his captivity, a mood of cynicism and profound distrust came upon him whereupon he undertook to inflict irreparable damage upon the one who uncorked him from his aqueous cell.

A salutary fable and one that I always enjoyed. Mentally, I began brushing up on it, thinking I might tell it to the Consul. A moment or so before I went for this throat. By God, it was tedious sitting on that bench; the room stifling hot, men and boys passing to and fro, bumping against one's legs, one man depositing a sack of putrid onions near our feet for an hour or so. Small wonder, then, that when David, noticing my fatigue, suggested that I take a walk to clear my head, advising that he would hold the fort, I accepted the invitation gladly, intending to be away for only a short period, not giving the slightest thought to what might be the consequences of our separation, entirely unable to foresee the interpretation which would later be placed on his suggestion.

142

Chapter 12

My night of temptation. Keeping the powder dry in the flesh-pots of Egypt. Ah, the mask of flippancy; the armour-plate of farce. How often have I described the episode? How often has my own identity perished in the flames of fabrication.?

Once, dining with the Dean of the faculty, he drew me aside shortly before the guest of honour, a visiting professor, was due to arrive. 'Try and keep it within reason, tonight,' he said. I asked him to explain. But all he would say, shushing me and looking furtive, was: 'The Egypt thing — just keep it within reason.'

Perhaps he thought he was talking to Mark Antony. Certainly, I resented his remarks. I was tempted to retrieve my bottle of wine and leave. But that would have meant facing his wife, a woman for whom I have a great deal of respect.

'There is nothing especially filthy about my Egypt "thing",' I replied, refusing to be shushed, but wondering what he would say if he ever heard the full story. That would be something for our visiting professor to feast his ears upon; something to force the Dean back into private practice with.

My night of temptation. Perhaps I should begin by saying that it happened during the day. Not long after I left David at the consulate. And of temptation — there was none. Only stark terror. No wonder I've had to embellish the anecdote. But what still startles me about it when I consider the matter privately, is how on earth I let myself be drawn into the affair. I can only suppose that my encounter with Isobel, my night-time fantasies, had left me restless, in a mood to receive a proposal of the kind put to me.

'American?' That was the first thing the girl said.

I was standing outside a shop in one of the main streets, still not far from the Consulate, fingering the coins in my pocket, wondering whether it would be risky to walk inside and buy a couple of the flat, oval-shaped loaves of bread on display in the window, conscious that it was now midday and that neither of us had had anything to eat since setting out at dawn.

'No,' I replied, and turned back to the window, thinking she must have mistaken me for someone. She looked a rather ordinary girl; olive-skinned and dressed in European clothing. A trifle 'dressed up', perhaps; but otherwise rather ordinary. My guess was that she was employed by the Consulate.

'Canadian?' She smiled at me, waiting for an answer.

I shook my head again, turning to look at her directly.

'I am from the American Club,' she said in halting English, gesturing towards the next street, and smiling. 'We have everything there for you.'

She was only about nineteen and seemed quite friendly; looking at me with earnest eyes. It was broad daylight. A tram was lumbering along the street. Two men were seated on their bicycles at the kerb nearby, talking loudly and gesticulating. There was nothing in the scene to put me on my guard.

'Food?' I asked cautiously, not sure how much English she spoke.

She laughed. 'Sure thing,' she said, tossing her head, the expression sounding somewhat strange in her mouth. 'Sure thing. Canned food. Coca Cola. Everything is there. No questions asked.'

I fingered the coins in my pocket, not really sure how far my money would take me. I had a few pound notes in my hip pocket but was not quite sure what they were worth. It was all very well to trade them in for local currency on the black market which seemed to exist in every port. But you had to have some idea of the rate of exchange and, in that respect, I was completely at sea.

'Bread?' I asked, rapping the shop window beside me to indicate what I had in mind.

'Sure thing. Bread. Canned food. Coca Cola. Everything you want at the American Club.'

'Far from here?' I found that I myself was lapsing into a kind of pidgin English.

'I will show you.' She took my wrist and commenced to lead me towards the corner. Still feeling self-conscious about my peeling skin I wriggled free of her grasp. She smiled and beckoned me to follow.

From what she had said, I had the impression that the American Club was just around the next corner. It took me by surprise, therefore, when, beyond the first corner, she began leading me into side streets away from the main thorough-fares, walking briskly, and no longer talking. But as happens so often, once committed, one tends to persevere long after it becomes apparent that it's unwise to do so, simply out of embarrassment, for fear of seeming anti-social, contradictory, or just plain gutless.

So I went on following her, even though, now that she had entered a laneway which ran along the rear of a number of buildings, I was becoming increasingly apprehensive. The staircases tottered crookedly downwards from the upper storeys, and the shuttered windows of the area, some of them smashed in, splintered, gap-toothed, presented a forbidding picture. An old man with a barrow full of rubble leading a donkey staring at me impassively from the shelter of his robes.

'How far?' I called to my guide, coming to a halt.

'Not far now,' she said, coming back and taking my arm lightly, and smiling pleasantly, her teeth, I noticed for the first time, yellowish, suggesting that she might have been older than she looked. 'Sure thing. Not very far now.' She applied a slight pressure to my arm and led me on.

I followed, but unwillingly, knowing that if we didn't reach our destination in the next few minutes I would start back. It was beginning to concern me that I had been away for so long, having left David alone.

The girl stopped outside the rear entrance to one of the tall buildings overhanging the laneway. There was no one in sight. A rust-coloured mongrel was rooting round in some boxes of garbage stacked up a few feet away from the entrance. A painted board tacked up over the entrance said simply: 'The American Club.'

Although faded, the lettering on the sign had clearly been done by a professional signwriter. Which made it all the more grotesque, being entirely out of keeping with the dingy sur-roundings, there being no other signs or indications of com-mercial activity nearby. It was only a small piece of board and quite portable. It looked to me like the sort of sign which had been and would be carried from one doorway to the next, probably at short notice.

'Chicago style,' the girl said with a smile, drawing me forward.

This note of jocularity did little to allay my fears. It simply suggested that some previous patron, equally disconcerted by the undercover appearance of the premises, had tried to keep his heart afloat with a feeble quip. And the way she said it, confidently, almost as a matter of routine, but without really appearing to understand what it meant, made it quite clear that, confronted by the notice, nervous laughter was the rule rather than the exception.

'Here we are then.' Before I could decide what I should do, I found that she had parted the curtain over the entrance and drawn me inside.

With that, as if by magic, the girl disappeared from my side. She just seemed to vanish, the precise moment of her disappearance being impossible to tell. I myself was left standing at the head of a small flight of steps looking downwards into a dimly-lit basement room which had been set up to resemble a cocktail bar.

There were no windows, the walls being covered from ceiling to floor by thick drapes. A single bulb in the ceiling, concealed by a chintz shade, illuminated the room with a feeble, yellowish light. The floor was concrete, warmed in places by threadbare rugs. There was a scattering of tables and chairs in the room. In one corner there was a street musician standing up playing some kind of flute. At his feet, cross-legged, an old Arab with glazed eyes sat, spasmodically slapping a pair of skin drums. On the other side of the room there was a counter, an unsuitable length of wood which looked as though it had seen service in a railway booking office. There was a miscellany of bottles on the counter and, behind it, nothing more than some large travel posters pinned to the drapes depicting the skyscrapers of Manhattan.

At the counter, literally 'at it' in the sense of being the representation of three random points, showing no more interest in their surroundings than if they were, indeed, in a geometric sense the termination of some arbitrary configuration, there were three women — perched on bar stools, each dressed up so as to bear a bizarre resemblance to New York sophisticates as seen in the films or fashion magazines.

Each had hair swept up into stiff piles which were held in place by jewelled hairpins. Each was wearing a tight satin

evening dress. Each had an ivory cigarette holder. Each had a
sequin-covered purse, the purses nestling in their respective
laps as if flung into position by a props and costumes
manager as an afterthought. They sat there, looking at the
posters set opposite them without expression.

Before I could flee, something in a tuxedo with a swarthy,
pock-marked face materialized from the shadows at my side.
'Monsieur!' the man said; affecting an air of bonhomie, his
face compressed into a smile; the fat smile only serving to
emphasize the hardness in his eyes; a rigid black bow tie
planted in the folds of flesh beneath his chin. 'It is so very
good to see you. Chicago style, eh? You must have champagne.'

As he spoke, he had been herding me down the steps and
into the room. It was quite apparent that I was the only customer. More precisely, the only member of the club.

'I'll just have the Coca Cola,' I said nervously, wondering
how I could get out. He pulled a chair out from the nearest
table and stood directly in my path until I sat down. 'Chicago
style, eh,' he said again; compressing his face into another
smile. I could feel the windy city breathing down my neck.
And at that moment, one of the women at the bar — the first
off the rank — tottered over to my table on high-heeled shoes
while simultaneously a waiter appeared from behind a
curtain at my left holding a bottle swaddled in a dirty napkin
and two glasses.

'Champagne?' the waiter muttered thickly, pouring what
appeared to be muddy orange juice into the two glasses, a
second before the counter-woman sat on my lap and put an
arm around my neck and reached for one of the glasses. I had
been in the room all of thirty seconds. The drummer began
working at his instruments with increased fervour, the
membrane fluttering rapidly but irregularly, like a cardiac
valve in its last throes.

'Drink up, you bad boy,' the woman said tonelessly, letting
me have a ravishing wink. 'What do you think of Mrs
Simpson?'

She drained her glass with one gulp and put it back on the
table. The thick-set waiter lurched out of the shadows and
filled it again.

'We are all for Mrs Simpson here,' she added. 'We are
right behind her all the way.'

She opened her sequin purse and fished about inside it, producing a lipstick and a small mirror. Pouting her lips at the mirror, scrubbing each lip in turn with her tongue, she began applying the paste to her mouth as though she was touching up the lips of Jean Harlow. It was hard to tell what nationality she was or her age. She spoke with a pronounced accent. Forty, perhaps. Lebanese.

'You bad boy,' she said, putting away her lipstick and leering at me. 'I bet you never stop at that.'

Apart from shifting my legs so as to be better able to support her weight, which was considerable, I hadn't actually done anything. So I found it hard to decipher what she meant. I smiled weakly and picked up my glass, trying to think straight. The drink didn't help me. It tasted like vinegar. I put it back on the table.

No sooner had my glass been returned to the table-top than the woman's confederate in the shadows stepped forward and aimed another splash at it, most of which spilled on to the table. The proprietor of the premises himself had moved across to the counter and was making a pretence of polishing glasses, but watching me all the time.

'Chicago style, eh?' the woman said, picking up her glass again, some of the liquid spilling down my shirt front as she moved it to her lips. The notion entered my head that it was all a dream; that I was on a turntable crazily running anti-clockwise, every few seconds hurdling a crack in the record which swept towards me like a lighthouse beam echoing 'Chicago style . . . Chicago style . . . Chicago style.' But it was no dream. The woman put her glass down again. She appeared to have left one of her lips on the rim. 'You are looking for a good time, you bad boy,' she stated, summarizing the position for me. The waiter filled her glass again.

'What does all this cost?' I gasped, wondering how I could slow things down; retard the mechanisms of the production which now seemed to be functioning like clockwork.

'The hell with money,' she said, muscling in on what was obviously my side of the dialogue. 'Let's have ourselves a good time. You want the back room?'

'Do you have any bread?' I asked.

'Bread?' This seemed to take her by surprise. She looked at the proprietor for reassurance. He gesticulated at her impatiently, apparently urging her to get on with it.

'Bread.' I attempted to trace the outline of an oval-shaped loaf in the air with one hand, she having already draped my other arm around her waist.

I don't exactly know what my one-handed aerial display meant to her but, certainly, for the first time, she looked at me with what seemed to be a real interest. 'You bad boy,' she crooned, leaning back to examine me, reaching forward and lightly placing a playful fingertip on my spectacles, leaving a moist tear of liquid on that lens.

She stood up and, taking me by the hand, commenced to lead me through the doorway nearby in which the waiter had been lurking. He stood aside to let us pass. She pushed through a curtain of beads, still holding me firmly by the hand, and I found that we were standing in a short corridor servicing four open doorways, terminating in a heavier door at the far end of the corridor.

It is at this point, of course, that my story, or the story of 'what happened to a friend of mine,' or the story of some anonymous protagonist, is usually wound up; at best, hilariously, but even at worst, wound up efficiently, leaving no loose ends lying about, no mess.

He thought she was referring to bread but she had in mind the other, and there it was, he scuttled out with them all behind him, so have another drink and I'll tell you about the campsite in Dubrovnick, et cetera . . .'

But how can I gloss over it in that way now? How can I attempt to avoid the truth, knowing that in order to tell the whole story of our quarantine, in order for you to understand how exactly it was that David met his death, there is no course available to me other than to set down the full facts of my degradation, to disclose fully my state of mind, because it is only then, only when you have shared my folly, appreciated the dilemma which in turn it forced me into, that you can hope to comprehend the circumstances underlying his betrayal.

It is true, in a general sense, that when she took me into the first room in the corridor, a room containing no more than a divan and a narrow window above us at ground level, the woman softly shutting the door, that if someone had handed me a loaf of bread, even a mere crust, and offered me the opportunity to leave, I would have left immediately, and left gladly. But what need would there be for morality if life was

149

as bountiful as that? Despite my confusion, my sense of being enmeshed in matters of which I wanted no part, I would be less than honest if I failed to confess that while the woman had been sitting on my knee my thoughts had not been fixed on bread alone.

She was not so unattractive as to prevent me thinking: 'Here is an opportunity. Here is a chance to disgrace yourself and nobody will ever know. To put aside fantasies and tackle reality. It will be over and done with quickly and there will be no repercussions.'

Ah, the insidious voice of desire; the secret, whispering voice — so often at odds with the conscious mind. Even at its weakest, even when not strong enough to prompt direct action, strong enough to paralyse the will, to encourage one to linger. 'Just stay long enough to see what happens. You can always leave if you want to.' The secret voice; holding one back, creating a vacuum to be occupied by events.

And, therefore, in that mood of indecision, intending to leave but in fact remaining, repelled but fascinated, knowing that to leave was to have to run the gauntlet of the outer room. When she drew me towards the divan, encouraging me to sit down, I made no protest but sat down nervously, still determined to leave, wondering how it was that I had reached this point already, still determined to make my escape even as she began removing her clothes, her arms raised, fumbling at the cross-over shoulder straps of her dress, and then wriggling her shoulders free, naked beneath her dress, her slumbrous breasts, her body, appearing from beneath the smooth satin, her hands working the dress downwards with slow coaxing movements, easing her hips free of it, stepping out of her clothes, all the time her eyes provocatively fixed on mine.

The dress left there on the floor. Still in her high-heeled shoes she approached the bed, easing me over to make room for her and, almost in the same motion, kicking off first one shoe and then the other, and lying there pulling me down beside her, her hands beginning to work gently at the buckle of my belt, softly chuckling, almost making a game of it.

My mouth felt dry. The absurdest notions kept flashing into my head. The narrow window above us, I kept wondering, are the cops going to come bursting through there, any moment, Chicago style? Her hair. The ornate hairpins. Will she remove them? Or is that her hallmark, her specialty? Notorious throughout the Middle East?

My mind racing in this way, seeming to belong somewhere else, to be having nothing to do with the struggle beneath it reluctantly gaining momentum on the bed, the absurdest notion of all, perhaps, the notion that I could still escape, that there was still time to leave, but even as I began to persuade myself, and to persuade myself that this was so, and that there was still time to leave, feeling the glow, the woman's body beneath me, her soft thighs coaxing me towards her, and persuading myself now that there was no time, had never been, not now that I was there, unable to open my eyes, and all of me there, and there, now knowing there was no escape, the time for, the notion of now gone, all time, all notions fixed on this one point, that window, the jewelled hairpin molten in my mind, the window shattering, all notions gone, gone utterly into this darkness of closed eyes and perspiration and bodies lapsing into languid stillness, immediately a kind of horror coming upon me, and the woman chuckling softly, and knowing then that there would never be any escape from it, this flesh, not now, not ever.

But now, it having happened so quickly, appalled at myself, disgusted, already wondering what madness had prompted me to enter this room, like an ugly shadow, the thought suddenly forced its way into my mind, the recollection of Johnno; the truculent transport driver sitting on the verandah, his friends unwilling to look him in the eyes. 'It's not my fault,' he said. 'How was I to know?'

'We warned you not to.' Bricky's harsh reply, echoing in my mind, forced me upwards. 'I'm mad,' I said aloud. 'I must be mad.' Frantically, I began adjusting my clothes, my hands trembling, fumbling to find the buckle of my belt.

'Money,' the woman said, straightening up. The softening I had detected in her manner as we lay together, now being replaced by a note of shrillness. 'Where are your dollars?'

'How much?' I asked, struggling to my feet. I emptied out all the coins in my pocket on to the bed.

'Where are your dollars?' she demanded. She rolled out of the bed and scooped up her dress from the floor, pulling it on with incredible speed, pulling it up over her buttocks, scrabbling at the straps.

I reached into my hip pocket and pulled out the notes I

had. She looked at them suspiciously and then quickly crossed over to the door, wrenching it open. 'Osman!' she shouted into the corridor.

I stepped past her into the corridor but was immediately intercepted by the proprietor who appeared through the beaded doorway leading into the bar. I held out my notes. 'How much?' I asked.

He snatched them off me, counting the four of them quickly and testing them with his fingers. 'Where are your dollars?' he demanded angrily.

'That's all,' I said becoming scared. 'That's all I have. And the money on the bed.'

'Ai,' he bellowed, over his shoulder, then gripped my shirt and swung me against the wall with staggering force. 'Where are your dollars?' he snarled. 'You owe us money, you pig. Keep quiet,' he shouted brutally at the girl, who was now jabbering at me from the doorway of the small room.

The waiter came blundering into the corridor from the bar. While Osman held me fiercely against the wall, without waiting for directions, as if carrying out a well-established routine, the waiter began searching me, turning my pockets inside out, patting me all over with his clumsy paws, roughly kneeling down and pulling off my shoes, stripping away the linings with his fingers. He flung them down and grunted something at Osman.

'Where is your hotel?' Osman said. 'Where is the rest of your money?'

'I am staying with the Consul,' I said, finding it difficult to draw breath, his hold on my shirt being so tight. 'I am leaving tomorrow.'

'Liar!' he screamed, battering me against the wall again spitting in my face. 'English pig.'

'I have nothing else,' I blubbered. 'Nothing else.' My legs gave way beneath me out of sheer fright. But Osman hauled me back up to my full position.

Osman scowled at me savagely. 'You are a cheat,' he said.

'I don't know the price of things . . .' I began to say.

'You are a cheat,' he screamed. My words had obviously provoked him. Then, he quietened down. 'I let you go on one condition,' he said. 'You will meet me outside the Consulate tomorrow with twenty dollars. Twenty dollars, you hear me?' His voice had become shrill again.

'I will,' I said. 'I'll get the money somehow.'

'You promise?' he screamed, spitting in my face again.

'I promise,' I replied, almost whimpering.

Abruptly, he let me go. Looking at the four pound notes still in his hand, he screwed them up and stuffed them in his pocket. He signalled to the waiter to make room for me to pass. Cautiously, I bent down and picked up my shoes. I edged my way along the wall of the corridor, half expecting some fresh assault, through the beads and into the cocktail bar. My legs were trembling so much I almost doubted that I could make it across the room to the way out. The drummer and flute-player were squatting in their corner of the room talking in undertones, apparently unmoved by the shouting in the corridor. There was no sign of the other two girls.

'You meet me tomorrow,' Osman rapped out at me, just as I finally reached the door

'I will,' I stammered. 'I will.' Then, groped my way quickly through the curtain into the open air, still trembling all over.

I ran wildly down the laneway and kept on running for two blocks before pausing for breath. Then, still panting, I sat down on a stone wall beside a row of bicycles.

My tie had come adrift. I straightened it. Some of the buttons on my trousers were still undone. I did them up. If that lot were for Mrs Simpson, I decided, she had a fighting chance. Chicago style. The more I thought about it, the clearer it became that I had been played for a sucker from the start. Being on my own, I had been terrorized as part of a calculated plan. What were their usual prices? Twenty American dollars sounded fantastic.

But one thing was certain, I wouldn't be going back to the Consulate the next day. Nor on any other day. Not in a lifetime. The mere possibility that Osman might keep a watch on the place was enough to deter me. No, I decided, henceforth, I would stay put at the Quarantine Station. I shuddered, feeling filthy all over, utterly degraded, unclean. I despised myself, beginning to be haunted by the certainty that I had contracted some loathsome disease. If only the quarantine could be brought to an end. Surely we have been through enough, I thought. Surely we must have served out our time.

After a short rest, I began walking again. The inners having been torn loose, my shoes were uncomfortable, my heels chafing against the leather. It took me a while to find my way

153

back to the Consulate. Several times I had to retrace my steps when it became apparent I was proceeding in the wrong direction. It was now well after midday and I could feel the sun's heat aching into my bare head. Sometimes, feeling dizzy, I had to pause and rest again. But mainly I was worried that David might have gone without me, presuming I had deserted him.

But my fears turned out to be groundless. Limping towards the Consulate, I saw him standing on the steps of the portico. It was a relief to see him. Indeed, I was so relieved to see him, so anxious to explain away my long absence, that it was not until I was quite close that I noticed that the thin figure standing near him in the shadow of one of the columns supporting the portico was Shewfik's Arud's purchaser.

Catching sight of me, David hurried forward, brushing aside my hesitant attempt to tell him where I'd been. 'That's all right,' he said, testily, without really listening. 'That's all right. I've seen the Consul and I've got a lot to tell you. But the main thing is to get moving. If we leave right now we can get a lift out to the Station with Shewfik's purchaser. He's been seeing the Consul too and I've lined him up for a lift as long as we leave right now.'

Without hesitation, I agreed. As far as I was concerned, the sooner we left the precincts of the Consulate the better. Accordingly, without David having to say anything more, I limped forward to meet Shewfik's purchaser.

At close quarters, he seemed even thinner than when seen at a distance; his eyes dark and parsimonious, his black suit, I noticed, on closer inspection, worn and shiny in places, his shirt collar frayed. But whatever the state of his finances, he certainly assumed the pose of a person of consequence, viewing my approach disdainfully, making no attempt to alter his position on the steps.

'So,' he said, a sarcastic whine to his voice, 'you are the one we have been waiting for. Had it been for myself I would have left you.'

He shrugged, signifying the matter was of no importance to him. 'Your friend must have much patience, waiting here in the sun even before I have come. But that is his business. I fetch my car to the front.'

The three of us walked down the steps together, David and I waiting by the gates of the Consulate while the Purchaser, crossed over to the far side of the street.

'It's as bad as I thought,' David said, turning to me. 'The Consul has been away. If the Ship's Officer hadn't left a message for him he wouldn't have known anything about it. Certainly, he's seen no medical reports. And as for Magro, apparently he's notorious. Competent years ago but nowadays practically a drunk. No one in the local administration takes any notice of him.'

David's voice was becoming excited. He bustled me forward to the kerb as we saw the Purchaser's car pull out into the centre of the road from the kerb opposite and halt there, waiting for an opportunity to edge his way through the congestion of bikes and pedestrians which flowed in all directions across the intersection.

'It was a stroke of luck recognizing Shewfik's Purchaser,' David said. 'He wasn't intending to go out there until tomorrow but I managed to talk him into it. It saves waiting all night for the water-carrier.'

'David,' I said, butting in on his remarks, trying to create another opportunity to explain where I'd been, not really wanting to tell the story in detail but feeling I had to, just in case Osman made trouble at the Consulate.

But David wasn't in a mood for listening. 'The Consul doesn't really have jurisdiction in the matter,' he went on, returning to his main theme. 'But what he wants us to do is to get a petition together signed by all the passengers so that he's got some leverage with the Canal company and the government. Something to hang his hat on. He wants you and me to get back to him with it tomorrow. That's why we've got to get back to the Station quick smart and call a meeting.'

'Why doesn't he go out to the Quarantine Station and make some inquiries for himself?' I asked. I couldn't put my finger on it but there seemed to be something ambivalent about the Consul's attitude to the matter. Besides which, I certainly had no intention of presenting myslf at the Consulate in the morning with or without a petition.

'Because of the problem with jurisdiction,' David said irritably. 'The Consul can't go trespassing on other people's territory. That would create more problems than it solves. The approach has to come from us to give him the leverage. He's going away again in a few days' time and wants to get straight on to it.'

155

'Magro may be a drunk,' I said sarcastically. 'But at least he stays on the spot.'

'We can forget Magro,' David said with determination. 'The main thing is to get the petition signed and get it in to the Consul — just as quick as we can.'

The Purchaser found his opening in the traffic and moved his car briskly across the street, pulling into the kerb in front of us. 'So there you are,' he called out to us, leaning across the front seat to release the catch on the passenger's door. 'Here is my car for your service. Quick now. I do not wish to be especially seen with people from the Quarantine Station.'

David climbed into the front seat. I scrambled into the back. 'And your money?' the Purchaser asked, holding his hand out to David, making it clear that he did not intend to move until he received whatever the price was that had been agreed between them. It confirmed my impression that the Purchaser was not the sort of person to offer lifts as a matter of charity.

'That is more like it,' the Purchaser said, giggling softly to himself as he pocketed the money. 'For myself, I am a man who drives better across the desert on a full stomach.'

He set the car in motion and soon found his way to the main thoroughfare leading past the market area on the way out of the city. Mid-afternoon, the market was now bustling with throngs of people, wagons humped high with merchandise; maize, carpets, leather goods. Men and women wandering backwards and forwards across the boulevard, forcing our driver to concentrate his attention upon the road.

But once we had bumped our way across the tram tracks and begun our trip towards the Quarantine Station across open country, the beige-coloured ground relieved only by stragglings of camel-thorn and glinting rock fragments, the Purchaser began to relax. He lit up a thin, black cheroot and slouched himself into a comfortable position behind the wheel, half-turning towards the back seat so as to include me in the conversation, not that I was especially interested in what he was saying, still troubled by my experience at the American Club, wondering at what stage I should seek medical advice, almost certain that my chafed heels were an early symptom of whatever it was that I was bound to get, convinced that I would be introduced to my tutor seething with unsightly carbuncles, incurable warts.

'Let me put it to you in that way,' the Purchaser said, giggling to himself, determined, apparently, to justify his fee. 'A man who is not paid before he drives into the desert makes a desert for himself. He deserves nothing more than this. Empty wastes.' The Purchaser flapped a hand at the surrounding terrain. 'Empty as his empty pocket. His empty head. Pah! Do I look like a man who would drive out here for pleasure? Would I come out here for Shewfik Arud and his Station full of rats?'

He giggled again and dragged deeply on his cheroot. 'Shewfik Arud. What a stupid man. What a little man. Un petit homme. Do you imagine I would pay good money for his flea-pit? His daughter — now, there is something I would pay money for. I have had my eye on that one. But his concession? What do you think, gentlemen? Would anyone in his right mind do such a thing? You have seen the place, have you not? It has a sour smell of a tomb.'

The Purchaser shifted his position again as the car bumped over a pot-hole. 'Let me tell you a little joke, gentlemen,' he said, giving a wink as he caught me staring at him in the rear-vision. 'Let me tell you a little joke that you in turn will be able to tell your friends.' He giggled again. Then laughed out loud. 'Oh, this is a fine joke, gentlemen. And you are the only chance I have to tell it aloud. And a pity it comes to an end today. But nothing goes on forever.'

'Do you want to hear my joke?' He leaned across and tweaked David's arm. 'You have noticed, of course, that Shewfik thinks I am about to buy his concession. Pah. Am I in a position to buy his concession? Look here.' He opened a glove-box in the centre of the dashboard and, keeping an eye on the road, pulled out a manilla folder. 'Do you know what goes in there? Can you guess? Monthly reports. Nothing more. Matters of routine. There is my joke, gentlemen. I am no purchaser. I am no rash businessman putting money into Shewfik Arud's pocket. I am just an official; an inspector of premises. That is my job. An inspector of premises. But how would Shewfik ever guess? That little man with all his snobberies. His education in the embassy. Do I astonish you? Do I take you by surprise?

'Gentlemen, I have had a laugh to myself for months, visiting this place, posing as a man of business. Such a fine joke. Such a pity not to share it. But now I go south to a new position. I must leave my joke behind, gentlemen. I will have to put my joke behind me, now. Such a fine joke. So good to laugh at. But not before I squeeze the last ounce out of it. To be sure, I will come within one piastre of Shewfik's price. But then — what is this? Is this heater in need of repair? Is that ceiling sagging down? I am very sorry, Shewfik, my friend, I much regret.

'Come gentleman, where is your English humour? Your practical joking? Isn't this a fine memory for me to take away with me? And if Shewfik ever finds out and reports me, I shall deny his accusation. Pah. Who would believe Shewfik Arud?' He held up the manilla folder again. 'There they are, gentlemen. The monthly inspections. There is no sign of my joke in there. There is no room for jokes in official files, gentlemen. You can be sure that my file is as empty of jokes as this desert. But are you not laughing with me, gentlemen? Sitting there with all your long faces. I am surprised at you. You amaze me. Such a good story for your friends. Come, you must rouse yourselves. Where is your humour? Where is your looking on the bright side? Such a small thing to make your face open up in a smile. Come, gentlemen, let me see your hearty laughing.'

Chapter 13

When we arrived at the Quarantine Station, I went straight to
my room. I brushed David aside, hands over my ears, refusing
to even listen to his fulminations, his programme of action,
his plans. I couldn't speak to him. I felt filthy all the way
through, utterly exhausted, painfully isolated. 'Do what you
please,' I snapped at him on the stairs. 'Do whatever you
please. I have to get some sleep.'

And I went straight to my room, collapsing on my bed
without changing; lying there staring at the grimy ceiling,
wondering what was to become of me, closing my eyes to
shut out the sight of that oppressive chamber.

I must have fallen asleep immediately, but I wasn't to be
left to myself for long. Only a few hours later, I was wakened
abruptly; awakened by shrieks that were like the rending of
metal. Shewfik was at the end of my bed; gripped by a seizure
of rage; the light above his head blazing; the verandah in
darkness.

'Filthy effendi!' he screamed at me. 'You pig! You are worse
than garbage. You dirty dog.' He gripped the metal rail at the
end of the bed and heaved at it. 'You pervert! I am blinded by
the sight of you, effendi.' He covered his eyes for a moment,
then gripped the rail more furiously, rattling the bed with his
fury. 'You are a worm in the belly eating at my bowel. The
scarab-beetle is nothing to you, effendi. You live on dung.
You have dung for eyes. You have dried dung for a mouth.'

The bed gave way beneath his onslaught, the foot of it
bumping to the floor, leaving me propped up beneath my
sheet on an incline. Shewfik shrieked again and stamped his
foot. 'I will teach you to meddle with my purchaser, effendi.'
A flick-knife appeared in his hand and he slashed wildy at
me, gashing the sheet. 'Do you know what it is to spend ten
years in a rat-trap? A rat-trap in the desert?' He stood above

me panting, his knife at the ready. 'Do you know, effendi?' he screamed, making a quick thrust at me with his knife.

'It is a torture. A torture which has no end to it. Year after year. And always the signs of sickness passing through these doors. And now, when I have a chance to end it, a chance to put it behind, you come with your friend and bring my contract crashing down around me. You are a monster, effendi. A barrow full of dung. Like this.'

He squatted in mid-air, grunting, teeth bared, hands on hips. 'Like that,' he snarled. 'You and your friend. Like that. One barrow full. There. Heaped up.'

And he came at me again, bounding on to the collapsed bed, his knife and fingers snatching at me.

'I have your gizzards. Your guts for garters. All over the floor. Sruss. Sruss. Blood. Finish. I tell you that. No joking. This time, no joking. I tell you.'

His voice raised to screaming pitch again, he slashed out wildly with the knife. As I pushed the sheet out to protect me, the blade ripped into the linen again.

'You have talked him out of it. You have turned him against me. The only heart you have is made of stone and that stone is made of dung. You are constantly devouring your heart, effendi, I can see it in your eyes. The shame. The guilt. You are rotten all the way through. You walk upright but you are sick to the core. You are diseased. Your words are poison. A leper is nothing beside you. Nothing.'

'What have you to say?' he screamed, slashing at me again as I kept retreating, struggling free of the bedclothes, kicking out at him, worming myself on to the floor.

'It's all wrong,' I gasped. 'You've got the story wrong. I'm not to blame. I've done nothing.'

'You are lying.' Shewfik followed me across the bed. The remaining bedstand gave way beneath his weight and the incline crashed to the floor. Shewfik took no notice. 'Do not lie. You rode back from the city with him. I saw you step out of the car.'

'But it wasn't me. I said nothing to him. Nothing at all. Believe me. We never spoke.'

'Ah,' Shewfik exclaimed, stepping backwards off the mattress. 'Of course, your friend is the one who does the talking. Yes, I see it now. He is the one to blame. He is the stronger of the two.'

'No,' I said, scrambling to my feet, still clutching the sheet for protection. 'You've missed the point. The Purchaser himself. He's the one to blame. He's been playing a joke.'

'Filthy effendi,' Shewfik roared, springing on to the mattress and leaping at me with his knife, pursuing me across the room as I struggled backwards, smothering his wild strokes with the sheet. 'Do you dare to call my contract a joke? Do you dare to attack my Purchaser? Do you spit on his name with your mouth of dried dung? But you are nothing?' Having forced me into a corner, Shewfik suddenly paused, and snapped his knife shut. 'You are nothing,' he repeated. 'Your friend is the one I want. He is the one who has done me in.'

Shewfik became thoughtful, turning away from me as he began to think, the rage draining out of him as quickly as it appeared. 'Yes, he is the one,' he muttered. 'Your friend is the one who has turned him against me. I can see them both talking, getting out of that car together. Yes, he is the one. Without doubt. Without a question of it.'

He picked up the bed end from the place where it had fallen and gazed at it absentmindedly, tentatively trying to balance it into an upright position. 'I will send the girl to clean this up,' he said vaguely, his mind obviously on other things. 'You will have no inconvenience.' Turning on his heel, he scuttled out of the room, leaving me breathless, the tangle of bedclothes all round me, the bed in ruins.

Giving Shewfik a few minutes' start, getting control of myself, I went in search of David, hoping I could find him first, so that I could warn him against Shewfik. But he was nowhere to be found. Not on the verandah nor in the bathroom. As I moved downstairs to the foyer, the sick child, who had now been moved to a corner room at one end of the corridor, began to wail, its thin cry of misery seeming to set up echoes in every niche of the building. Anxiously, Mrs Stacey, the child's mother, brushed past me on her way to comfort her daughter, harassed, scarcely acknowledging my offer of assistance.

Some of the passengers were seated in the foyer. But not David. I went out to the back-yard of the Station and poked my head in the laundry; sometimes the passengers made use of it at odd hours. Finding nothing, I went upstairs again and collected my torch. As I passed David's camp stretcher, I noticed that the clothes he had worn to the city lay on the end of the bed in a bundle, which suggested he had changed his clothes since his return from the city.

Armed with my torch, I left the Station by the main entrance and worked my way towards the clinic. Outside, it was utterly dark, the stars radiant in the night sky, but no moon. Offshore, the steamer rode at anchor; a ghostly outline, faint lights at the stern and on the bridge, some of the portholes aglow. Someone on deck was idling with a concertina; the tin sound of the instrument whining softly across the black water. Otherwise, everything was stillness. The light of the torch fossicking across the broken ground in front of me.

Finding the clinic in darkness, I moved further down the steps and went out along the jetty, conscious of the low, restless sound of water lapping at the piles. In the course of my excursion round the interior of the Station I had met a good many of the passengers. But not Isobel. Indeed, passing through the foyer, Mrs Walker herself, sitting in one of the chairs, thumbing irritably through a magazine had asked me that very question. Where is she? Accordingly, the thought had occurred to me that David and Isobel might have gone for a walk together. But it only took me a moment to establish that they were not on the jetty.

I turned back from the end of the jetty, wondering where to try next. Ahead of me, in dark silhouette against the starstrewn sky was the squat, forbidding bulk of the Quarantine Station, lighted windows appearing at random and at different levels throughout the building. As I moved back along the jetty, I considered the possibility of making my way along the pale road beside the parapet wall to the escarpment and thence to the vantage point. But the prospect made me shiver. It wasn't a trek I wanted to make alone, not with Shewfik Arud in his present mood.

Eventually, unable to think of any other places outside where David and Isobel might be, I returned to the foyer of the Station. Jack Morley and the two beefy young planters were beginning to set out chairs in preparation for a further meeting. I relaxed inwardly, presuming that David, in accordance with his stated intention, must have summoned the meeting. As I had not seen Burgess either in the course of my travels, quite probably, David and he were sitting down somewhere in a quiet corner, settling their differences.

Feeling more comfortable about the situation, I abandoned my search and made my way into the downstairs room leading off the foyer which, because a makeshift table-tennis table had been set up in it, had come to be known as the 'The Games Room'.

My feeling of well-being soon dissipated. Bricky and Murph were at the table, taking it in turns to play each other. But it was immediately obvious to me that Bricky, who was usually so laconic, so matter-of-fact, so totally in command of every situation, was nervy and bad-tempered; swinging wildly at the ball, cursing his partner under his breath. When he finished his game he chucked the bat down abruptly on the table. 'Shewfik Arud is a cunt,' he said bitterly, almost to himself, leaving a dented, dead ball in my hand, so that there was no point in my looking for a partner to play with.

I followed Bricky and Murph out into the foyer. There was no sign of Johnno. Upstairs, the child had begun to cry again, the thin, feverish wailing from the upper room almost ethereal, belonging to a world of anguish beyond the reach of its bewildered, suffering parent.

The room was filling up; people taking their seats in readiness for the meeting. I hesitated, leaning against the reception desk. I didn't really want to take any part in the meeting. I kept wondering whether Osman would find out that I was from the Quarantine Station. Whether I should seek medical attention. The overhead light in the centre of the room cast a dull, yellowish light on the ranks of armchairs set out below. The hessian drapes hung lifelessly from their rods.

'We've got trouble on our hands.'

I found that I was being addressed by Burgess. He had quietly slipped in beside me at the reception desk, glancing warily around the room as he spoke, keeping his voice low.

'David Shears has gone behind our backs,' he whispered, his grey eyes looking into mine for confirmation of his disapproval. 'He sneaked into the city and made some sort of approach to the Consul. He's cutting across our tracks. He's quite open about it. He saw me when he got back. Even had the audacity to demand some sort of signed authority from all the passengers to go again. The man's cracking up. I told him so. He doesn't seem to realize the effect all this is going to have on the others. Ruining whatever chance we've got of getting out. Making wild allegations about Dr Magro. But what's worse, apparently he's done some sort of deal with the fellow Arud's been bargaining with. Arud is livid about it. Quite violent, in fact. It took me half an hour to pacify him. Shears must have had a breakdown. God knows what this will do to morale. But we've got to tell them. I've called a meeting at short notice. Shears doesn't know about it. We'll have to decide what to do with him . . .'

At that point, I interrupted his hurried whispering to say simply: 'I was with him.'

'What?'

'I was with him. David Shears. He asked me to go with him to the city. I went.'

'You were with him?' Burgess couldn't believe it.

'Yes.'

'You sneaked in with him?'

'I went to the city.'

Burgess stared at me flabbergasted, as if suddenly realizing that the situation might be more complicated than he had first suspected — that David might have an ally. That it might not be enough simply to discredit his opponent by heaping ridicule on his head; by treating the incident merely as an act of aberration. Indeed, that might have been the moment at which Burgess came to the conclusion that if order was to be preserved, it was necessary to silence his opponent altogether, that a mere motion of censure would not be enough, that more drastic action was required.

Burgess was breathing heavily. He placed one hand on the counter for support. But his eyes remained expressionless. 'You saw the Consul together?' he asked warily.

'We went to the Consulate together.'

'But were you present when Shears spoke to the Consul?' Burgess snapped. Then lowered his voice. 'Were you with him all the time?' Burgess had a quick look round the room. It was almost full. The passengers settling themselves into their chairs; the chairs all facing towards the central desk. Clearly, any decision Burgess made would have to be made within the next few minutes.

I looked at Burgess without replying. The use to which he would put the answer was not quite clear to me. But I suspected that in some way it would be used against David.

He seized my wrist, looking excitedly into my eyes. 'Were you present when Shears spoke to the Consul? Answer.'

'No,' I replied.

'It was Shears who suggested the trip?'

'Yes.'

'Shears saw the Consul alone?'

'Yes.'

'Where were you?'

'I went for a walk.'

'And Shears saw the Consul while you were away?'

'Yes.'

Slowly, Burgess released his grip on my wrist. Suddenly, he looked bold; in command of himself again. He had the kind of look I have often seen on the faces of inexperienced chess-players confronting me across the board; the look of a person who is about to initiate an important stratagem, an almost imperceptible nervousness betraying an awareness that the move is not without hazard, but this, overborne by a suggestion in his manner of inner exultation, a belief that, in the final analysis, the move would be decisive.

He continued to look at me, studying my face intently, as if the solution to his problem was to be found there. To me, the protracted silence was awkward and embarrassing. I looked around to see whether anyone was watching us. But when I turned back to Burgess, he was still looking at me, directly in the eyes.

'Of course, Shewfik Arud has got the wrong end of the stick about the Purchaser,' I stammered, defensively. 'That's all a mistake. I think we can sort that one out.'

"Did you enjoy your walk?' Burgess asked, his voice low, soothing, almost intimate.

'It was okay,' I replied flushing. 'It was just a walk. A breath of fresh air. Something like that.'

Burgess nodded sympathetically. 'And Shears saw the Consul and arranged a trip back to the Station with Arud's Purchaser while you were gone. Is that how I understand it?' He resumed his business-like voice. 'You realize that it's important we get the facts straight for the sake of everybody present.' He waved a hand in the direction of the passengers.

I nodded; feeling uncomfortable, certain that he was up to something.

'Well, then, let's get the meeting under way.' He spoke briskly, confidently moving away from me as he uttered the words, heading towards his place at the central desk.

Upstairs, the sick girl kept on crying. From time to time, some of the passengers looked uneasily at the staircase as if half expecting the child to appear. I edged myself into a chair in the back row of the meeting; troubled by a feeling of emptiness, wishing there was someone I could confide in.

At the front of the meeting, Burgess tapped the table with his pen. Only a few quick taps. Only a small sound. But immediately there was complete silence in the room. 'Ladies and Gentlemen,' he began. 'I am afraid I have some disturbing news to put before you. Since we last met . . .'

But he could get no further. The mother of the sick child jumped up from the second row, her eyes blazing, leaning forward on the chair in front of her, haranguing the room at large. 'Nothing has happened since we last met. Nothing is happening at all.' She pushed away her husband's hands as he reached out trying to calm her, urging her to sit down.

'I'm not going to sit down and be silent,' she cried out, almost weeping. 'I've got the most to lose. All of us sitting here at meetings and nothing getting done. Why do we have to wait for Mr Burgess to do something? I want my husband to go to the city. So he can see the authorities. He's as good a man as Mr Burgess. I can't wait for any more meetings.' Breaking off in mid-sentence, she covered her face with her hands and started weeping, allowing her husband to draw her downwards into her seat. Around the room there were murmurs of sympathy but also of embarrassment. Some of the passengers looked at the floor. Some at the ceiling. Some at Burgess.

Burgess kept nodding gravely as if he was intent on giving full consideration to the point. When complete silence was restored to the room he resumed. 'All of you will readily appreciate that Mrs Stacey has my fullest sympathy. She and her husband have had to suffer more than any of us during this confinement.' This remark was endorsed by a murmur of approval from several quarters, although I noticed that the two elderly sisters who I suspected of being the authors of the rumour that the child's illness was responsible for keeping us in quarantine, kept silent.

'And for that reason,' Burgess continued, 'I respect her viewpoint. And far from taking her remarks personally, I would be willing to resign right away if that was the wish of the meeting.' There was no sound in the room.

166

'But before I did so,' Burgess said, raising his voice slightly, 'As my last action as your chairman, as it were, I would be obliged to disclose to you that one amongst us, without prior reference to the meeting, has taken certain steps which will quite probably prejudice the negotiations your committee got under way almost from the first day we were here. Now, would you like me to develop that point further or would someone prefer to put a motion of no confidence to the vote?'

There was complete silence in the room. 'I am referring to the activities of Mr David Shears,' Burgess said bluntly. 'Without prior reference to us he has made a journey to the city. As you know, no one is allowed to go to the city. That would be in breach of the terms of our confinement.' He paused, letting the information sink in.

'Damn fool,' the scrapbook man said from near the front.

Burgess quickly held up his hand, commanding silence. 'I will tell you what I know,' he said. 'And I might add, that as to what I do know — and there may, of course, be other evidence which hasn't yet come to light — we are indebted to our secretary who took it upon himself to keep an eye on Mr Shears once it was clear he was determined to go his own merry way.'

'Good lad,' the scrapbook man said, turning round stiffly to examine the faces of the audience behind him, eventually catching my eye.

But now Jack Morley was on his feet. 'Before you go on,' he said, a troubled look on his face, 'Mr Shears doesn't appear to be present. He ought to have a chance to hear what's being said. It may be he can explain.'

'Thank you,' Burgess said coldly, waiting for Morley to sit down. 'Thank you for the timely reminder. It is most important that we observe the proper formalities. Perhaps our secretary will ask Mr Shears if he would be good enough to join us.'

'I don't see why we have to wait for *him*,' one of the sisters interposed, tossing her grey head angrily.

'I notice that Miss Walker is also missing,' Burgess added.

Bricky and Murph, sitting at the back of the room, guffawed. Johnno was hunched up in his chair in sullen silence. Mrs Walker, who was sitting close to me, flushed at the sound of the laughter. I could see her hand stiffening on the arm of the chair, with vexation.

I rose to my feet uncertainly, not knowing where to start my search. 'Try upstairs,' Morley called across to me, sensing my dilemma. Having already made one search upstairs, I was doubtful that this would produce any result, although it did occur to me that I hadn't checked Isobel's room.

'As time is short,' Burgess said, once again focusing attention on the central table, 'I'm sure our secretary won't mind it if we proceed in his absence. If you wish, I can briefly summarize what I know of the matter.'

I started up the stairs, not knowing what was the best thing to do. On the one hand, I wanted to find David quickly so he could get to the meeting to defend himself. But on the other hand, I couldn't afford to be away from the meeting for long, not if Burgess was going to start putting his own gloss on the facts. My keeping an eye on David! That had taken me by surprise. But, admittedly, that was one way of looking at it. I had certainly kept in mind that, in some sense, I was a representative of the other passengers.

Where was David, I thought, impatiently, as I reached the top of the stairs? All the time, the nagging worry in my mind that Shewfik Arud, in his present mood, might not stop at anything. I shivered at the thought. Not Shewfik, surely. He was excitable. But he wouldn't go that far. He wouldn't be rash enough, not with all these people in the building.

There was a naked yellow bulb burning at the top of the stairs, making it difficult to tell whether the light in Isobel's room was on. Complete darkness would have revealed a splinter of light beneath the door. At the far end of the corridor I could hear the sick child whimpering.

The straightforward thing, I suppose, would have been to have knocked. But finding David was the main point of my search. I wasn't keen for Isobel to attend the meeting, especially if the matter of my movements came into question. If she was asleep then let her go on sleeping — that was my thought.

While I hesitated outside her door, it suddenly occurred to me that there was an easy way of finding out. Stealthily, I crept along the corridor to the next door, and, turning the handle carefully so as to raise the latch quietly, I let myself into the scrapbook man's room.

I stood there in the darkness, and then crept forward, moving closer to the thin partition at the head of the bed. But

168

then, as I listened, as I heard what was happening in the room next door, I stood there transfixed, almost paralysed, scarcely able to draw breath, fearing detection, but knowing that I had to move; that I had to escape. It was, perhaps, the worst moment of my life.

On the other side of the partition, I could hear the rhythm of their bodies. In the darkness on the far side of the partition, the movement of bedsprings, the unbridled flesh sounds, the joyous undercurrent of whispers and their frantic breathing, the quick gasps — oblivious to everything but their own passion; undoubtedly, a man and woman making love.

It was unbearable. The sense of having trespassed, the sense of having blundered into some dimension beyond one's understanding, of having briefly glimpsed, experienced, another level of reality, but being cut off from it, foreign to it; an alien.

Feeling faint, I groped my way back to the door, letting myself out and closing the door gently behind me. Standing in the corridor, perspiration broke out all over my body. Supposing they had heard me? Suppose they thought I was spying on them? But then that ceased to worry me as the full horror of the situation struck me. The fools, I thought. Not now. Not at this very moment when all the others are beginning to take sides. Not at the very moment when David had to protect himself; when his character had to be beyond reproach.

Distraught, scarcely able to cope with what I had overheard, I worked my way down to the end of the corridor, throwing myself onto David's camp stretcher, my mind reeling, tormented; cursing the Quarantine Station with all my heart, now, for the first time, feeling utterly diseased, stranded in surroundings from which there was no escape. And all the time, in the room nearby, the child whimpering, bringing me almost to the verge of tears as I pitied it, the sick child, an inhabitant of this void in which we had been abandoned.

Who was responsible? Who was to blame for our plight? These questions; these dark ganglions surrounding us. Had David not been determined to press his point of view, if he had not persuaded me to journey to the city, I would never have debased myself. But nonetheless, the fault was mine. And now, only a short distance away, two bodies joined in the darkness; clinging together, innocence now denied to them, to me. And David himself, unconscious of the allegations being made against him. This void. This void surrounding us. Less than a month ago, how safe we had seemed on the steamer. David and Isobel in their makeshift swimming pool. Tears came to my eyes at the memory of it. And now it had been reduced to this — this empty corridor with its threadbare carpet leading away from me to a blank wall, a single light at the head of the stairs casting shadows into the doorways. To be released. To be released from Quarantine. At least, to be able to think of oneself as clean again. Was it so much to ask?

I compelled myself to rise; forced myself back on to my feet; terrified at the thought of remaining alone in that corridor a second longer. To rejoin the others, that was my only thought. To join my fellow passengers. To find myself some position amongst them, no matter how unsatisfactory their company might be, or how unworthy their deliberations.

'David,' I called out loudly, rapping my knuckles firmly on the door. 'Are you in there? There's a meeting on. You're wanted at the meeting. Shall I say you're on your way down? You must come.'

I walked away from the door and paced up and down; the physical activity itself seeming to restore my confidence. I tried to prevent my thoughts straying; knowing that if I was once again obliged to confront my innermost feelings, I could never go on. 'David,' I called out, approaching the door. 'There's no time.'

As I turned towards the stairs, I heard the door open behind me. David appeared in the doorway, his clothes dishevelled. We faced each other, separated by only a few yards. There was nothing to be said. There was only an uneasiness between us; a kind of hesitation. It was as though we both knew instinctively that something had come between us; some circumstance, some shadow — that we both had to follow our own course, to make our own way.

'It's Burgess,' I blurted out. 'He's called a meeting. Behind our backs. You have to get down there. Tell them what you've found out. Everything.'

I hesitated. As I spoke he had just begun adjusting his clothes, straightening himself up. He made no attempt to explain himself. I put one hand up to the wall for support. 'I don't know what to do,' I stammered. 'I feel . . . cut off.'

He frowned, not understanding what I was trying to say. 'Don't worry,' he rapped out. 'We'll get rid of Burgess, once and for all. I'll be down in a moment. Tell them that if they ask. Say I was sleeping.'

He closed the door, leaving me in the corridor. Our conversation had done nothing to reassure me. The small lie he wanted me to carry back to the meeting left me more confused than ever.

Slowly, I turned away from the door and made my way back down the stairs, trying to compose myself, trying to control the turbulence within me. David. Johnno. Burgess. The closer you came to any of them, the further away from you they seemed to be, always beyond reach, but close enough to be constantly involving you in their affairs. I paused at the foot of the stairs, looking at the people in the room at their meeting. My own relationship to them — what was that?

Burgess caught sight of me standing at the foot of the stairs. 'The very man to answer our queries,' he said drawing attention to my return. Mr Horwood had been addressing the meeting. Burgess asked him if he would stand down for a moment. Then he beckoned to me to come forward.

'Mr Shears was resting,' I said, making my way though the chairs, directing my remarks to Burgess. 'Apparently, he was tired out by his journey and had fallen asleep. He says he'll be down in a moment.'

'Certainly. Certainly,' Burgess said, drawing up a chair for me at the central table. 'Whenever he's ready. But in the meantime, perhaps you can assist us on one or two matters of procedure.'

'Our secretary,' Burgess explained for the benefit of the meeting, 'in case any of you weren't aware of it, is a legal man. I would suggest we take advantage of his expertise and have him take charge of the formalities. To make rulings on any points of law which crop up.'

'What exactly are you doing?' I asked; wondering what on earth had gone on in my absence. 'You realize, of course, that I'm only a student. I'm not qualified to make rulings of any kind.' I licked my lips nervously, not knowing what was expected of me.

'Of course. Of course,' Burgess said, affecting an air of geniality. 'I think we all agree that these proceedings are entirely informal. But, after all, we live in the age of the expert and most people would prefer your help to none.' He looked at the elderly sisters with the kind of faint smile which invites a murmur of accord.

'Now, then,' he said. 'The position is that Mr Morley expressed some concern about the regularity of our meeting. He seemed to think that any allegations about the conduct of any member of our party should be the subject of a proper investigation. Personally, I couldn't agree more. It's most important that we observe the formalities. Fortunately, it transpires that Mr Horwood has had some experience with judicial inquiries in the course of his duties as a city councillor. Appeals against the issue of building licences and so forth. Accordingly, on his suggestion we've convened what might be loosely described as an *ad hoc* court of appeal. Is that the correct expression, Mr Horwood?'

Mr Horwood rose ponderously from the body of the meeting. 'That's right, Mr Chairman,' he said. 'An *ad hoc* committee of the whole. On the second Tuesday in every month, we used to...'

'Thank you, Mr Horwood,' Burgess said, cutting him short. 'Now then, the subject matter of our complaint is really the misconduct of Mr Shears. Firstly, in going to the city without proper authorization. Secondly, in having prejudiced our existing dealing with the authorities. Thirdly, in having jeopardized the welfare of the passengers by interfering with Mr Arud's commercial activities.' Burgess ticked the points off his fingers, briefly glancing at the rough notes set out in the pad in front of him. 'Were those the three main points?' he asked, looking in Mr Horwood's direction for confirmation.

Mr Horwood stood up again. 'In having prejudiced our dealings with the authorities while such matters were still *sub judice* was my wording,' Mr Horwood said. 'And my suggestion was that he be confined to his quarters as soon as the hearing is over.'

'*Sub judice*,' Burgess said, repeating the words aloud as he jotted them down. 'But I think we all agreed,' he added, looking up, 'that as Mr Shears doesn't have a room of his own, he would be moved in with our friends at the back.' He concluded his remarks by pointing at Bricky and the boys so that everyone would be clear who he was talking about. 'Mr Morley? Are you happy with that?'

172

'It's all very informal, of course,' Morley said, hesitantly, without rising in his place.

'I think we agree it has to be,' Burgess replied. 'Now then,' he continued, turning to me. 'Where should we begin?'

'Well,' I said. 'I think we should be very careful about taking it for granted that he's guilty. You can't talk about confining someone to quarters before the hearing has started.'

'Of course. Of course,' Burgess said, testily. 'That goes without saying. Now, what should we do first?'

Mrs Stacey jerked up on to her feet, eluding her husband's attempt to restrain her. 'Why do we have to go through all this?' she said in a shrill voice. 'If he's got us into trouble then he should be punished. Why should the rest of us have to suffer?'

'Thank you, Mrs Stacey,' Burgess said. 'But I think Mr Morley does have a point. As Mr Horwood rightly said — justice must not only be done. It must also be seen to be done. Now, I think we've all heard the evidence. It's really only a question of hearing what Mr Shears has to say. Would that be the correct procedure?' He turned to me for confirmation.

But at that moment, before I could answer, David himself appeared at the foot of the stairs. All heads turned in that direction. 'Mr Shears,' Burgess called out sternly. 'Come forward, please.'

'Are you asking me, or telling me?' David called out provocatively from his position at the foot of the stairs, hands on his hips.

One of the elderly sisters jabbed at the floor with her cane. 'Do as you're *told*, young man,' she snapped. And there was a murmur of approval from those nearby.

David hesitated, but then began edging his way along the wall to the front desk.

'We are offering you a chance to explain your actions in going to the city without the authority of this meeting,' Burgess said, when he reached the front, challenging him. 'Have you anything to say?'

This is absurd, I kept thinking to myself. This whole business is hopelessly absurd. But I knew it was fruitless to attempt to halt the proceedings.

David began talking; revealing his doubts about Magro, indicating the reasons for his decision to go to the city. As he talked, he became more excited, especially when he began describing his interview with the Consul. But Burgess interrupted at that point. 'Tell me one thing,' he asked. 'Were you alone when you saw the Consul?'

'Yes,' David replied.

'Is it true,' Burgess persisted, 'that shortly before seeing the Consul you suggested to the gentleman presently seated on my left that he should absent himself?'

'Yes,' David replied, not appreciating the significance of the remark.

There was a murmur of astonishment around the room that he should be so frank about it.

'The Consul is prepared to act on our behalf if the two of us can get back to him tomorrow morning with a petition signed by you all.' David spoke eagerly, pointing to himself and then to me as the two people would carry out this line of action.

'This is right, actually,' I chipped in, rising to my feet, trying to relax the meeting. 'You see, what happened was basically a mix up. I wasn't actually there when we found out that Dr Magro isn't much use to us. But that was my fault. Not being there to get it straight from the horse's mouth, as it were.'

No one laughed at my small pleasantry. They were all staring at me. I sat down. But then I stood up again. I felt that I hadn't got my point across.

'I realize that in one sense I'm speaking as a witness now rather than as a judge, or legal adviser, I should say. And it's true, in a general sense, that corroboration of what took place would be best. That's a rule of evidence in hard cases where it all depends on the work of one person.'

Everyone was still staring at me. I couldn't seem to think straight. 'Corroboration,' I added. 'In other words, one person backing up what another has said. But be that as it may, basically David's plan is a good one. Although it would be better if someone else but me went back to the Consul with him next time.'

I sat down feeling uncomfortable. Some of the audience were shifting in their chairs restlessly.

'You see,' David exclaimed, appealing to them. 'He came with me and he knows what's best. We have to get back to the Consul.'

'I have a little point.' Mrs Walker was on her feet, a dainty hand hoisted to shoulder level, her eyes on the chairman.

174

Burgess gave her leave to proceed. She coughed discreetly. All eyes turned in her direction.

'Like Mr Morley, I just want to see fair play. I would have been most upset if we hadn't done things according to the rules. But as Mr Burgess says, fortunately we have a legal man in our midst. And I think it's jolly lucky we do.'

Eloquently, she stretched the palm of her hand out towards me; holding the gesture for a moment longer than was necessary. 'Now,' she continued, 'as I understand it, under this rule of corroboration, boiling it all down to tin tacks, we shouldn't believe a thing Mr Shears says. I move that he be confined to quarters.'

'Just a minute,' David shouted as Mrs Walker sat down. 'He didn't say that at all. He thinks like me. That we have to get back to the Consul.'

'Point of order, Mr Chairman.' Mr Horwood rose in his place, stony faced. He waited until he had the attention of everyone in the room. 'The witness has ceased giving evidence as to what actually happened at the time in question,' he said, speaking in a monotone. 'He is beginning to refer to what he intends to do rather than what he has actually done.'

'Good point,' the scrapbook man said from the second row. 'Point well taken.' He turned round and nodded encouragement to Mr Horwood.

But Burgess was following up another point. 'I doubt that our secretary would be prepared to go back to the Consul with you,' Burgess said, addressing himself to David.

'He will.'

'I doubt it!'

'He will because he knows what I've done is right. That everything I've done has been for the benefit of all of us. This talk about witnesses. I'm not on trial here. I'm trying to prevent you making a mistake. This is the quickest way to get out. We've got to get back to the Consul. It's the only way. He'll come with me because he knows I'm right.'

As David spoke, I found that a fluttering had started in my stomach which I couldn't control. I began trembling, trembling inwardly, and all over. I was aware that all eyes in the room were gradually turning towards me to see how I would answer. Why had David put me in this position? How can people be so foolish as to think that a public forum is the place to find out what is in a man's heart; the complex mixture of loneliness, aspirations and experience which determines how a man will act, how far he will go for another? And all the time, to the forefront of my mind, the horror of having to return to the Consulate, possibly to be confronted by Osman, subjected to his demands, involved in some scene, ostracized by my fellow passengers even if we were released.

The room was quite silent. Deathly still. 'Will you go with him?' Burgess asked, so that all could hear, turning to me; staking everything on the turn of a single card.

'No,' I replied.

And at that answer, Mrs Stacey rose to her feet, her face contorted with grief, pointing directly at David, accusing him, threatening him with her outstretched hand. 'He's the cause of them keeping us here,' she cried, hysterically. 'He's the cause.'

Burgess raised a hand and beckoned to the back of the room. I saw Bricky give a nod to Johnno. The big man blundered up out of his chair. People made way for him, pulling their chairs aside, as he limped towards David.

Chapter 14

'The *lex Pompeia de parricidiis* imposes a singular punishment on a terrible crime, enacting that if any man has hastened the death of a parent or a son or of any other person close to him, secretly or openly, or has procured the same, or been privy to such a crime even though unrelated to the victim, he is not to be punished by sword or flame or any usual process, but is to be sewn up in a sack with a dog, a cock, a viper and a she-ape, and in this hideous cell is to be cast into the sea, so that living he shall be denied all use of the elements, and while he yet survives the air of heaven, and when he is dead, the boon of earth shall be withheld from him.'

Does it surprise you that my Borthwick has remained a secret; containing, as it does, my only record of our quarantine, and that grotesque passage from the *Institutes* underlined in my own hand; seeming to conclude the narrative? Now that you have the truth of the matter set before you, do you understand my agitation? Looking up from your work, looking out to sea from the verandah of your peaceful bungalow, can you forgive my folly? Do you know why I have argued so passionately, so extravagantly, and on so many occasions, often to the prejudice of my own case, to the detriment of my own reputation, that unless we are preparing our students for independence of thought and action, their minds fortified by history, philosophy, the lessons of the past, our work is wasted?

Can you imagine how it has been for me — the memory of that Quarantine Station, that final meeting, being always in my mind? The spectre of it always in my mind? On sleepless nights, those bailiff shadows of the old transaction rifling through my mind with wallet fingers saying: 'We are reality.'

And yet, when I awoke at the Quarantine Station on the

morning after the final meeting, strangely enough, my initial feeling of remorse was soon replaced by a mood of hope, a sense of well-being. Everything having been brought to a point of crisis, it almost seemed as though the period of anxiety was over, as though the fever had subsided.

I can remember the feeling distinctly. Waking up, still tired, but becoming conscious of the sun at the verandah door, thin slivers of it visible through the shutters; aware that for the first time in many nights I had slept soundly, noticing immediately that, for the first time in many mornings, the sick child was no longer whimpering. And getting dressed in a mood of determination; preparing myself for action.

I was deeply troubled by the events of the previous night. The proceedings at the meeting had been outrageous. We had all been overwrought. We had behaved badly. The matter had to be put right. With that thought in mind, I set off down the corridor with a resolute step; determined to take the matter up with Burgess.

That David should be confined to quarters, that Bricky and the boys had, in effect, been appointed to stand guard over him, was too absurd. I wanted the matter put right; especially as it was now clear to me that I had let David down at the moment he needed my support most. If necessary, I thought, a further meeting must be called. I was sure I could achieve something.

That was my frame of mind, my plan of action. But when I got downstairs, I was disconcerted to find that the foyer was utterly deserted. Chairs were still grouped in a wide arc round the central table, having been left in position from the previous night's meeting. But there was no one to be seen. Not even in the kitchen, or in the laundry.

Returning to the foyer again, I looked at the clock near the reception desk. Worn out by the previous day's events, I apparently slept longer than I thought. It was almost midday. But no sign of anyone. The scrapbook man's album lay open on a chair in his usual corner; the shoe-boxes nearby. But no sign of the man himself. Feeling almost panicky, fearing that the others might have left without me, I rushed across to one of the windows, being relieved to find that the steamer was riding at anchor, its position unaltered.

Still puzzled by the strange silence which seemed to have settled down on the Quarantine Station, I stepped outside to

178

get a better view of the steamer, hoping to see some indication of activity on its decks. Outside, the sky was pale, drained of colour by the noonday heat. There was no sign of anything happening aboard the steamer; the dilapidated old vessel sombre, motionless in the grey water; beyond it, on the far side of the lake, the outline of the distant shore providing a backdrop of featureless rock and sand like the edge of some rugged moon-crater. But when I turned to go indoors again, the cause of the Quarantine Station's emptiness became immediately apparent to me.

Beneath the ridges of the escarpment, directly below the lookout, at the point where the dusty road leading away from the Station narrowed and passed between the rocky outcrop and the inlet, half a mile away, perhaps, there was a cluster of people gathered together on the road. An assembly of people and of vehicles. And on the pathway up to the look-out itself, fossicking through the boulders and scraggy camel-thorn, stretched out along the track, I could see figures dressed in khaki moving across the face of the escarpment, apparently searching the ground for something.

I began walking towards the assembly, then broke into a jog-trot. The sight was so unusual that I knew instinctively that something was wrong — seriously wrong. Coming towards me along the road, I saw the two elderly sisters, accompanied by their brother and the scrapbook man, cautiously making their way back to the Quarantine Station; their frail parasols erected above them.

'What's wrong?' I called out, as I approached them, but not breaking my stride, fearing to waste a single moment. 'What's happened?'

The sisters and the brother, walking almost as if they were in a trance, took no notice of me. But the scrapbook man paused and looked up as I passed. 'There's been some trouble,' he muttered clumsily, his eyes and voice bewildered. 'Some terrible trouble. Down there on the road.'

He looked so shocked that I didn't stop to question him further. Instead, I quickened my pace; hurrying towards the escarpment, bare-headed, feeling the dry heat rising from the road ahead of me, the heat pressing itself into my face like rough cloth, the sun exhausting me, my damp shirt an irksome poultice on my shoulders, my shadow on the road beside me contracted into a hobbling dwarf.

179

'All these people,' I said almost breathless, accosting Burgess on the outskirts of the gathering, at the foot of the escarpment. 'What are they looking for?' Above us, on the track up to the vantage point, I could see three men in khaki uniforms at different points, still searching amongst the rocks. The road itself was blocked off by a number of vehicles parked at random — one of them a black van; one of them, I noticed, Dr Magro's car, pulled in nearby. A canvas awning had been set up at the rear of the van, so as to create a makeshift tent, one wall of which was the van itself. There was a man in a khaki uniform standing beside the van talking to Mr Horwood. He was taking down notes on a small pad, using the side of the van as a support.

'His passport,' Burgess snapped. 'He must have lost it before he fell. The bloody fool.'

'But what's happened? I haven't heard.'

'Shears,' Burgess rapped out, impatiently. 'David Shears. Where on earth have you been? They found him hours ago. He's dead. Fell off the rocks. What he was doing out here by himself, I can't imagine. The bloody fool. Scuttling out of it, I suppose.' Burgess took a handkerchief out of his pocket and mopped his brow. 'And now we've got this.' He jerked his hand at the awning. 'Questions. Perhaps an inquest. More complications.'

I felt like my stunted shadow in the dust; speaking with its voice, my words drawn from somewhere in its bruised heart. 'Complications,' I stammered. 'You're worried about complications? What was he doing here? It's obvious.' My words were painful gasps, becoming shrill. 'We forced him out. We've killed him.'

'Don't be ridiculous,' Burgess said, grasping the front of my shirt. 'Don't be ridiculous.' He looked round nervously and then let go of me. 'Keep your voice down. There's nothing we can do. It was an accident.'

I felt the tears coming to my eyes and couldn't look at him. My shadow lurched away from his.

'Don't be a fool,' Burgess said; taking me tightly by the arm, following me. 'Don't be a bloody fool.'

'This is his friend?' I found that I was being addressed by the Egyptian officer; a short, neat figure in khaki, looking at me dispassionately. Mr Horwood was beside him. The other passengers had parted to let them through.

'Captain Shurbagi, sir,' the officer said, speaking to me directly and offering me a perfunctory handshake. 'Please come with me.'

He turned on his heel briskly and moved back towards the van. I fell in behind him, the other passengers making way for us. He paused outside the canvas awning and addressed me again, speaking with the same clipped voice; a voice with only a slight suggestion of a foreign accent in it. 'Others have told me,' he said, quickly identifying Burgess and Mr Horwood who had followed us across, 'that you went to the city with your friend.'

'Yes,' I said, swallowing nervously, but determined to be truthful no matter what the cost.

'Yesterday, was it?'

'Yes.'

'When did you leave?'

'Just before dawn. At daybreak.'

I had thought that he was about to charge me with the offence. But he didn't seem to be interested in what we had done in the city or why we had gone to the city.

'How did you get to the city?' he asked.

'With the water-carrier.'

'At what point did you board his truck?'

Somewhat surprised by the question, I looked around me. 'At this point,' I replied, startled by the coincidence. 'Almost exactly at this point.'

'That's what we told you,' Mr Horwood interjected, putting his view of the matter to the Egyptian officer with an air of indignation. 'Obviously, that's what happened. The man came out here to wait for the water-carrier and slipped from those rocks.' Mr Horwood pointed to the overhanging crags above us. 'From those rocks up there.'

Captain Shurbagi looked at him coolly. 'I will ask the questions, please,' he said. He took my arm to guide me under the tent-flap but then hesitated. 'How did the man get into the water, then?' he said, turning his attention back to Mr Horwood; his face expressionless — but an edge of sarcasm in his voice; a slight note of hostility.

Well, I imagine he hit the ground and then rolled in,' Mr Horwood said, blustering, tumbling his hands around to suggest a rolling action.

The officer looked up at the rocks. Then at the width of

roadway where we were standing, occupied by the length of the van and the tent — before he allowed his eyes to move on to the edge of the inlet, at this point, swampy ground consisting of reeds and shallow water leading into the mud-flats; the mud-flats themselves forming part of the oasis half a mile away where the fishermen's huts were situated.

'The width of a road. A long way for a dead man to roll, don't you think?'

'Exactly,' Burgess said, breaking in, speaking rapidly, more rapidly than was usual for him. 'Which was why I said that having had the fall he probably blundered into the water while semi-conscious. He didn't know what he was doing.'

Captain Shurbagi gave a short, dry laugh. 'Well, then,' he said. 'I am surprised you say there is no need for an investigation. To find out if what you say is true we must know whether he died by the fall or by drowning. Surely you must agree? I myself am not a doctor, gentlemen. But we have the Doctor with us for that very purpose. I'm sure you do not object.'

Burgess bit his lip. 'Look here,' Mr Horwood said. 'We don't want any trouble about this. All we expect is fair play. But we can't be held up indefinitely. We have certain rights.' Some of the others murmured support for this proposition.

'In this country, we are not so very much interested in your rights,' Captain Shurbagi said. 'But that is another matter. Another matter altogether. For the moment, I am interested in that rock. The road we are standing on and the water. But I am also interested by what is in your minds. And, therefore, your theories have been put in my notebook. They are not without importance. Your theories have always been of interest to us in this country. A matter of constant interest. I am privileged to have the benefit of some new ones.' He patted his pocket. 'But please,' he continued, 'let me be content with what I have. In this country, for many years, we have learned to keep our stomachs small. I shall make do with what I have.' He bowed quickly, but as if he was mocking them by his courtesy. It was obvious he meant no respect. 'You may go now,' he said, straightening up, and calling out loudly so that the others standing some way back could hear. 'All the passengers may go.'

'And him?' Burgess asked, pointing at me.

'He will stay for one moment,' Captain Shurbagi replied.

'He must identify the body also. We must be certain. The head is badly battered.'

The Captain turned away from them and, stooping down, led the way into the tent, allowing the tent-flap to fall into position, closing us off from the others remaining outside.

The light inside the tent was greenish; the canvas acting as a filter for the sun's rays. Dr Magro was sitting on a small stool scribbling notes on a pad supported by his knees, hunched over his work. He looked up as I entered and nodded to me. The doors of the van had been opened outwards beneath the awning. A body was lying on a stretcher inside the van, the face of the inert figure being covered by a blood-stained towel loosely draped across the head and shoulders. The clothing on the body was sodden wet, dirtied by mud and grime, fragments of reed still clinging to the shirt and trousers.

'The clothes aren't his,' I blurted out, noticing immediately that the sandals, the dungarees and the faded blue shirt on the corpse resembled nothing I had ever seen David wearing, hoping, for a moment, that there was some mistake; that the victim of the mishap was a stranger.

'Yes,' Captain Shurbagi said, 'that is puzzling. Very puzzling to us. His passport missing also. And very little money on him. We can only think that he wanted to travel in disguise. Where these clothes came from — impossible to tell.'

He drew the stretcher forward and casually lifted the blood-stained towel away from the face.

I turned away from the sight, shuddering. It was him. One side of the face lacerated into pulp almost beyond recognition. But quite clearly it was David.

'Is that your friend?' the Captain said from behind my shoulder.

I couldn't answer; my whole body trembled. Dr Magro got quickly to his feet and supported me on to the stool he had been sitting on. 'Don't upset yourself, my friend,' he said; his voice kindly. 'Death is not such an unexpected thing.'

'Especially at a Quarantine Station such as this,' Shurbagi added, uttering a small, mirthless laugh.

'Yes,' Dr Magro added for my benefit. 'Captain Shurbagi and I have worked together on many reports. All of them adding up to the same sort of certificate in the end. Try and understand that it is not such an unexpected thing.'

183

'Look again please, sir,' Captain Shurbagi said briskly, and without wasting his time on sympathy. 'Let us be certain so that we won't trouble you any more.'

Steeling myself to do so, I looked again. But when I inspected David's broken features for the last time, I had eyes only for the leech, the leech which had concealed itself in the wet curls of his head, and wormed its way on to his brow; the blind slug, easing its way forward, oblivious to my horror-stricken cry, my wretched tears, my wild hysteria, attacking Dr Magro with my hands, my nails, my feet, begging them to stop that slug, to cover my dead friend's face, to bring him back to life, to set me free.

Chapter 15

Mrs Walker and Isobel went back to the city with Dr Magro. I never saw her again. According to the others, at the news of David's death she became uncontrollable; distraught with grief. She accused us all.

Those who saw her agreed that, in her condition, she never would have been able to complete the voyage; that Mrs Walker's decision to break their journey with a period of recuperation was the most sensible course. The rest of us left the Quarantine Station two days later. We never found out how far Captain Shurbagi went with his inquiries. What he said in his report, we never knew. The reason for our detention was never revealed and seldom discussed. The passengers had ceased to be curious about such matters. We simply accepted the assurance from the ship's officer that we had been given 'a clean bill of health'. We weren't inclined to probe further.

Somehow, from the day on which Captain Shurbagi made his inquiry, we all seemed to know, instinctively, that we would soon be leaving. There was no need for discussion. We accepted that there was no further need for meetings or negotiations. It was as though some cure had been effected. People became cheerful again. Even Shewfik Arud appeared amongst us on the day following the inquiry; more restrained than before, but polite and willing to be of service, accepting commiserations about the loss of his Purchaser with a shrug and a nervous smile, rubbing his hands occasionally and saying: 'It has been a bad time. Please. You will not think badly of me. My accommodation.'

'I had a feeling we'd come through in the end,' the scrapbook man said to me on the day of our departure.

Our luggage had already gone out to the steamer and we were waiting in the foyer of the Station for our turn to be ferried out to the ship.

'Mind you, it was a shame about that David Shears,' he continued. 'Nice young chap really. Bit excitable, perhaps. But having an accident just on the last leg of his trip. It's a rotten shame. I shall probably drop a note to his parents. Although it's a bit hard to think of anything to say. But what a rotten thing to happen. Still, we lost a lot of good men in the war.'

He passed his album to me as we moved down the jetty to take our place in the stern of one of the lifeboats. 'Here,' he said. 'Hang on to that, there's a good chap. Not enough free hands for everything.'

We settled down in our seats and waited for the others to clamber in. Mr Horwood helped the two elderly sisters into their seats in the centre of the boat and then moved forward to take a seat beside his wife.

'Yes,' the scrapbook man said as we pushed away from the jetty, the boat's inboard motor chugging steadily. 'There's always one or two hitches on a trip like this. But I knew we'd make it at the end of the day. Whenever there's a spot of bother, it's just a question of keeping a bit of pressure on in the right places and things soon sort themselves out. Jolly lucky we had a chap like Burgess around, though. Don't you agree? You know, to put in the leg work, as it were. Of course, you played your part. I haven't forgotten that.'

He tapped the album I was holding across my knees. 'Wouldn't be surprised if I didn't put a bit of what happened into there.' He delved into the breastpocket of his flannel suit and extracted a few scraps of paper. One was a photograph of the Quarantine Station. There was also a piece of the Station's yellow notepaper with the vivid sun emblem on it. 'I asked that Shewfik Arud chappie to sign it,' he said, turning the photograph over. 'But he wasn't willing. Probably can't write his name in English although he seemed quick-witted enough.'

I was the last person out of the boat. In fact, the last passenger to come aboard. By the time I had been down to my cabin, checked that all my belongings had arrived safely and gone back up on deck again, the steamer was under way; the heavy muscle of its engines making the steel frame of the vessel shudder, an experience which, undoubtedly, we would soon become accustomed to but which, after our weeks on shore, was unfamiliar.

I stood at the rail watching the Quarantine Station gradually recede — the masts of the fishing vessels, the dhows, the palm trees comprising the small oasis at the far end of the inlet, the low escarpment, the Quarantine Station itself, resembling a faded postcard, all beginning to slip quietly away behind us.

At a distance, the building was not impressive, I reflected. Placed in a row of buildings in a city street it would look downright ugly, squalid even. But in isolation, here, on the edge of the desert, the one building of any size for several miles, it had a kind of decaying grandeur about it. And now it had become part of me. Of that I was quite certain. Not merely a memory, some passing episode which could easily be described without exposing anything of one's self. No, much more than that. A segment of one's being. Something I had taken possession of and it of me. To describe it properly, without dissembling would necessarily be to reveal one's mind; to reveal the multiplicity of experiences, influences and fantasies which lie behind an attitude, thereby permitting one to find some position in reality, and hold to it.

But as the Station drifted away from us, drifting into the brown featureless landscape, becoming no more than an apparition, a cardboard structure on the horizon, I suddenly became conscious of all the unanswered questions. Why had we been brought there? Why had they allowed us to leave? And above all — the enigma of David's death. It was too much. And for some reason, I couldn't help calling Dr Magro's words to mind — that sometimes, among primitive peoples, the patient was discharged during a period of temporary improvement so that he wouldn't taint the reputation of the hospital with his death.

But how much could one believe what Dr Magro said — that bitter, disappointed man? These thoughts troubled me for many hours. Indeed, still ruminating about such matters, the next night, after we completed our journey through the canal and reached the open sea, I was prompted to go down to my cabin after dinner to look at my Borthwick once again; the one passage of translation continuing to reverberate in my mind.

'Also things captured in war, and an island arising in the sea, and gems, stones, and pearls found on the shore become the property of him who has been the first to take possession of them. Now one can acquire possession in person. A madman, and a ward without his tutor's authority, cannot begin to possess since they have not the intention to hold, however much they are in physical contact with the thing, as though one put something in the hand of a sleeper.'

I closed the book, bemused by the passage. The scrapbook man had his photograph and a few scraps of paper. But did he have the intention to hold? The Quarantine Station. Did any person have the capacity, the wisdom, to encompass the whole structure, its inhabitants, to take possession of the entirety? Or was each of us, with his own limited viewpoint, restricted to being merely in physical contact with the thing, incapable of seeing more than what was put in front of him, not really comprehending of what was in his hand? And how were we to take possession of the gifts held out to us, or found, or rediscovered? The gift of friendship; the gift of understanding.

But, as always, the attempt to generalize becomes confounded by events. Some fresh mystery reveals itself, throwing a new light on what has gone before, the embers transform themselves into flame.

Uncomfortable in my cabin, oppressed by the smallness of it, some mood of restlessness in me, feeling the ship steadily surging forward into the night, I put aside the book and made my way up to the deck. It was a warm night; a light breeze ruffling my shirt, spasmodically flapping the canvas of random deck-chairs. No sign of the moon. The stars spread throughout the blackness above the ship in radiant clusters; fragments, vestiges of a pre-existing order deep in space.

I worked my way along the rail, sometimes stopping to admire the phosphorescence of the ship's track rollicking outwards from its keel in white combers, becoming wavelets rippling into the darkness and subsiding. In this way, idly having in mind to stroll right round the ship before turning in, my mind still preoccupied with the events which had taken place at the Quarantine Station, my attempt to unravel what had occurred, I came to a portion of open deck at the very rear of the ship; an area which was used as a sports deck — a deck tennis court marked out on the boards.

There, sitting at one of the low tables immediately outside the folding doors which, in daylight, open inwards to create the aperture which was euphemistically described as 'The Sportsmen's Bar', Bricky and the boys were playing a desultory game of cards; the only illumination for their game a bright, unshaded bulb projecting out from the stepped deck above them, their three shadows slanting away from them starkly. There was no one else on the deck. The night sky a dark backdrop to their game. As usual, glasses set out in front of them.

I intended to move on without speaking. Since the night of the meeting, the night they had taken David into their custody, I had had little to do with them. I hadn't been able to find it in me to approach them. According to Burgess, their story was that they had moved David's camp stretcher into their dormitory but otherwise had taken no steps to restrict him. In the morning they had found him gone and were, so they said, as surprised as anyone else to find that he had set off for the city only to meet his death on the escarpment.

But I was still suspicious of them. I had no idea what Captain Shurbagi had put in his report. But if he was anything like Dr Magro, it was quite possible that his report did not necessarily correspond with what he truly thought. And in that respect, whether the official verdict was an accident or not, I found it impossible to forget the scepticism with which he had greeted the theories put forward by Burgess and Mr Horwood as to how David met his death. Nor could I forget the strange bond which seemed to exist between Shewfik Arud and the three transport drivers.

Accordingly, although I had no reasonable grounds for my suspicion, nor even any real theory as to how or to what extent the three of them might have been implicated in David's death, having myself been threatened with a knife by Shewfik, and having, as I say, observed a nexus between Shewfik and these three, I felt, instinctively, that they had played some part in the tragedy which hadn't been revealed. At the very least, they were the last people to see David alive. I had no concrete evidence on which to base any allegation. I was not in a position to condemn them having myself, in my own way, been instrumental in bringing about David's death. But since the inquiry, I had resolved to give them as wide a berth as possible.

So as not to make my withdrawal too apparent, I lingered at the rail for a moment, making a pretence of studying the horizon. But it was never really possible to keep out of their reach. They always had that surly street-corner manner about them which meant that if you looked at them directly more than once they took it as provocation — while consciously minding your own business was interpreted as disdain, an act of defiance which called for some form of retribution.

Most often, being aware of these extremes, I would compromise, half looking at them and half looking at something else. I suspect this only made matters worse; that a shambling, sideways-looking fellow like myself was regarded not only as weak, but as weak and disdainful — practically an outright invitation to assault; it mattering little whether such assault was physical or verbal.

'Come 'ere, Professor,' I heard Bricky say, in a thick, slurred voice, just as I was about to move back along the rail to leave them behind me.

'How's y'r cough, Prof,' Murph chipped in, displaying, as he often did, a penchant for idiotic doggerel.

I was tempted to keep on walking, pretending I hadn't heard. But, of course, I knew what the consequence of that line of action would be. At worst, if they were especially drunk, it could involve an uproarious physical pursuit followed by more belligerent bantering. At least, in my experience, it would end with them hilariously shouting abuse after me of such crudity that I would be identified in the minds of the other passengers, unfairly but inevitably, as the cause of constant disturbances. Accordingly, on this occasion, as I had done on others, I settled for a middle course. I had found that if I chatted for a minute or two they usually lost interest in me and let me go on unmolested. So I took a few steps towards them, moving cautiously.

'Nice night,' I said.

Bricky and Murph guffawed as they always did, treating my remark as an astonishing piece of repartee.

'Bullshit,' Bricky said, abruptly cutting his mirth short. Beside him, Johnno, the heaviest of the three, sat silent, staring morosely at his hand of cards, hunched up, utterly still. Even the sight of him made me feel uncomfortable, wondering what was preying on his mind, reminded of my own folly, that we might both be sharing the same secret, the same burden; and not wishing to be reminded of it.

'Complete and utter bullshit,' Bricky repeated, throwing down his hand of cards and lounging back in his deck-chair to look at me. 'You're always up to some bullshit.'

'Hot from the cow,' Murph piped in illogically.

'What about a drink, Professor?' Bricky asked, stretching his powerful arms out above his head and yawning. 'One for the road.'

'One for the salty brine,' Murph added.

I shook my head. 'Not for me,' I replied, wondering if it would be safe to leave, having gone through the motions of a conversation.

'Take one down to the Contessa, Professor,' Murph said, chuckling a bit, and looking round the table for an answering laugh.

Bricky seemed to sense that the conversation was wearing thin. 'Do you know where we keep our grog, these days?' he asked. 'Do you want to see something?'

I shook my head.

'Shall we show him?'

'Why not?' Murph replied. 'No harm done. We'll know who to come looking for if we find any gone.'

Bricky bent over and groped beneath the table. He produced a large wooden box covered with ornate carvings. 'Look at this,' he said proudly, setting it up on the table like a child demonstrating a toy. 'Just the right size for hip flasks. Shewfik gave it to us.'

'A genuine Arabian casket,' Murph commented. 'A real dazzler.'

I stepped closer. Sure enough, it was the same box Shewfik had shown me in the laundry.

Bricky opened the box and invited me to look in. There were two small flasks of brandy inside it. He took them out and put them on the table. Johnno slowly put his cards down flat on the table and stared at the box, the yellow light overhead making his face shadowy, almost brutal.

Bricky winked at Murph. 'Suppose you want some cigarettes, Professor,' he said, holding the box up to show me that it was empty except for the silken lining. 'Suppose you want to get some cigarettes through customs. Where do you think they might be?'

I couldn't resist the temptation. To Bricky's surprise, I casually took the box from him and felt for the knob in the centre of the wooden flower. I pressed it and the hidden drawer popped open. I extended it to its full length, exposing some packets of cigarettes.

'There,' I said, trying to keep a tremor of glee out of my voice, feeling that I had at last bested them at their own game.

Bricky put the box down on the table and looked across at Murph. He, with the brow furrowed, looked back. 'What a card!' Bricky said, trying to carry it off casually, but sounding crestfallen. 'What a bloody card.'

'That's not all,' I said, keeping my voice steady, but in fact made reckless by my success. 'There's another drawer for matches. Or keeping money.'

'Money,' Johnno said, starting suddenly. Bricky and Murph went quiet, looking at each other across the table.

'Another drawer?' Johnno said, taking an unsuspected interest in the box, stretching out a hand to touch it.

'Yes,' I said uneasily, taken aback by the tension which had suddenly developed around the table.

'Show us,' Bricky said, looking up at me, a peculiar expression on his face.

I crouched down beside him and began levering up the row of studs holding the silken lining in place, using my fingernails. I was still bewildered by their interest. I sensed that it was more than just a game now. That it was important to them to know if there was anything else in the box.

'I could do with some matches,' Murph said, giggling nervously. But no one else said anything.

I laid the lining back, exposing the concealed compartment beneath the hinge. I poked my fingers into the thin compartment. Then, faltered, and drew back; knowing immediately by the feel of it what was inside.

'What's there?' Johnno said, his voice hoarse, becoming anxious. 'What's in there?' He snatched up the box and jammed one of his fingers into the crack and quickly levered up the passport concealed in the compartment, extracting it with his thumb and forefinger, dropping the box on the table as he fumbled to open the passport, beginning to breathe heavily.

He opened it. And we stared at David's face, looking out at us full of vigour. Johnno dropped it like something contaminated, giving a sharp cry as he did so. The smiling eyes kept staring at us, looking upwards at us from the table-top.

'Shewfik Arud,' Johnno mumbled. He picked up the box again and ripped the lining out of it with one quick stroke; the silk tearing free from its fastenings with an angry sound.

192

'Shewfik Arud,' he cried out, ignoring the rest of us, and smashing the box against his knee, and then smashing it on to the deck violently until it began to splinter, pounding it against the deck until it was in fragments, all the time his fingers groping at the wreckage as if expecting it to confront him with some other secret.

He staggered to his feet, clutching the debris of the broken box to his chest and kicking at the fragments which remained on the deck with his shoes, kicking them towards the ship's rail and then hurling the remnants of the box wildly over the rail and into the blackness as far as he could. 'Shewfik Arud,' he screamed. 'You swine.' He fumbled in his pocket and pulled out a tiny bottle. 'I don't need you,' he moaned, and flung the bottle into the darkness after the box, as though he was pelting refuse at the invisible presence of Shewfik himself somewhere beyond the rail. 'Take your bloody medicine back, you swine. I don't need you. I don't need you.'

He moaned again and turned to face us with a pitiable cry. Standing there panting, enraged, but his face contorted with pain, his arms bent back behind him almost to the point of dislocation, clutching the rail. 'I don't need him,' he shouted at us. 'I don't need him. I don't need his medicine. I never did. I'm all right. Do you hear me? I'm all right. I'm the same as I ever was. I'm the same man. I'm the same as the rest of you. You're in it as much as me. I'm not the only one.'

Then, he staggered away from us along the rail, forced to use his hands, lurching along the rail, limping badly on one leg, like a weakened giant, and disappeared into the shadow of the promenade deck running alongside the cabins.

Bricky and Murph looked at each other, paying no attention to me. 'Shit,' Bricky said. 'He's cracking up. He can't handle it.'

'We'd better get him,' Murph replied, looking around uneasily. 'We'd better go get him.' He pushed back his chair.

With that, leaving the cards, the open passport, their glasses, the bottles, scattered on the table, they went after their friend, breaking into a run as they reached the line of shadow separating the sports area from the promenade deck. I heard them calling after him as they disappeared into the shadows.

I looked round me. After such a commotion, I was certain

that people would begin converging on the deck at any moment from all sides. I looked at David's photograph on the table. It was impossible to tell what had brought him to this. I didn't hesitate. There was no time. I picked the passport up and walked quickly to the rail, flinging it overboard, the dark binding of the document immediately lost in the blackness.

There was still no movement on the deck. Only the empty table and the bottles on it under the harsh, yellow light, and the ship surging restlessly forward, its huge engines throbbing, pushing us towards the horizon. And beyond its rail, the darkness — out there, earth and heaven merging in one tide of darkness, the gentle wind blowing in off the Aegean, a faint pulse at my shirt collar.

This *faszad*, I thought to myself, alone at the rail, gripping the metal for support, feeling the blistered paintwork of the ship's rail beneath my hands, this intolerable *faszad*, this affliction — will there ever be an end to it?

THE BELLARMINE JUG
Nicholas Hasluck

In Holland to study at the mysterious Grotius Institute, Leon Davies is accosted by a student linked to foreign radicals.

The encounter plunges him into an intrigue which will haunt him for a lifetime – leading finally to his interrogation by a counter-espionage expert who confronts him with evidence gathered in Amsterdam, Indonesia and Australia.

The questions probe deep. Doubts, fears, myths, betrayals, utopian illusions, are all relentlessly exposed, then stripped away.

At the centre of the affair, stands the Bellarmine Jug, the strangely inscribed curio which seems to hold the key . . .

'Here is compelling reading . . . Better than most novels and superior to any week of television'
      Humphrey McQueen, *Sydney Morning Herald*

'Detective thriller or history mystery. Nicholas Hasluck's latest novel is an adventure on the high seas of Higher Education'
                Hugh Barnes, *The Times* (London)

MORE ABOUT PENGUINS AND PELICANS

For further information about books available from Penguin please write to Dept EP, Penguin Books Ltd, Harmondsworth, Middlesex UB7 ODA.

In the U.S.A.: For a complete list of books available from Penguin in the United States write to Dept DG, Penguin Books, 299 Murray Hill Parkway, East Rutherford, New Jersey 07073.

In Canada: For a complete list of books available from Penguin in Canada write to Penguin Books Canada Ltd, 2801 John Street, Markham, Ontario L3R 1B4.

In Australia: For a complete list of books available from Penguin in Australia write to the Marketing Department, Penguin Books Australia Ltd, P.O. Box 257, Ringwood, Victoria 3134.

In New Zealand: For a complete list of books available from Penguin in New Zealand write to the Marketing Department, Penguin Books (N.Z.) Ltd, Private Bag, Takapuna, Auckland 9.